PENGUIN CLASSICS

BEAUTY AND THE BEAST

MARIA TATAR is the John L. Loeb Professor of Folklore &
Mythology and Germanic Languages & Literatures at Harvard
University. She is the author of many acclaimed books, as well as
the editor and translator of *The Annotated Hans Christian
Andersen*, *The Annotated Brothers Grimm*, *The Classic Fairy
Tales: A Norton Critical Edition*, *The Grimm Reader*, and *The
Turnip Princess and Other Newly Discovered Fairy Tales*. She
lives in Cambridge, Massachusetts.

D0724776

WITHDRAWN

WITHDRAWN

Beauty and the Beast

CLASSIC TALES ABOUT ANIMAL BRIDES AND GROOMS FROM AROUND THE WORLD

Edited by
MARIA TATAR

PENGUIN BOOKS

PENGUIN BOOKS

An imprint of Penguin Random House LLC
375 Hudson Street
New York, New York 10014
penguin.com

Introduction, notes, and selection copyright © 2017 by Maria Tatar
Penguin supports copyright. Copyright fuels creativity, encourages diverse voices, promotes free speech, and creates a vibrant culture. Thank you for buying an authorized edition of this book and for complying with copyright laws by not reproducing, scanning, or distributing any part of it in any form without permission. You are supporting writers and allowing Penguin to continue to publish books for every reader.

Grateful acknowledgment is made for permission to reprint the following copyrighted works:

"Zeus and Europa" from *Mythology* by Edith Hamilton. Copyright 1940, 1942 by Edith Hamilton, renewed © 1969 by Doris Fielding Reid, Executrix of the will of Edith Hamilton. Reprinted by permission of Little, Brown and Company.

"The Muskrat Husband" from *Cev'armiut Qanemciit Qulirait-llu: Eskimo Narratives and Tales from Chevak, Alaska* compiled and edited by Anthony C. Woodbury (Alaska Native Language Center, University of Alaska, 1984/1992). Used by permission of Anthony C. Woodbury.

"A Boarhog for a Husband" from *African American Folktales: Stories from Black Traditions in the New World* by Roger Abrahams. Copyright © 1985 by Roger D. Abrahams. Used by permission of Pantheon Books, an imprint of the Knopf Doubleday Publishing Group, a division of Penguin Random House LLC. All rights reserved.

"The Monkey Bridegroom" and "Urashima Taro" from *Folktales of Japan* by Keigo Seki, translated by Robert J. Adams. Used by permission of Chicago University Press.

"Tale of the Girl and the Hyena-Man" from *Tales Told in Togoland* by Allan Wolsey Cardinall. First published for the International African Institute by Oxford University Press. Used by permission of the International African Institute.

"The Girl Who Married a Dog" from *Indian Tales of North America* by Tristam P. Coffins. Used by permission of American Folklore Society.

"The Turtle and the Chickpea" from *Folktales of Greece*, edited by Georgios A. Megas, translated by Helen Colaclides. Used by permission of University of Chicago Press.

"The Frog Maiden" from *Burmese Folk Tales* by Maung Htin Aung. Copyright © 1948 by Oxford University Press. Reprinted by permission of Oxford University Press India.

"The Peasant and Zemyne" from *The Serpent and the Swan: The Animal Bride in Folklore and Literature*, translated by Boria Sax (McDonald & Woodward, 1998). Used by permission of Boria Sax.

Source information for all of the selections in this book appears on pages 191–196.

LIBRARY OF CONGRESS CATALOGING-IN-PUBLICATION DATA
Names: Tatar, Maria, 1945— editor.
Title: Beauty and the beast: classic tales about animal brides and grooms
from around the world / edited by Maria Tatar.
Other titles: Beauty and the beast (Penguin Books)
Description: New York: Penguin Books, [2017]
Identifiers: LCCN 2016040960 (print) | LCCN 2017000535 (ebook) |
ISBN 9780143111696 | ISBN 9781101992951 (ebook)
Subjects: LCSH: Fairy tales. | Human-animal relationships—Fiction.
Classification: LCC GR552 .B43 2017 (print) | LCC GR552 (ebook) |
DDC 398.2—dc23
LC record available at https://lccn.loc.gov/2016040960

Printed in the United States of America
1   3   5   7   9   10   8   6   4   2

For the Blums:
Jason, Lauren, and Roxy

Contents

Animal Grooms

Animal Brides

Introduction: The Odd Couple in Tales as Old as Time

"Beauty and the Beast" may be our culture's love story about the transformative power of empathy, but it also has a dark side. It is not just that the tale has a high coefficient of weirdness, with monkeys, goats, lizards, and bears courting beautiful young women, and with cats, tortoises, dogs, and frogs revealing their talents to enraptured young men. It also has an emotional ferocity that encodes messages about how we manage social and cultural anxieties about romance, marriage, and "the other." Beauty and the Beast stories speak a universal language—the story is as ubiquitous as "Cinderella"—but with messaging that is nearly always culturally inflected. Like all good folkloric memes, the tale migrates and morphs into new versions of itself, becoming entertaining in its heterogeneity, especially to readers familiar with other versions. It may be the tale as old as time, but it is never the same old story.

"Beauty and the Beast" ranks among the most popular of all fairy tales. It has been retold, adapted, remixed, and mashed-up by countless storytellers, writers, filmmakers, philosophers, and poets. Rich with implications about matters both aesthetic and existential, as its title implies, it derives its power in part from the mysterious mismatch between its two protagonists, with the one not only classically beautiful but also instinctively generous, the other grotesquely ugly and desperately needy. In a move rare in fairy-tale worlds, it gives us a double trajectory in its standard version, a cursed Beast in search of redemptive love, and a captive Beauty who discovers that essences transcend appearances.

The genius of "Beauty and the Beast" lies in its engagement with the cultural contradictions that riddle every romantic relationship, as well as the perils of leaving home and the possibilities of new family constellations. How do power and wealth figure in the calculus of marriage? What is the value of beauty? Of charisma? Of charm? What are the limits to forgiveness and compassion? How does marriage change family dynamics and vice versa? What is the right balance between compromise and dignity?

As we shall see, there are just as many handsome men and beasts as there are beautiful women and beasts. The two antithetical allegorical figures in the title have traditionally resolved their differences in what can be seen as a heteronormative myth of romantic love, yet the story's representational energy is also channeled into the tense moral, economic, and emotional negotiations that complicate all courtship rituals and do not yield to easy solution.

There is something unapologetically contrived, if not perverse, about choreographing human courtship rituals using a human and a beast. And yet nearly every storytelling culture maps out dating practices with animal partners. Are the animals reminders of our fundamentally primitive nature? Are they proxies for the "beastliness" of sex? Are they remnants of a totemic purpose that once captured the spirit of a clan, family, or tribe? And why the stunning variety of beasts, with creatures ranging from snakes and warthogs to cranes and pigs?

"Animals are good to think with." That is the wisdom of Claude Lévi-Strauss and countless other anthropologists. "Beauty and the Beast" illustrates that truism supremely well, combining animal magnetism with human charms to create a symbolic story about what it means to form a partnership both passionate and principled. The odd couple featured in "Beauty and the Beast" may not be so odd after all, for the two embody the mind/body problem, along with the many other binaries that shadow it, including the hierarchy that sets *zoe* over *bios*, instinct over intellect, social life over brute animal existence, rational consciousness over intuitive know-how. Beauty and the

Beast stories are, then, not just about marriage, but also about our relationship and connection to the social world we share with other living beings.

There are also sound pragmatic reasons for storytellers to pair humans with beasts. Tales are always better with animals in them, as Yann Martel tells us in *Life of Pi*. And a curved mirror, one that distorts and takes us into the fun house, is always more compelling—and often more true—than a purely reflective one. That every culture seems to tell "Beauty and the Beast" in one fashion or another suggests that it is part of our DNA. We make the story new so that we can think more and think harder about the stakes in partnerships and marriages, as well as about a world that today is not merely anthropocentric but also biocentered with an ecophilosophical orientation. There is good reason to keep hitting the refresh button, and this volume offers an opportunity to pause and reflect on different versions of the story and on how it has changed as it migrates across time and place.

"Beauty and the Beast" is so deeply entrenched in our thinking about tales featuring a companionate/romantic pairing of beasts and humans that we are often unaware that it is a mere nostalgic remnant of a vast repertoire of stories about animal grooms and animal brides. Beast was not always a suitor living in regal isolation; Beauty was not always kept in a castle. Sometimes a young man will court an enchanted cat living in a castle. Or he will take home a crane disguised as a beautiful woman. Empathy and compassion are not always the answer to the challenges faced by Beauty/Handsome and Beast. Some spells are broken when animal skins are burned. Some beasts are disenchanted when their repulsed partners hurl them against walls. And decapitation also often succeeds in restoring a Beast to the human condition. And, finally, tragedy often haunts these stories, with animals that follow the call of the wild and return to nature rather than endure life in the "civilized" world.

This volume seeks to create a fuller spectrum of stories that commonly go by the name of "Beauty and the Beast." It will explore plots, broadly speaking, about what folklorists call animal grooms and animal brides. It will reach into the long ago and far away, and it will also consider how those tales operate in a global network and make their way today through multiple media channels. And, finally, it will draw attention to the slipstream, stories that continue to glide along and make themselves visible in brief flashes, even as the classic "Beauty and the Beast" dominates the mainstream, continuing to surge in popularity.

THE ORIGINS OF OUR "BEAUTY AND THE BEAST"

Before mapping out the terrain of tales about animal grooms and animal brides, it is worth interrogating the terms of a version that has received the lion's share of public attention and lives on vigorously in the cultural imagination, constantly recycled and renewed. The animal-groom story most familiar to Anglo-American audiences was penned in 1756 by Madame de Beaumont (Jeanne-Marie Leprince de Beaumont) for her *Magasin des Enfants*, designed to promote good manners in the young. Based on a baroque literary version of more than one hundred pages written in 1740 by Gabrielle-Suzanne de Villeneuve, Madame de Beaumont's child-friendly "Beauty and the Beast" reflects a desire to transform fairy tales from adult entertainments into parables of good behavior, vehicles for indoctrinating and enlightening children about the virtues of fine manners and good breeding, often by strategically inserting standard-issue platitudes into the narrative.

The lessons and moral imperatives encoded in Beaumont's "Beauty and the Beast" serve as an ethical antidote in some ways to the outrageous subject matter of the tale—innocent girl incarcerated by a ferocious beast. They pertain almost exclusively to the young women in the story, who, in a coda, are showered with either praise or blame. As Angela Carter points out, the moral of Madame de Beaumont's tale has more to do with "being good" than with "doing well": "Beauty's happiness is founded on her abstract quality of virtue."[1] With nervous pedagogical zeal, Madame de Beaumont concludes her tale in a frenzy of plaudits and aspersions. Beauty has "preferred virtue to looks" and has "many virtues" along with a marriage "founded on virtue." Her two sisters, by contrast, have hearts "filled with envy and malice."

What exactly makes Beauty virtuous? To begin with, she seems possessed of a yen for acts of self-sacrifice. After discovering that Beast is willing to let her father go as long as one of his daughters shows up at the castle, she declares: "I feel fortunate to be able to sacrifice myself for him, since I will have the pleasure of serving my father and proving my feelings of tenderness for him." To be sure, not all Beauties are such willing victims, valuing subordination over survival. In the Norwegian "East of the Sun and West of the Moon," the heroine has to be coaxed into submission with promises of wealth. She agrees to marry Beast (a white bear) because her father badgers her: "[He] kept on telling her how rich they would be and how well she herself would do. Finally, she agreed to the exchange."[2]

That the desire for wealth and upward mobility motivates parents to turn their daughters over to beasts points to the possibility that these tales mirror social practices of an earlier age. Many an arranged marriage must have felt like being tethered to a monster, and the telling of stories like "Beauty and the Beast" may have furnished women with a socially acceptable channel for providing advice, comfort, and the consolations of imagination. Written at the dawn of the Enlightenment, Madame de Beaumont's tale attempted to steady the fears of young women, to reconcile them to the custom of arranged marriages, and to brace them for an alliance that required effacing their own desires and submitting to the will of a "monster."

It is easy to see why "Beauty and the Beast" managed to survive at the expense of its folkloric cousins. By pairing two figures renowned for their spectacular looks, the story created endless possibilities for aesthetic collisions, emotional conflict, and cognitive wobbles. It also produced opportunities for talking about the moral and financial economies at stake in domestic arrangements. And it provided the consolation of happily ever after in a story that seems to be racing toward a tragic denouement. What is not to love about the romance in "Beauty and the Beast," a story that turns antagonists into allies and brings out the best in both human and beast?

CLASSIFYING ANIMAL BRIDES AND ANIMAL GROOMS

Once we look at the entire array of stories featuring the romantic entanglements of humans and beasts, the phrase "absurd neglect" comes to mind. Why have we sacrificed richness and complexity for regimented predictability? To be sure, there is some melodic diversity and tonal variation in our reorchestrations of "Beauty and the Beast," but why choose less when you can have more in the repertoire? And why, in particular, miss the opportunity to reflect on the full range of possibilities that once characterized the many narratives told by our ancestors, who each added new ingredients to improve the flavor and zest of the stories?

Folklorists long ago recognized that classification systems can be clarifying and that they help us understand what is at stake in clusters of tales with shared affinities. Beyond that, they shed light on the origins and dissemination of tales, on gender roles and generational conflicts, as well as on which elements of a story are universally relevant and which are culturally specific. What folklorists call a tale type provides a useful tool for broadening our understanding of "Beauty and the Beast." A tale-type name offers a shorthand designation of a global theme or set of characters, and it is used as a category for collecting international variants that enable the study of how the tale is inflected at the local level.

"Beauty and the Beast," as it turns out, is a subset of the tale type ATU 425 The Search for the Lost Husband. And that tale type is a mirror image, with genders reversed, of ATU 400 The Man on a Quest for His Lost Wife. However problematic those designations may be (note that the woman "searching" is not named as agent in ATU 425, and the man is on a "quest" rather than a mere search in ATU 400), they offer a convenient pair of categories for sorting out the standard features of the two tale types. It would not be out of line to rename them "The Woman in Search of Her Lost Husband" and "The Man in Search of His Lost Wife."

The latest edition of the tale-type index, published in 2011 under the title *The Types of International Folktales*, gives us an inventory of the variants of the two different types of stories, both of which are the subject of this volume. Below is an abbreviated version of the subheadings in the two categories:

ATU	400	The Man on a Quest for His Lost Wife
	401A	The Soldiers in the Enchanted Castle
	402	The Animal Bride
	403	The Black and the White Bride
	404	The Blinded Bride
	405	Jorinde and Joringel
	406	The Cannibal
	407	The Girl as Flower
	408	The Three Oranges
	409	The Girl as Wolf
	410	Sleeping Beauty
	411	The King and the Lamia
	412	The Maiden (Youth) with a Separable Soul in a Necklace
	413	The Stolen Clothing (Marriage by Stealing Clothing)
ATU	425	The Search for the Lost Husband
	425A	The Animal as Bridegroom
	425B	Son of the Witch
	425C	Beauty and the Beast
	425D	The Vanished Husband
	425E	The Enchanted Husband Sings a Lullaby
	425M	The Snake as Bridegroom
	426	The Two Girls, the Bear, and the Dwarf
	433B	King Lindorm
	440	The Frog King, or Iron Henry
	441	Hans My Hedgehog
	444	Enchanted Prince Disenchanted

What is the use of the folkloristic typology? For one thing, it enables us to see immediately that an animal partner in a romantic relationship with a human constitutes the backbone of the two tale types. And that concept—an animal bride or an animal groom—is packed with sensational scandal. All other variations on the tale types are just that: variations that swirl around the notion of a beastly spouse, at times literally so, at times figuratively so. The trope of a beastly mate captures the heart and soul of both tale types, and it challenges us to make sense of something that we do not encounter in real life. In our anthropocentric, rational, "enlightened" universe, animals stand in an asymmetrical relationship to humans. They may, in their domesticated form, be our companions, but only in the pornographic imagination are they anything more than that. As our dark doubles, they stand for everything we disavow in ourselves—ferocity, bestiality, and untamed urges. Because our relationship to them is saturated with mysterious desires and projected fantasies, our stories about them enable us to probe what remains uncivilized, unruly, and undomesticated in us.

In an analysis of sexual decadence in Western literature and art, Camille Paglia tells us that the point of contact between "man and nature" is sex, and that "morality and good intentions" fall there to "primitive urges." She describes this intersection as an "uncanny crossroads," both "cursed and enchanted."[3] Paglia's observations go far toward explaining the staying power of Beauty and the Beast stories, tales that invoke the mind/body problem and lead us into the fraught territory of beauty and charisma as a challenge to ethical aspirations. Where do we draw the line when it comes to desire, and how and why do we set limits on it?

Tales of animal brides and animal grooms have suffered neglect today in part because we have new ways of figuring the monstrous other. In the twentieth century, we feared beasts like King Kong and Godzilla, along with aliens from other planets, more than anything else. Today our anxieties about creatures that will take over the planet are embodied more often in cyborgs, robots, and androids than in animals. Wolves, bears, and lions figure less as predators than as endangered species in our cultural imaginations. In some ways, life in a posthuman era has intensified our anxieties about machines while reducing our fears about beasts.

In the tale type known as "The Man on a Quest for His Lost Wife," an adventurous young man must break the magic spell cast on the woman who will become his bride. Devoted and doting, he keeps the faith despite the manifest "otherness" of the beloved, who is divided in her allegiance to nature and to civilization. Two types of animal brides haunt the folkloric imagination, with the first as the victim of abduction or seduction. These are the selkies, mermaids, seals, and swan maidens who marry mortals and become human, bearing children and keeping house until one day they are seized by a powerful sense of nostalgia. Putting their sealskins back on or donning their feathers, they abandon their families and follow the call of nature. Rooted in the idea that women have mysteriously close ties to nature, these stories reveal the dangers of what anthropologists call exogamy—marrying outside the tribe—as well as of consorting with outsiders in general. They form a sharp contrast with another set of animal brides, the many toads, birds, fish, monkeys, mice, tortoises, and dogs that seek men who can break the magic spell binding them to an animal state. Frequently these creatures excel at domesticity, spontaneously and effortlessly carrying out prodigious tasks that demonstrate their clear superiority to the human competition.

"The Man on a Quest for His Lost Wife" is something of a misnomer, for rather than find their brides, the men who marry creatures of the earth, air, and sea often stumble upon them or are part of an elaborate plan orchestrated by those metamorphic women. In the Filipino "Chonguita," the protagonist does nothing but agree to marry a monkey, and he liberates her through an act of brutal force, hurling her against a wall. The Indian "The Dog Bride" features a youth who resolves to marry a beautiful maiden after witnessing her shed her dogskin before bathing. The Russian "Princess Frog" gives us an amphibious bride who is so resourceful, enterprising, and accomplished that she succeeds in earning the devotion of a husband who does little more than burn her animal skin, and too soon at that: The burning of the skin leads to a second phase of action that demonstrates the husband's willingness to go to the ends of the earth for his wife's sake and stages the joyous reunion of the pair.

One cultural variant of animal-bride stories is particularly powerful in its representation of the painful burdens of social masquerades and domestic responsibilities. "The Swan Maiden," a tale widespread in Nordic regions, discloses the secretly oppressive nature of marriage, with its attendant housekeeping and child-rearing duties. Swan maidens, domesticated by acts of violence, eventually seize the opportunity to return to a primordial, natural condition. In Henrik Ibsen's play *A Doll's House*, the tormented Nora, a figure identified again and again as a bird or creature of nature, was clearly inspired by the mythical swan maiden and her domestic tribulations. Instead of donning feathers (as swan maidens do), Nora rediscovers a diaphanous dancing dress and, after executing a frantic tarantella, takes leave of her dour husband, Torvald. The symbolic nexus connecting animal skins, costumes, and dancing is so prominent in this tale type that it points to a possible underlying link with Cinderella, Donkeyskin, and Catskin stories, showing us the dark side of what happens in a post–happily-ever-after phase.

Tales about swan maidens, selkies, seals, and mermaids may once have been far more widespread than they are today. One critic has argued that the tales can be found "in virtually every corner of the world," because in most cultures "woman *was* a symbolic outsider, was the *other*, and marriage demanded an intimate involvement in a world never quite her own."⁴ Yet some animal brides lure their mortal husbands into their own worlds, hermetic spaces of timeless beauty where husbands partake of untold pleasures even as they are aware of an uncanny edge to their carefree bliss. Like Tannhäuser, who in medieval lore becomes Venus's captive in the caverns of her mountain abode, the Japanese fisherman Urashima and his many folkloric cousins dwell in a realm where they are emphatically the outsiders.

Like tales about animal brides, stories about animal grooms display an interesting bifurcation, with one set of stories going viral and mainstream, the other going dormant and, if not underground, then under the radar. The "classic" version of "Beauty and the Beast" gives us a compassionate heroine who redeems Beast with her tears. Its less prominent counterpart (the best-known example of which is "East of the Sun and West of the Moon") features an adventurous heroine on a mission to lift the curse that has turned a man into a beast. These are the stories that show us the heroine as determined agent—wearing out iron shoes or racing to the back of the north wind to liberate men kept prisoner by ill-tempered trolls or diabolical vixens. Both sets of tales bleach out details about the animal groom and give us a heroine enviable in the determined gusto with which she undertakes tasks. As if to compensate for the lack of verbal descriptors for Beast, illustrators and animators have turned him into an alluring chimera with a commanding sense of mystery and authority. In recent remediated versions, he has gained much in terms of nobility, status, and dignity, in part because we have renewed respect today for the beauty and spiritual power of animals.

Terri Windling, whose literary fairy tales for adults are powered by a deep understanding of myth and history, writes with vivid sympathy about how a switch has been flipped in our contemporary rescriptings of "Beauty and the Beast":

One distinct change marks modern re-tellings however—reflecting our changed relationship to animals and nature. In a society in which most of us will never encounter true danger in the woods, the bear who comes knocking at our window is not such a frightening creature; instead, he's exotic, almost appealing. Where once wilderness was threatening to civilization, now it's been tamed and cultivated (or set aside and preserved); the dangers of the animal world now have a nostalgic quality, removed as they are from our daily existence. This removal gives "the wild" a different kind of power; it's something we long for rather than fear.[5]

ANIMALS AS SELF AND OTHER: THERIANTHROPY AND TERATOLOGY

There is poetry in the notion of Beauties encountering Beasts, yet there is also a reductive binarism at work in the pairing, something that Jacques Derrida, in a moment of deep philosophical insight, referred to as intellectual *bêtise*.[6] With that brilliant phrase he both undid the divide between humans and animals and at the same time reinforced it. What we are discovering today is that the bifurcation of living beings into human and animal is not a universal feature of thought. Rather, that particular binary derives from Enlightenment thinking, from a post-Cartesian moment in which humans are decreed to exist in a different mode of consciousness and being from all other living creatures: Cogito ergo sum.

A look at the *Oxford English Dictionary* reveals that the term "animal" hardly appears at all in English before the end of the sixteenth century. Instead, there are "beasts" and "creatures," beings differentiated topographically (inhabiting the earth, the waters, or the air) and also sentient and capable of communication, as in this Bible passage: "Aske now the beasts, and they shall teach thee, and the foules of the heaven, and they shall tell thee: Or speake to the earth, and it shall shewe thee: or the fishes of the sea, and they shall declare unto thee. Who is ignorant of all these, but that the hande of the Lord hath made these? In whose hande is the soule of every living thing, and the breath of all mankinde" (Job 12:7–10).

Shakespeare tells us in *As You Like It* that there are "tongues in trees, books in the running brooks, / Sermons in stone, and good in everything."[7] Less pantheistic than offering a cosmic vision of connectedness, the passage reminds us, with its biblical partner, of fairy-tale paracosms, worlds in which nature in all its manifestations is voiced, vocal, and animated. The fish of the sea respond to catch and release by granting wishes; a stream warns that drinking its waters will transform you; and a trickster cat wins a kingdom for his master by telling tall tales. Partnerships and collaborations exist alongside predator/prey relationships marked by domination and submission.

The word "animal" contains within it an odd cultural contradiction. Although we define animals by their lack of a soul, we use a word derived from the Latin noun *anima*, meaning "soul, spirit, or breath," to refer to them. Artistotle's *De Anima* endowed all living creatures with a soul even as it created hierarchies by ranking them. Fairy-tale worlds tap into this kind of thinking and feed on it, creating universes in which living beings exist in a state of connected enmity or empathy. If Little Red Riding Hood frames the relationship between humans and beasts in terms of predators and prey, then Beauty and the Beast stories contrastingly tell us that, in a heartbeat, humans can become beasts and vice versa.

Therianthropy is the term used by folklorists to describe what happens in tales like "Beauty and the Beast." Derived from the Greek *therion*, meaning "beast," and *anthropos*, meaning "human being," the word captures both hybridity (humans who believe that they possess the soul of an animal) and shapeshifting (humans changed into animals). Lycanthropy, or the transformation of humans into wolves, is perhaps the most prominent form of therianthropy, but both feral and domestic forms of dogs and cats also figure frequently in the therianthropic imagination of cultures from the East and West. There are many variations on therianthropic beings: skin-walkers, for example—men and women who turn themselves into animals by putting on their pelts.

Pantheistic forces surge and ebb in the fairy-tale universe, animating rivers, rocks, and trees, but also endowing everything from bones and mirrors to birds and frogs with the power to sing and speak. Fairy-tale plots are fueled by magic and transformation, and they recruit those forces to animate a universe in which sudden shifts in the narrative circuits move us headlong from the sublime to the monstrous and back again. Much as wisdom and power are distributed democratically across the animal, vegetable, and mineral worlds, hierarchies remain and install the sovereign human subject as the heroic, redemptive force in the fairy-tale world.

Monsters, as Rosi Braidotti has pointed out, are inherently "epistemophilic."[8] In other words, they arouse our curiosity about origins and causes. "How could this happen?" we ask, when a talking muskrat comes courting or when a crane starts talking and decides to abandon her aquatic home to marry a mortal. Ruptures in the natural order of things are always charged with significance. But they do more than fascinate, for, despite the fact that they are *physically* other, they challenge us to explore the *moral* transgression from which the monstrous—a breaching of the laws of nature—seems to emerge. Teratology—the study of monsters—helps us understand who we are and how we define ourselves, by distancing ourselves from the pathologies we project onto difference. Monsters unsettle boundaries, reminding us that the distinctions we make between nature and culture, the human and the nonhuman, or reason and instinct are both fragile and fraught.

Monstrosity arouses curiosity, invites speculation, and has helped us shape moral landscapes, even as it remains a general placeholder for alterity, any and all deviations from dominant social norms. Representing more than otherness, monsters come to embody threats and dangers, tapping into our fears about invasion, contamination, and wholesale consumption. As one theologian points out, the Greek word for monster, *teras*, captures a paradox, designating something both repulsive and attractive. Monsters may be awful, but they also inspire awe, making us stare with enraptured attentiveness.

"Monsters are our children," Jeffrey Cohen tells us in a study about how the monsters we create invite us to meditate on the fragile and indeterminate boundaries we set up when it comes to race, gender, and sexuality.[9] We make the mistake of locating the origins of monsters in exotic regions and terrain, but they cohabit the world with us, as alter egos that capture all the anxieties we disown, disavow, and project onto creatures who are *different* from us. They challenge us to ask how we created them, as Cohen observes, and by following their cues, we can begin to discover in our projections exactly who we are and what makes us as ferocious, predatory, and cruel as the monsters out there.

THE MYTHICAL BACKGROUND: BRUTE APPETITES AND SOUL MATES

Fairy tales mix history, myth, and psychology to produce compelling narratives that get us talking and thinking about our values. While it is impossible to identify an Ur-narrative—a primal Beauty and the Beast story that laid the foundation for cultural variants—there are many early versions that are telling in their own way. Legends about animal deities and their sexual congress with humans can be found in ancient cultures the world over—Sumerian, Indian, Chinese, Egyptian, and Babylonian. The ancient sources best known to occidental cultures are the Greek myth of Zeus and Europa and the Roman tale of Cupid and Psyche, stories that frame encounters between gods and humans in very different ways. One is a narrative of abduction and sexual assault, despite the efforts of painters, poets, and philosophers over the centuries to capture the moment of "rapture" in it. The story of Zeus and Europa remains a rape, with a young virgin taken away from her companions by a bull, against her will. The other is a story about the union of Eros and Psyche, with allegorical figures for carnal desire and soulful yearning confidently forming a perfect union.

The Greek myth and the Roman tale both have a rich history of translation and transmission, in story, song, sculpture, painting, and other media. Zeus and Europa figured prominently in the imaginations of countless European artists, with painters ranging from Titian and Giordano to Noël-Nicolas Coypel and Gustave Moreau giving us scenes of erotic abandonment and oceanic ecstasy in paintings with "rape" and "abduction" in their titles. Few artists and even fewer viewers registered alarm at the mismatch between the revels on the canvases and the perils spelled out in their titles, as well as the story behind the painted scene. (Rembrandt is almost the exception to the rule in portraying a Europa whose features register trepidation rather than ecstasy as her white mount charges through the waters, tail raised high.)

The story of Zeus and Europa remained remarkably durable, migrating into books designed for children as well as adults. The Greek poet Moschus, living in the second century B.C., preserved the account in his poem *Europa*, which was retold for English-speaking audiences by Thomas Bulfinch in his popularization of Greek mythology published in 1855. Bulfinch's tightly ordered narrative remained the standard retelling of the myth in Anglophone cultures until Edith Hamilton published her *Mythology: Timeless Tales of Gods and Heroes* in 1942.

Given the shock value of a story that shows a young woman abducted by a bull in preparation for a sexual assault, it seems astonishing that the myth of Zeus and Europa found its way into literary channels that transmitted the tale to multigenerational audiences. Nathaniel Hawthorne somehow believed that he had created a child-friendly version for his *Tanglewood Tales* (1853), in which Europa, "a very beautiful child," encounters a bull described as "gentle, sweet, pretty, and amiable."[10] The tale is not entirely steeped in treacle, for the bull turns "treacherous" when it leaps into the waves and carries the girl off, leaving her three brothers to gaze at the "sad spectacle." It is perhaps our misplaced reverence for ancient Greece and its sacred myths that led Hawthorne and others to consider the story as "pure" as the children to whom it is told. Tales from a time described as "the pure childhood of the world" are perfectly suited—and this was an article of faith for Hawthorne—for young "auditors," marked by "childish purity." "The objectionable characteristics of the plot seem to be a parasitical growth, having no essential connection with the original fable," the folksy narrator insists in the introduction, as if the central events—abduction and rape—were not the backbone of the "original fable."

There may be pragmatic reasons for Zeus to conceal his identity (Hera has her spies, after all), but they seem a mere pretext for putting on display the spectacularly incongruous pairing of young woman and bull, a pairing that does more than border on the pornographic. How do we explain the powerful afterlife of a story this offensive? Why would artists come back to the story again and again, in a nearly desperate effort to re-create scenes of carnal and spiritual ecstasy from stories that in reality depict abduction and rape?

Human sexuality has at its core a basic conflict between tenderness, affection, and compassion on the one hand and violence, aggression, and rough-and-tumble play on the other. That the language of love so often draws its power from the language of combat and the hunt reveals exactly how divided we are when it comes to considering the operation of sexual desire. Discomfort with the cruder, animal-like aspects of human sexuality can easily lead to disavowal, with projections of the ferocity of assaults onto either gods or beasts and only rarely onto normal human subjects. In the story of Zeus and Europa, the divine and the beastly both become culprits, larger than life and twice as unnatural.

Quod licet Iovi, licet bovi. Perversely, in the arena of storytelling, beasts have the same license as gods to commit acts of atrocity. In projecting brute sexual force onto gods, centaurs, and beasts, the ancients in a sense also licensed its representation and enabled debate about its legitimacy or lawlessness. Verbal and visual depictions of erotic pursuit throw us into a hermeneutic crisis precisely because they invoke cultural anxieties about defining and maintaining the lines we draw between nature and culture, between brute beasts and caring humans. The mechanism of disavowal, combining denial and displacement, is a powerful manifestation of the rich mix of shame and desire about the beastly aspects of human sexuality. And, in some mysterious way, it also stimulates the storytelling instinct.

Passion can be a volatile and combustible emotion, consuming itself as quickly as it is ignited. Zeus, we recall, is not only a serial rapist, moving from Io to Europa to Leda, but also polymorphously perverse, abducting youngsters like Ganymede. Our modern-day tales about Beauties and Beasts do not do away with passion altogether, but, with their emphasis on an enduring happily ever after, they demonstrate that domestic partnerships have something going for them—the affection, stability, and longevity absent from the short-lived couplings of the mythic tales. Our versions of "Beauty and the Beast" reveal a cultural investment in privileging companionate pairings over passionate couplings that are made culturally acceptable by the divinities who participate in them.

Antecedents can be found in the ancients for the caring, compassionate union of soul mates. Back in the second century A.D., Lucius Apuleius included the tale of Cupid and Psyche in *The Golden Ass*. The story displays a distinct kinship with earlier myths about gods and mortals, with a hero who is the son of Venus paired with a woman so beautiful that she is not meant for ordinary men. Psyche, as obedient as she is beautiful, consents to follow the decree of the oracle and to marry a creature who may be a monster. Tempted by her sisters to turn disobedient, Psyche lights a lamp while her husband is asleep and discovers the true meaning of love at first sight. Cupid becomes as flighty as Zeus, and leaves his beloved on real wings, only to return when Psyche has completed a series of "impossible tasks" as a sign of her devotion. The two are married by Jupiter, who is tired of hearing tales about Cupid's "lechery and riot" and decides to put an end to his "intemperance" with the "bonds of matrimony."

Apuleius's fairy tale, told by a drunken and half-demented old woman, shows us the marriage of spiritual love (in Greek mythology, Psyche incarnates the human soul and is often portrayed as a butterfly) with physical passion (Cupid is the god of erotic love, born of the union of Venus and Mars, and it is no accident that he shoots arrows to inspire love). The rich irony of channeling our iconic story about the union of passion and spirituality through a crazed crone comforting a young woman abducted by vicious robbers powerfully reminds us of the gulf between fairy tale and real life. As important, it brings to mind the etymology of the German term for fairy tales. Märchen are misrepresentations, rumors, untruths connected to the practice of lying. Apuleius's "Cupid and Psyche" may be closer to our hearts and minds than the story of Zeus and Europa when we indulge in fantasies about romance and courtship, but, as Apuleius suggests in the tale's frame, it may be nothing but a set of beautiful lies designed to distract from horrifying realities. More likely, Apuleius, like all great storytellers, uses his art to give us a mix of beastliness and beauty, to show how they intersect, and how their collision compels us to think hard about the *human* condition. No wonder Einstein is reputed to have said that if you want intelligent children, read them fairy tales. And if you want more intelligent children, read them more fairy tales. These are the stories that challenge us to figure things out.

MACHINES, MONSTERS, AND CULTURAL ANXIETIES

"Beauty and the Beast" has become a kind of dense palimpsest of narratives, with so many layers that it becomes almost impossible to sort out the many different cultural stakes in the narrative. In the future, the Beast may take the form of an android or cyborg, machines that embody our anxieties and phobias about what the future holds for man-made devices. For now, our animal brides and animal grooms function as mediators between nature and culture, enabling us to think through our relationship to "otherness." They are "impossible" hybrid creatures that help us to negotiate that divide, to construct our own realities and identities through the dialectical interplay between the animal and human kingdoms. Stories featuring these creatures, often as charismatic as they are monstrous, take up matters both primal and mythical as well as domestic and down to earth. As humans, we have distanced ourselves from nature, set ourselves apart as a separate breed, and yet we are perpetually drawn to the wild side, searching for an understanding of what we share with beasts even as we try to discover what makes us human.

These days we have begun to recognize the downside to being at the top of the food chain. In a curious twist, anthropocentric ideologies have backfired to turn us into the monsters, with animals as our innocent victims. And the symbolic calculus has shifted in significant ways, as new technologies make it attractive to invest more cultural work in our relationship to androids, cyborgs, and other high-tech wonders. Still, our need to understand the "beauty and infinite complexity of the co-adaptations between all beings," as Darwin put it, is more than likely to keep replenishing the broad, deep, and capacious reservoir of stories about Beauties and Beasts.

MARIA TATAR

NOTES

1. Angela Carter, "About the Stories," in *Sleeping Beauty and Other Favourite Fairy Tales*, ed. Angela Carter (Boston: Otter Books, 1991), 128.

2. "East of the Sun and West of the Moon," in *The Blue Fairy Book*, ed. Andrew Lang (Harmondsworth: Penguin/Puffin Books, 1987), 2.

3. Camille Paglia, *Sexual Personae: Art and Decadence from Nefertiti to Emily Dickinson* (New York: Vintage, 1991), 3.

4. Barbara Fass Leavy, *In Search of the Swan Maiden: A Narrative on Folklore and Gender* (New York: New York University Press, 1994), 2.

5. www.endicott-studio.com/articleslist/married-to-magic-animal-brides-and-bridegrooms-in-folklore-and-fantasy-ii-by-terri-windling.html.

6. Jacques Derrida, "The Animal That Therefore I Am (More to Follow)," trans. David Wills, *Critical Inquiry* 28.2 (Winter 2002): 369–418.

7. The passage is cited, along with the Bible passage, by Laurie Shannon in "The Eight Animals in Shakespeare; or, Before the Human," *PMLA* 124:2 (March 2009): 472–79.

8. Rosi Braidotti, "Signs of Wonder and Traces of Doubt: On Teratology and Embodied Differences," in *Between Monsters, Goddesses and Cyborgs: Feminist Confrontations with Science,*

    Medicine, and Cyberspace, eds. N. Lykke and R. Braidotti (London: Zed Books, 1996), 135–52.

9. Jeffrey Jerome Cohen, "Monster Culture," in *Monster Theory: Reading Culture,* ed. Jeffrey Jerome Cohen (Minneapolis: University of Minnesota Press, 1996), 20.

10. Nathaniel Hawthorne, "The Wayside," introduction to *Tanglewood Tales* (Chicago: Rand McNally, 1913), 7–14.

Suggestions for Further Reading

Bacchilega, Cristina. *Postmodern Fairy Tales: Gender and Narrative Strategies*. Philadelphia: University of Pennsylvania Press, 1997.

———. *Fairy Tales Transformed? Twenty-First Century Adaptations and the Politics of Wonder*. Detroit: Wayne State University Press, 2013.

Baker, Ronald L. "Xenophobia in 'Beauty and the Beast' and Other Animal/Monster-Groom Tales." *Midwestern Folklore* 15 (1989): 74–80.

Barchilon, Jacques. "Beauty and the Beast." *Modern Language Review* 56 (1961): 81–82.

———. "Beauty and the Beast: From Myth to Fairy Tale." *Psychoanalysis and the Psychoanalytic Review* 46 (1959): 19–29.

Bettelheim, Bruno. *The Uses of Enchantment: The Meaning and Importance of Fairy Tales*. New York: Knopf, 1976.

Block, Francesca Lia. "Beast." In *The Rose and the Beast*. New York: HarperCollins, 2000, pp. 133–49.

Bottigheimer, Ruth B. "'Beauty and the Beast': Marriage and Money—Motif and Motivation." *Midwestern Folklore* 15 (1989): 79–88.

———. "Cupid and Psyche vs. Beauty and the Beast: The Milesian and the Modern." *Merveilles et Contes* 3 (1989): 4–14.

Bryant, Sylvia. "Re-Constructing Oedipus Through 'Beauty and the Beast.'" *Criticism* 31 (1989): 439–53.

Burton, Anthony. "Beauty and the Beast: A Critique of Psychoanalytic Approaches to the Fairy Tale." *Psychocultural Review* 2 (1978): 241–58.

Canepa, Nancy. *Out of the Woods: The Origins of the Literary Fairy Tale in Italy and France*. Detroit: Wayne State University Press, 1997.

Canham, Stephen. "What Manner of Beast? Illustrations of 'Beauty and the Beast.'" In *Image and Maker: An Annual Dedicated to the Consideration of Book Illustration,* edited by Harold Darling and Peter Neumeyer. La Jolla, Calif.: Green Tiger Press, 1984.

Carter, Angela. *The Bloody Chamber.* New York: Penguin, 1993.

Cashdan, Sheldon. *The Witch Must Die: How Fairy Tales Shape Our Lives.* New York: HarperCollins, 2000.

Cunningham, Michael. "Beasts." In *A Wild Swan and Other Tales.* New York: Farrar, Straus and Giroux, 2015, pp. 101–16.

Darnton, Robert. "Peasants Tell Tales: The Meaning of Mother Goose." In *The Great Cat Massacre and Other Episodes in French Cultural History.* New York: Basic Books, 1984.

Datlow, Ellen, and Terri Windling. *The Beastly Bride: Tales of the Animal People.* New York: Viking, 2010.

Davidson, Hilda Ellis, and Anna Chaudhri. *A Companion to the Fairy Tale.* Cambridge, U.K.: D. S. Brewer, 2003.

DeNitto, Dennis. "Jean Cocteau's *Beauty and the Beast.*" *American Imago* 33 (1976): 123–54.

Donoghue, Emma. "The Tale of the Rose." In *Kissing the Witch: Old Tales in New Skins.* New York: HarperCollins, 1997, pp. 27–37.

Edens, Cooper. *Beauty and the Beast.* San Diego, Calif.: Green Tiger Press, 1989.

Erb, Cynthia. "Another World or the World of an Other? The Space of Romance in Recent Versions of 'Beauty and the Beast.'" *Cinema Journal* 34 (1995): 50–70.

Estés, Clarissa Pinkola. *Women Who Run with the Wolves: Myths and Stories of the Wild Woman Archetype.* New York: Ballantine, 1992.

Fine, Gary Alan, and Julie Ford. "Magic Settings: The Reflection of Middle-Class Life in 'Beauty and the Beast.'" *Midwestern Folklore* 15 (1989): 89–100.

Frus, Phyllis, and Christy Williams, eds. *Beyond Adaptation: Essays on Radical Transformation of Original Works.* Jefferson, N.C.: McFarland, 2010.

Galef, David. "A Sense of Magic: Reality and Illusion in Cocteau's *Beauty and the Beast.*" *Literature-Film Quarterly* 12 (1984): 96–106.

Griswold, Jerry. *The Meanings of "Beauty and the Beast."* Peterborough, Ontario: Broadview Press, 2004.

Haase, Donald, ed. *The Reception of Grimms' Fairy Tales: Responses, Reactions, Revisions.* Detroit: Wayne State University Press, 1993.

———. *Fairy Tales and Feminism: New Approaches.* Detroit: Wayne State University Press, 2004.

————. *The Greenwood Encyclopedia of Folktales and Fairy Tales*. Westport, Conn.: Greenwood, 2007.

Hallet, Martin, and Barbara Karasek. *Fairy Tales in Popular Culture*. Peterborough, Ontario: Broadview Press, 2014.

Harries, Elizabeth Wanning. *Twice upon a Time: Women Writers and the History of the Fairy Tale*. Princeton, N.J.: Princeton University Press, 2001.

Hawkins, Harriet. "Maidens and Monsters in Modern Popular Culture: *The Silence of the Lambs* and *Beauty and the Beast*." *Textual Practice* 7 (1993): 258–66.

Hearne, Betsy. *Beauties and Beasts*. Phoenix, Ariz.: Oryx Press, 1993.

————. *Beauty and the Beast: Visions and Revisions of an Old Tale*. Chicago: University of Chicago Press, 1989.

Heinen, Eglal. "Male and Female Ugliness Through the Ages." *Merveilles et Contes* 3 (1989): 45–56.

Heiner, Heidi Anne. *Beauty and the Beast: Tales from Around the World*. N.p.: Surlalune Press, 2013.

Hood, Gwyneth. "Husbands and Gods as Shadowbrutes: 'Beauty and the Beast' from Apuleius to C. S. Lewis." *Mythlore* 15 (1988): 33–43.

Hopkinson, Neil, ed. *Theocritus, Moschus, Bion*. Cambridge, Mass.: Harvard University Press, 2015, pp. 455–65.

Jeffords, Susan. "The Curse of Masculinity: Disney's *Beauty and the Beast*." In *From Mouse to Mermaid: The Politics of Film, Gender, and Culture,* edited by Elizabeth Bell, Lynda Haas, and Laura Sells. Bloomington: Indiana University Press, 1995.

Joosen, Vanessa. *Critical and Creative Perspectives on Fairy Tales: An Intertextual Dialogue Between Fairy-Tale Scholarship and Postmodern Retellings*. Detroit: Wayne State University Press, 2011.

Leavy, Barbara Fass. *In Search of the Swan Maiden*. New York: New York University Press, 1994.

Lee, H. Chuku. *Beauty and the Beast*. New York: HarperCollins, 2014.

Lee, Tanith. *Red as Blood; or Tales from the Sisters Grimmer*. New York: DAW Books, 1983.

Lüthi, Max. *The European Folktale: Form and Nature,* translated by John D. Niles. Philadelphia: Institute for the Study of Human Issues, 1982.

McKinley, Robin. *Beauty: A Retelling of the Story of Beauty and the Beast*. New York: HarperCollins, 1978.

————. *Rose Daughter*. New York: Greenwillow Books, 1997.

Manley, Kathleen E. B. "Disney, the Beast, and Woman as Civilizing Force." In *The Emperor's Old Groove: Decolonizing Disney's Magic Kingdom*. New York: Peter Lang, 2003, pp. 79–89.

Murai, Mayako. *From Dog Bridegroom to Wolf Girl: Contemporary Japanese Fairy-Tale Adaptations in Conversation with the West.* Detroit: Wayne State University Press, 2015.

Pallottino, Paola. "Beauty's Beast." *Merveilles et Contes* 3 (1989): 57–74.

Pauly, Rebecca M. "Beauty and the Beast: From Fable to Film." *Literature-Film Quarterly* 17 (1989): 84–90.

Roche, Thomas. "Beauty and the Beast." In *Happily Ever After: Erotic Fairy Tales for Men*, edited by Michael Ford. New York: Masquerade Books, 1996.

Sax, Boria. *The Serpent and the Swan: The Animal Bride in Folklore and Literature.* Blacksburg, Va.: McDonald and Woodward Publishing, 1998.

Shell, Marc. "Beauty and the Beast." *Bestia: Yearbook of the Beast Fable Society* 1 (1989): 6–13.

Steptoe, John. *Mufaro's Beautiful Daughters.* New York: Lothrop, Lee and Shepard, 1987.

Swahn, Jan-Ojvind. "'Beauty and the Beast' in Oral Tradition." *Merveilles et Contes* 3 (1989): 15–27.

Swan, Susan Z. "Gothic Drama in Disney's *Beauty and the Beast*: Subverting Traditional Romance by Transcending the Animal-Human Paradox." *Critical Studies in Mass Communication* 16 (September 16, 1999): 350–69.

Tatar, Maria. *The Annotated Classic Fairy Tales.* New York: W. W. Norton, 2002.

———. *Off with Their Heads! Fairy Tales and the Culture of Childhood.* Princeton, N.J.: Princeton University Press, 1992.

Teverson, Andrew. *Fairy Tale.* London: Routledge, 2013.

Tiffin, Jessica. *Marvelous Geometry: Narrative and Metafiction in Modern Fairy Tale.* Detroit: Wayne State University Press, 2009.

Walker, Barbara. "Ugly and the Beast." In *Feminist Fairy Tales.* New York: HarperCollins, 1996, pp. 49–51.

Ward, Donald. "'Beauty and the Beast': Fact and Fancy: Past and Present." *Midwestern Folklore* 15 (1989): 119–25.

Warner, Marina. *From the Beast to the Blonde: On Fairy Tales and Their Tellers.* New York: Farrar, Straus and Giroux, 1994.

———. *Stranger Magic: Charmed States and the Arabian Nights.* Cambridge, Mass.: Harvard University Press, Belknap, 2012.

———. *Once Upon a Time: A Short History of Fairy Tale.* Oxford: Oxford University Press, 2014.

Wilson, Susan. *Beauty.* New York: Simon and Schuster, 1997.

Yep, Lawrence. *The Dragon Prince: A Chinese Beauty and the Beast.* New York: HarperCollins, 1997.

Zipes, Jack. *Beauties, Beasts and Enchantment: Classic Fairy Tales.* New York: New American Library, 1989.

———. *Beauty and the Beast and Other French Fairy Tales.* New York: Signet Classics, 1997.

———. *The Oxford Companion to Fairy Tales.* Oxford: Oxford University Press, 2000.

———. *The Enchanted Screen: The Unknown History of Fairy Tale Films.* New York: Routledge, 2011.

———. *The Irresistible Fairy Tale: The Cultural and Social History of a Genre.* Princeton, N.J.: Princeton University Press, 2012.

Acknowledgments

It began to rain Beauty and the Beast stories once I set out on the hunt for a "tale as old as time" (that's Mrs. Potts in Disney's film version of the fairy tale). The story has been with us for centuries, and this volume aims to help us understand exactly why. I am grateful to John Siciliano for encouraging a project that required thinking broadly about fairy tales and understanding their global reach. "Beauty and the Beast," as I quickly discovered, is a narrative far more complex, fractured, and contested than I had imagined, and it is a story that has been preserved precisely because its cultural authority is forever being challenged. My thanks also go to Emily Hartley at Penguin for guiding the book through the intricacies of the production process and making sure that I did not lose my way in the forest of fairy tales, folktales, and wonder tales collected by those with a stake in understanding the eccentric ways of the popular imagination. With lightning speed, Doris Sperber brought me books and tracked down sources, solved puzzles and decoded mysteries, all the while keeping track of errors in my many "final" drafts.

Beauty and the Beast

MODEL COUPLES
FROM ANCIENT
TIMES

ZEUS AND EUROPA

Ancient Greece

Edith Hamilton, born in Dresden, Germany, and educated at Bryn Mawr College, studied briefly in Munich before returning to the United States to become head of the Bryn Mawr School for Girls in Baltimore. Her book Mythology *was published when she was in her seventies and remains the premier introductory text on the subject. Hamilton tried to capture the multiple voices behind each of the stories she retold. The source material for Hamilton's retelling of the story of Zeus and Europa can be found in Neil Hopkinson's* Theocritus, Moschus, Bion. *Moschus was a Greek poet who lived in Syracuse in the second century B.C. The poem about Zeus and Europa is one of his few surviving works.*

Io was not the only girl who gained geographical fame because Zeus fell in love with her. There was another, known far more widely—Europa, the daughter of the King of Sidon. But whereas the wretched Io had to pay dearly for the distinction, Europa was exceedingly fortunate. Except for a few moments of terror when she found herself crossing the deep sea on the back of a bull she did not suffer at all. The story does not say what Hera was about at the time, but it is clear that she was off guard and her husband free to do as he pleased.

Up in heaven one spring morning as he idly watched the earth, Zeus suddenly saw a charming spectacle. Europa had waked early, troubled just as Io had been by a dream, only this time not of a god who loved her but of two Continents who each in the shape of a woman tried to possess her, Asia saying that she had given her birth and therefore owned her, and the other, as yet nameless, declaring that Zeus would give the maiden to her.

Once awake from this strange vision which had come at dawn, the time when true dreams oftenest visit mortals, Europa decided not to try to go to sleep again, but to summon her companions, girls born in the same year as herself and all of noble birth, to go out with her to the lovely blooming meadows near the sea. Here was their favorite meeting place, whether they wanted to dance or bathe their fair bodies at the river mouth or gather flowers.

This time all had brought baskets, knowing that the flowers were now at their perfection. Europa's was of gold, exquisitely chased with figures which showed, oddly enough, the story of Io, her journeys in the shape of a cow, the death of Argus, and Zeus lightly touching her with his divine hand and changing her back into a woman. It was, as may be perceived, a marvel worth gazing upon, and had been made by no less a personage than Hephaestus, the celestial workman of Olympus.

Lovely as the basket was, there were flowers as lovely to fill it with, sweet-smelling narcissus and hyacinths and violets and yellow crocus, and most radiant of all, the crimson splendor of the wild rose. The girls gathered them delightedly, wandering here and there over the meadow, each one a maiden fairest among the fair; yet even so, Europa shone out among them as the Goddess of Love outshines the sister Graces. And it was that very Goddess of Love who brought about what next happened. As Zeus in heaven watched the pretty scene, she who alone can conquer Zeus—along with her son, the mischievous boy Cupid— shot one of her shafts into his heart, and that very instant he fell madly in love with Europa. Even though Hera was away, he thought it well to be cautious, and before appearing to Europa he changed himself into a bull. Not such a one as you might see in a stall or grazing in a field, but one beautiful beyond all bulls that ever were, bright chestnut in color, with a silver circle on his brow and horns like the crescent of the young moon. He seemed so gentle as well as so lovely that the girls were not frightened at his coming, but gathered around to caress him and to breathe the heavenly fragrance that came from him, sweeter even than that of the flowery meadow. It was Europa he drew toward, and as she gently touched him, he lowed so musically, no flute could give forth a more melodious sound.

Then he lay down before her feet and seemed to show her his broad back, and she cried to the others to come with her and mount him.

> For surely he will bear us on his back,
> He is so mild and dear and gentle to behold.
> He is not like a bull, but like a good, true man,
> Except he cannot speak.

Smiling she sat down on his back, but the others, quick though they were to follow her, had no chance. The bull leaped up and at full speed rushed to the seashore and then not into, but over, the wide water. As he went the waves grew smooth before him and a whole procession rose up from the deep and accompanied him—the strange sea-gods, Nereids riding upon dolphins, and Tritons blowing their horns, and the mighty Master of the Sea himself, Zeus's own brother.

Europa, frightened equally by the wondrous creatures she saw and the moving waters all around, clung with one hand to the bull's great horn and with the other caught up her purple dress to keep it dry, and the winds

> Swelled out the deep folds even as a sail
> Swells on a ship, and ever gently thus
> They wafted her.

No bull could this be, thought Europa, but most certainly a god; and she spoke pleadingly to him, begging him to pity her and not leave her in some strange place all alone. He spoke to her in answer and showed her she had guessed rightly what he was. She had no cause to fear, he told her. He was Zeus, greatest of gods, and all he was doing was from love of her. He was taking her to Crete, his own island, where his mother had hidden him from Cronus when he was born, and there she would bear him

> Glorious sons whose sceptres shall hold sway
> Over all men on earth.

Everything happened, of course, as Zeus had said. Crete came into sight; they landed, and the Seasons, the gatekeepers of Olympus, arrayed her for her bridal. Her sons were famous men, not only in this world but in the next—where two of them, Minos and Rhadamanthus, were rewarded for their justice upon the earth by being made the judges of the dead. But her own name remains the best known of all.

CUPID AND PSYCHE

Ancient Rome

This version of "Cupid and Psyche" comes from Bulfinch's Greek and Roman Mythology. *Its author, Thomas Bulfinch, declared his purpose to be an "attempt to popularize mythology, and extend the enjoyment of elegant literature," as well as to "teach mythology not as a study, but as a relaxation from study." He wanted to give his work the "charm of a story-book, yet by means of it to impart a knowledge of an important branch of education." Bulfinch was born in Newton, Massachusetts, the son of the architect who built the Massachusetts State House and parts of the U.S. Capitol in Washington, D.C.*

A certain king and queen had three daughters. The charms of the two elder were more than common, but the beauty of the youngest was so wonderful that the poverty of language is unable to express its due praise. The fame of her beauty was so great that strangers from neighboring countries came in crowds to enjoy the sight, and looked on her with amazement, paying her that homage which is due only to Venus herself. In fact Venus found her altars deserted, while men turned their devotion to this young virgin. As she passed along, the people sang her praises, and strewed her way with chaplets and flowers.

This perversion of homage due only to the immortal powers to the exaltation of a mortal gave great offence to the real Venus. Shaking her ambrosial locks with indignation, she exclaimed, "Am I then to be eclipsed in my honors by a mortal girl? In vain then did that royal shepherd, whose judgment was approved by Jove himself, give me the palm of beauty over my illustrious rivals, Pallas and Juno. But she shall not so quietly usurp my honors. I will give her cause to repent of so unlawful a beauty."

Thereupon she calls her winged son Cupid, mischievous enough in his own nature, and rouses and provokes him yet more by her complaints. She points out Psyche to him and says, "My dear son, punish that contumacious beauty; give thy mother a revenge as sweet as her injuries are great; infuse into the bosom of that haughty girl a passion for some low, mean, unworthy being, so that she may reap a mortification as great as her present exultation and triumph."

Cupid prepared to obey the commands of his mother. There are two fountains in Venus's garden, one of sweet waters, the other of bitter. Cupid filled two amber vases, one from each fountain, and suspending them from the top of his quiver, hastened to the chamber of Psyche, whom he found asleep. He shed a few drops from the bitter fountain over her lips, though the sight of her almost moved him to pity; then touched her side with the point of his arrow. At the touch she awoke, and opened eyes upon Cupid (himself invisible), which so startled him that in his confusion he wounded himself with his own arrow. Heedless of his wound, his whole thought now was to repair the mischief he had done, and he poured the balmy drops of joy over all her silken ringlets.

Psyche, henceforth frowned upon by Venus, derived no benefit from all her charms. True, all eyes were cast eagerly upon her, and every mouth spoke her praises; but neither king, royal youth, nor plebeian presented himself to demand her in marriage. Her two elder sisters of moderate charms had now long been married to two royal princes; but Psyche, in her lonely apartment, deplored her solitude, sick of that beauty which, while it procured abundance of flattery, had failed to awaken love.

Her parents, afraid that they had unwittingly incurred the anger of the gods, consulted the oracle of Apollo, and received this answer: "The virgin is destined for the bride of no mortal lover. Her future husband awaits her on the top of the mountain. He is a monster whom neither gods nor men can resist."

This dreadful decree of the oracle filled all the people with dismay, and her parents abandoned themselves to grief. But

Psyche said, "Why, my dear parents, do you now lament me? You should rather have grieved when the people showered upon me undeserved honors, and with one voice called me a Venus. I now perceive that I am a victim to that name. I submit. Lead me to that rock to which my unhappy fate has destined me." Accordingly, all things being prepared, the royal maid took her place in the procession, which more resembled a funeral than a nuptial pomp, and with her parents, amid the lamentations of the people, ascended the mountain, on the summit of which they left her alone, and with sorrowful hearts returned home.

While Psyche stood on the ridge of the mountain, panting with fear and with eyes full of tears, the gentle Zephyr raised her from the earth and bore her with an easy motion into a flowery dale. By degrees her mind became composed, and she laid herself down on the grassy bank to sleep. When she awoke refreshed with sleep, she looked round and beheld nearby a pleasant grove of tall and stately trees. She entered it, and in the midst discovered a fountain, sending forth clear and crystal waters, and fast by, a magnificent palace whose august front impressed the spectator that it was not the work of mortal hands, but the happy retreat of some god. Drawn by admiration and wonder, she approached the building and ventured to enter. Every object she met filled her with pleasure and amazement. Golden pillars supported the vaulted roof, and the walls were enriched with carvings and paintings representing beasts of the chase and rural scenes, adapted to delight the eye of the beholder. Proceeding onward, she perceived that besides the apartments of state there were others filled with all manner of treasures, and beautiful and precious productions of nature and art.

While her eyes were thus occupied, a voice addressed her, though she saw no one, uttering these words: "Sovereign lady, all that you see is yours. We whose voices you hear are your servants and shall obey all your commands with our utmost care and diligence. Retire, therefore, to your chamber and repose on your bed of down, and when you see fit repair to the bath. Supper awaits you in the adjoining alcove when it pleases you to take your seat there."

Psyche gave ear to the admonitions of her vocal attendants, and after repose and the refreshment of the bath, seated herself in the alcove, where a table immediately presented itself, without any visible aid from waiters or servants, and covered with the greatest delicacies of food and the utmost nectareous wines. Her ears too were feasted with music from invisible performers; of whom one sang, another played on the lute, and all closed in the wonderful harmony of a full chorus.

She had not yet seen her destined husband. He came only in the hours of darkness and fled before the dawn of morning, but his accents were full of love, and inspired a like passion in her. She often begged him to stay and let her behold him, but he would not consent. On the contrary he charged her to make no attempt to see him, for it was his pleasure, for the best of reasons, to keep concealed. "Why should you wish to behold me?" he said; "have you any doubt of my love? have you any wish ungratified? If you saw me, perhaps you would fear me, perhaps adore me, but all I ask of you is to love me. I would rather you would love me as an equal than adore me as a god."

This reasoning somewhat quieted Psyche for a time, and while the novelty lasted she felt quite happy. But at length the thought of her parents, left in ignorance of her fate, and of her sisters, precluded from sharing with her the delights of her situation, preyed on her mind and made her begin to feel her palace as but a splendid prison. When her husband came one night, she told him her distress, and at last drew from him an unwilling consent that her sisters should be brought to see her.

So, calling Zephyr, she acquainted him with her husband's commands, and he, promptly obedient, soon brought them across the mountain down to their sister's valley. They embraced her and she returned their caresses. "Come," said Psyche, "enter with me my house and refresh yourselves with whatever your sister has to offer." Then taking their hands she led them into her golden palace, and committed them to the care of her numerous train of attendant voices, to refresh them in her baths and at her table, and to show them all her treasures. The view of these celestial delights caused envy to enter their bosoms, at seeing their young sister possessed of such state and splendor, so much exceeding their own.

They asked her numberless questions, among others what sort of a person her husband was. Psyche replied that he was a beautiful youth, who generally spent the daytime in hunting upon the mountains. The sisters, not satisfied with this reply, soon made her confess that she had never seen him. Then they proceeded to fill her bosom with dark suspicions. "Call to mind," they said, "the Pythian oracle that declared you destined to marry a direful and tremendous monster. The inhabitants of this valley say that your husband is a terrible and monstrous serpent, who nourishes you for a while with dainties that he may by and by devour you. Take our advice. Provide yourself with a lamp and a sharp knife; put them in concealment that your husband may not discover them, and when he is sound asleep, slip out of bed, bring forth your lamp, and see for yourself whether what they say is true or not. If it is, hesitate not to cut off the monster's head, and thereby recover your liberty."

Psyche resisted these persuasions as well as she could, but they did not fail to have their effect on her mind, and when her sisters were gone, their words and her own curiosity were too strong for her to resist. So she prepared her lamp and a sharp knife, and hid them out of sight of her husband. When he had fallen into his first sleep, she silently rose and uncovering her lamp beheld not a hideous monster, but the most beautiful and charming of the gods, with his golden ringlets wandering over his snowy neck and crimson cheek, with two dewy wings on his shoulders, whiter than snow, and with shining feathers like the tender blossoms of spring. As she leaned the lamp over to have a nearer view of his face a drop of burning oil fell on the shoulder of the god, startled with which he opened his eyes and fixed them full upon her; then, without saying one word, he spread his white wings and flew out of the window. Psyche, in vain endeavoring to follow him, fell from the window to the ground. Cupid, beholding her as she lay in the dust, stopped his flight for an instant and said, "O foolish Psyche, is it thus you repay my love? After having disobeyed my mother's commands and made you my wife, will you think me a monster and cut off my head? But go; return to your sisters, whose advice you seem to think preferable to mine. I inflict no other punishment on you than to leave you for ever. Love cannot dwell with suspicion." So saying, he fled away, leaving poor Psyche prostrate on the ground, filling the place with mournful lamentations.

When she had recovered some degree of composure she looked around her, but the palace and gardens had vanished, and she found herself in the open field not far from the city where her sisters dwelt. She repaired thither and told them the whole story of her misfortunes, at which, pretending to grieve, those spiteful creatures inwardly rejoiced. "For now," said they, "he will perhaps choose one of us." With this idea, without saying a word of her intentions, each of them rose early the next morning and ascended the mountain, and having reached the top, called upon Zephyr to receive her and bear her to his lord; then leaping up, and not being sustained by Zephyr, fell down the precipice and was dashed to pieces.

Psyche meanwhile wandered day and night, without food or repose, in search of her husband. Casting her eyes on a lofty mountain having on its brow a magnificent temple, she sighed and said to herself, "Perhaps my love, my lord, inhabits there," and directed her steps thither.

She had no sooner entered than she saw heaps of corn, some in loose ears and some in sheaves, with mingled ears of barley. Scattered about, lay sickles and rakes, and all the instruments of harvest without order, as if thrown carelessly out of the weary reapers' hands in the sultry hours of the day.

This unseemly confusion the pious Psyche put an end to, by separating and sorting everything to its proper place and kind, believing that she ought to neglect none of the gods, but endeavour by her piety to engage them all in her behalf. The holy Ceres, whose temple it was, finding her so religiously employed, thus spoke to her: "O Psyche, truly worthy of our pity, though I cannot shield you from the frowns of Venus, yet I can teach you how best to allay her displeasure. Go, then, and voluntarily surrender yourself to your lady and sovereign, and try by modesty and submission to win her forgiveness, and perhaps her favor will restore you the husband you have lost."

Psyche obeyed the commands of Ceres and took her way to the temple of Venus, endeavoring to fortify her mind and ruminating on what she should say and how best propitiate the angry goddess, feeling that the issue was doubtful and perhaps fatal.

Venus received her with angry countenance. "Most undutiful and faithless of servants," said she, "do you at last remember that you really have a mistress? Or have you rather come to see your sick husband, yet laid up of the wound given him by his loving wife? You are so ill-favored and disagreeable that the only way you can merit your lover must be by dint of industry and diligence. I will make trial of your housewifery." Then she ordered Psyche to be led to the storehouse of her temple, where was laid up a great quantity of wheat, barley, millet, vetches, beans, and lentils prepared for food for her pigeons, and said, "Take and separate all these grains, putting all of the same kind in a parcel by themselves, and see that you get it done before evening." Then Venus departed and left her to her task.

But Psyche, in a perfect consternation at the enormous work, sat stupid and silent, without moving a finger to the inextricable heap.

While she sat despairing, Cupid stirred up the little ant, a native of the fields, to take compassion on her. The leader of the ant-hill, followed by whole hosts of his six-legged subjects, approached the heap, and with the utmost diligence taking grain by grain, they separated the pile, sorting each kind to its parcel; and, when it was all done, they vanished out of sight in a moment.

Venus at the approach of twilight returned from the banquet of the gods, breathing odors and crowned with roses. Seeing the task done, she exclaimed, "This is no work of yours, wicked one, but his, whom to your own and his misfortune you have enticed." So saying, she threw her a piece of black bread for her supper and went away.

Next morning Venus ordered Psyche to be called and said to her, "Behold yonder grove which stretches along the margin of the water. There you will find sheep feeding without a shepherd, with golden-shining fleeces on their backs. So, fetch me a sample of that precious wool gathered from every one of their fleeces."

Psyche obediently went to the riverside, prepared to do her best to execute the command. But the river god inspired the reeds' harmonious murmurs, which seemed to say, "O maiden, severely tried, tempt not the dangerous flood, nor venture among the formidable rams on the other side, for as long as they are under the influence of the rising sun, they burn with a cruel rage to destroy mortals with their sharp horns or rude teeth. But when the noontide sun has driven the cattle to the shade, and the serene spirit of the flood has lulled them to rest, you may then cross in safety, and you will find the woolly gold sticking to the bushes and the trunks of the trees."

Thus the compassionate river god gave Psyche instructions how to accomplish her task, and by observing his directions she soon returned to Venus with her arms full of the golden fleece; but she received not the approbation of her implacable mistress, who said, "I know very well it is by none of your own doings that you have succeeded in this task, and I am not satisfied yet that you have any capacity to make yourself useful. But I have another task for you. Here, take this box and go your way to the infernal shades, and give this box to Proserpine and say, 'My mistress Venus desires you to send her a little of your beauty, for in tending her sick son she has lost some of her own.' Be not too long on your errand, for I must paint myself with it to appear at the circle of the gods and goddesses this evening."

Psyche was now satisfied that her destruction was at hand, being obliged to go with her own feet directly down to Erebus. Wherefore, to make no delay of what was not to be avoided, she goes to the top of a high tower to precipitate herself headlong, thus to descend the shortest way to the shades below. But a voice from the tower said to her, "Why, poor unlucky girl, dost thou design to put an end to thy days in so dreadful a manner? and what cowardice makes thee sink under this last danger who hast been so miraculously supported in all thy former?" Then the voice told her how by a certain cave she might reach the realms of Pluto, and how to avoid all the dangers of the road, to pass by Cerberus, the three-headed dog, and prevail on Charon, the ferryman, to take her across the black river and bring her back again. But the voice added, "When Proserpine has given you the box filled with her beauty, of all things this is chiefly to be observed by you, that you never once open or look into the box nor allow your curiosity to pry into the treasure of the beauty of the goddesses."

Psyche, encouraged by this advice, obeyed it in all things, and taking heed to her ways traveled safely to the kingdom of Pluto. She was admitted to the palace of Proserpine, and without accepting the delicate seat or delicious banquet that was offered her, but contented with coarse bread for her food, she delivered her message from Venus. Presently the box was returned to her, shut and filled with the precious commodity. Then she returned the way she came, and glad was she to come out once more into the light of day.

But having got so far successfully through her dangerous task a longing desire seized her to examine the contents of the box. "What," said she, "shall I, the carrier of this divine beauty, not take the least bit to put on my cheeks to appear to more advantage in the eyes of my beloved husband!" So she carefully opened the box, but found nothing there of any beauty at all, but an infernal and truly Stygian sleep, which being thus set free from its prison, took possession of her, and she fell down in the midst of the road, a sleepy corpse without sense or motion.

But Cupid, being now recovered from his wound, and not able longer to bear the absence of his beloved Psyche, slipping through the smallest crack of the window of his chamber which happened to be left open, flew to the spot where Psyche lay, and gathering up the sleep from her body closed it again in the box, and waked Psyche with a light touch of one of his arrows. "Again," said he, "hast thou almost perished by the same curiosity. But now perform exactly the task imposed on you by my mother, and I will take care of the rest."

Then Cupid, as swift as lightning penetrating the heights of heaven, presented himself before Jupiter with his supplication. Jupiter lent a favoring ear, and pleaded the cause of the lovers so earnestly with Venus that he won her consent. On this he sent Mercury to bring Psyche up to the heavenly assembly, and when she arrived, handing her a cup of ambrosia, he said, "Drink this, Psyche, and be immortal; nor shall Cupid ever break away from the knot in which he is tied, but these nuptials shall be perpetual."

Thus Psyche became at last united to Cupid, and in due time they had a daughter born to them whose name was Pleasure.

For full translations of the story of Cupid and Psyche and its frame tale in Apuleius's The Golden Ass; or The Transformations of Lucius, *published in the second century* B.C., *see the following:*

Apuleius. *The Golden Ass*, translated by Jack Lindsay. Bloomington: Indiana University Press, 1932.

Apuleius. *The Transformations of Lucius, Otherwise Known as The Golden Ass,* translated by Robert Graves. New York: Farrar, Straus and Giroux, 1951.

Neumann, Erich. *Amor and Psyche: The Psychic Development of the Feminine,* translated by Ralph Manheim. New York: Bollingen Series LIV, Princeton University Press, 1956, pp. 3–53.

THE GIRL WHO
MARRIED A SNAKE

India

This story comes from the Panchatantra, *a set of five books of animal fables in verse and prose contained within a frame narrative. Compiled between the fourth and sixth centuries A.D., the stories were attributed to a wise man named Bidpai, a Sanskrit term for "court scholar." Boys of royal blood were the implied audience, and the stories were intended to teach them how to conduct exemplary lives. By the twentieth century, the* Panchatantra *had been translated into more than fifty languages. It reached Europe as early as the eleventh century, finding its way through Persian, Greek, Latin, and Arabic translations, and through oral channels of transmission.*

In the city of Rajagrha there lived a Brahmin named Deva Sarma. His wife, who had no children, wept bitter tears whenever she saw the children of her neighbors. One day the Brahmin tried to comfort her by telling her, "Dearest of wives! You can stop grieving at last. Just imagine, while I was making a sacrifice so that we would have a child, I heard an invisible being say to me in the clearest language, 'Brahmin, you shall have a son more handsome and virtuous than any other man, and good fortune will be his lot.'"

When she heard those words, the Brahmin's wife was overjoyed, and she said, "May those exhilarating words come true." Before long, the woman became pregnant and gave birth to—a snake. When her attendants, one and all, saw the snake, they advised her to toss it away, but she paid no attention to them and instead picked him up affectionately, bathed him, and made a home for him in a large, clean chest, where she fed him milk, butter, and all kinds of fine foods. In no time at all, the snake had grown to a mature state.

Once while the Brahmin's wife was attending the marriage festivities of a neighbor's son, tears began to stream down her face, and she turned to her husband and said, "You are showing nothing but contempt for me with your refusal to try to arrange a wedding for my darling boy!"

The Brahmin replied with these words, "Oh, noble wife! Do you really expect me to travel down into the depths of the underworld to ask Vasuki, King of the Serpents, for the hand of his daughter? Who else, oh, foolish woman, do you think would be eager to offer his beloved daughter to a snake?"

When he finished speaking, he realized that his wife looked utterly despondent. Because he loved her and wanted to make her feel better, he packed up some provisions and left on a long journey. After traveling for some time in distant lands, he reached a place known as the City of Warbling Birds. There, just as night was falling, he found shelter at the home of an acquaintance, a man with whom he had a respectful and affectionate relationship. At his home, he was given a bath, food, and everything he needed to restore himself for the night.

The next morning he was about to depart after thanking his host, when his host asked, "What brought you to this place, and where are you going now?"

The Brahmin replied, "I left my home to search for a woman who would make a suitable bride for my son."

After hearing these words, his host said, "If that is the case, then I have a very beautiful daughter, and I am yours to command. Accept my daughter as your son's bride!"

The Brahmin did not need to be asked twice, and he took the girl, who was accompanied by her retinue, back home with him. When the townspeople saw the girl and how beautiful, gifted, and charming she was, they opened their eyes wide with astonishment and said to her entourage, "How could anyone with any dignity at all deliver this priceless jewel of a young woman to a snake?"

After hearing those words, the girl's kinfolk, their hearts heavy with anxiety, began to whisper, "Let this girl be taken far away from a boy who seems possessed by some evil spirit." But the girl put an end to their chatter and said, "Enough! Stop that kind of talk and pay attention to the words of the verse:

> A monarch speaks just once;
> The wise and holy speak just once;
> A maid is promised in marriage just once:
> These three things are done once and once alone.

"And besides:

> An act is paired with its inevitable end,
> What is predicted must occur;
> Nothing can change that; even the gods
> Have no way of altering poor Little Blossom's fate. . . ."

Having spoken those words and told a tale about Little Blossom, she secured the permission of her attendants and married the snake. She showed him proper respect and waited on him with devotion, serving him milk to drink and performing other tasks.

One night the snake left the large chest where he slept and climbed into his wife's bed. She cried out, "Who is this creature in the form of a man?" Thinking it must be some stranger, she jumped up and, trembling in every limb, tore open the door and was about to dash off when the snake said, "Stay here, gracious lady! I am your husband." To convince her, he reentered the snakeskin he had shed and then left it again to return to his human state. He was wearing a magnificent diadem, gleaming earrings, flashing armlets, and beautiful rings. His wife fell at his feet. They embraced and the two of them experienced the raptures of love.

The Brahmin, who had woken up before his son, saw how

matters stood. He took the snakeskin out of the chest and threw it into the fire, saying, "He shall never enter it again." Later that morning, the Brahmin and his wife, their hearts bursting with joy, introduced their lovestruck young man and his beautiful bride to everyone there. It was all marvelous beyond what anyone could imagine.

HASAN OF BASRA

Iran

The tangled skein that makes up The Thousand and One
Nights *and the history of its translations into English means
that it is daunting to identify a standard version for any one
particular story. A polyvocal anthology, the* Nights *is a treasure
trove of tales put together from Persian fables, the culture of
medieval Baghdad, fairy tales from Egypt in the Mameluke
period, and other sources. The story of Hasan of Basra has been
reshaped by many translators and transmitters, most recently by
Marina Warner in her volume* Stranger Magic. *Warner retells
the story for us, turning its extravagant, overwrought style and
vertiginous lyrical outbursts into more accessible prose. As a
forerunner of the Swan Maiden story in Occidental cultures,
"Hasan of Basra" reminds us that the ocean of stories is vast
and deep, and that motifs, tropes, and memes that seem quint-
essentially "European" are in fact part of a vast global network.
The lengthy, convoluted narrative is summarized in what
follows by Edwin Sidney Hartland, a British folklorist who
wrote about the Swan Maiden story and its international
cognates back in 1891.*

Hasan is a worthless boy who falls under the influence of a
Magian, who professes to be an alchemist, and who at length
kidnaps him. Having used him with great cruelty the Magian
takes him fifteen days' journey on dromedaries into the desert
to a high mountain, at the foot whereof the old rascal sews him
up in a skin, together with a knife and a small provision of
three cakes and a leathern bottle of water, afterward retiring

to a distance. One of the vultures which infest the mountain then pounces on Hasan and carries him to the top. In accordance with the Magian's instructions, the hero, on arriving there, slits the skin, and jumping out, to the bird's affright, picks up and casts down to the Magian bundles of the wood which he finds around him. This wood is the means by which the alchemy is performed; and having gathered up the bundles the Magian leaves Hasan to his fate. The youth, after despairing of life, finds his way to a palace where dwell seven maidens, with whom he remains for awhile in Platonic friendship. When they are summoned away by their father for a two months' absence, they leave him their keys, straitly charging him not to open a certain door. He disregards their wishes, and finds within a magnificent pavilion enclosing a basin brimful of water, at which ten birds come to bathe and play. The birds for this purpose cast their feathers; and Hasan is favored with the sight of "ten virgins, maids whose beauty shamed the brilliancy of the moon." He fell madly in love with the chief damsel, who turns out to be a daughter of a King of the Jinn. On the return of the maidens of the palace he is advised by them to watch the next time the birds come, and to take possession of the feather-suit belonging to the damsel of his choice, for without this she cannot return home with her attendants. He succeeds in doing so, and thus compels her to remain with him and become his wife. With her he departs to his own country and settles in Baghdad, where his wife bears him two sons. During his temporary absence, however, she persuades her mother-in-law—who, unfortunately for the happiness of the household, lives with the young couple—to let her have the feather-suit which her husband has left under her charge. Clad with this she takes her two boys in her arms and sails away through the air to the islands of Wák, leaving a message for the hapless Hasan that if he loves her he may come and seek her there. Now the islands of Wák were seven islands, wherein was a mighty host, all virgin girls, and the inner isles were peopled by satans and marids and warlocks and various tribesmen of the Jinn, and whosoever entered their land never returned thence; and Hasan's wife was one of the king's daughters. To reach her he would have to cross seven wadys and seven seas and seven mighty mountains. Undaunted, however, by the difficulties wherewith he is threatened, he determines to find her, swearing by Allah never to turn back till he regain his beloved, or till death overtake him. By the help of sundry potentates of more or less forbidding aspect and supernatural power, to whom he gets letters of introduction, and who live in gorgeous palaces amid deserts, and are served by demons only uglier and less mighty than themselves, he succeeds in traversing the Land of Birds, the Land of Wild Beasts, the country of the Warlocks and the Enchanters, and the Land of the Jinn, and enters the islands of Wák—there to fall into the hands of that masterful virago, his wife's eldest sister. After a preliminary outburst against Hasan, this amiable creature pours, as is the wont of women, the full torrent of her wrath against her erring sister. From the tortures she inflicts, Hasan at length rescues his wife, with their two sons, by means of a cap of invisibility and a rod conferring authority over seven tribes of the Jinn, which he has stolen from two boys who are quarrelling over them. When his sister-in-law with an army of Jinn pursues the fugitives, the subjects of the rod overcome her. His wife begs for her sister's life and reconciles her husband to her, and then returns with her husband to his home in Baghdad, to quit him no more.

CHARISMATIC
COUPLES IN
THE POPULAR
IMAGINATION

BEAUTY AND THE BEAST

France

With one swift literary stroke, an entire oral storytelling culture, with its investment in grotesque, ribald humor and surges of violence, goes down for the count when Madame de Beaumont publishes her Beauty and the Beast tale about a marriage "founded on virtue." Inspired by Madame Gabrielle-Suzanne de Villeneuve's novel-length story of Beauty and the Beast, Madame de Beaumont's more compact narrative came to dominate the literary landscape even as it shifted the audience for the story from adults to the young.

Once upon a time there was a very wealthy merchant who lived with his six children, three boys and three girls. Since he was a man of intelligence and good sense, he spared no expense in educating his children and hiring all kinds of tutors for them. His daughters were very beautiful, but everyone admired the youngest more than the others. When she was little, people used to refer to her as "the beautiful child." The name "Beauty" stuck, and, as a result, her two sisters were always very jealous. The youngest daughter was not only more beautiful than her sisters but also better behaved. The two older sisters were vain and proud because the family had money. They tried to act like ladies of the court and paid no attention at all to girls from merchant families. They chose to spend time only with people of rank. Every day they went to balls, to the theater, to the park, and they made fun of their younger sister, who spent most of her time reading good books.

Since the girls were known to be very wealthy, many prominent merchants were interested in marrying them. But the two older sisters always insisted that they would never marry unless they found a duke or, at the very least, a count. Beauty (as noted, this was the name of the youngest daughter) very politely thanked all those who proposed to her, but she told them that she was still too young for marriage and that she planned to keep her father company for some years to come.

Out of the blue, the merchant lost his fortune, and he had nothing left but a small country house quite far from town. With tears in his eyes, he told his children that they would have to live in that house from now on and that, by working there like peasants, they could manage to make ends meet. The two elder daughters said that they did not want to leave town and that they had many admirers who would be more than happy to marry them, even though they no longer had money. But the fine young ladies were wrong. Their admirers lost all interest in them now that they were poor. And since they were disliked because of their pride, people said: "Those two girls don't deserve our sympathy. It's quite satisfying to see pride take a fall. Let them play the ladies while tending their sheep."

At the same time, people were saying: "As for Beauty, we are very upset by her misfortune. She's such a good girl! She speaks so kindly to the poor. She's so sweet and sincere."

There were a number of gentlemen who would have been happy to marry Beauty, even though she didn't have a penny. She told them that she could not bring herself to abandon her poor father in his distress and that she was planning to go with him to the country in order to comfort him and help him with his work. Poor Beauty had been upset at first by the loss of the family fortune, but she said to herself: "No matter how much I cry, my tears won't bring our fortune back. I must try to be happy without it."

When they arrived at the country house, the merchant and his three sons began working the land. Beauty got up every day at four in the morning and started cleaning the house and preparing breakfast for everyone. It was hard for her at first, because she was not used to working like a servant. At the end of two months, however, she became stronger, and the hard work made her very healthy. After finishing her housework, she would read for a while or sing while spinning. Her two sisters, by contrast, were bored to tears. They got up at ten in the morning, took walks all day long, and talked endlessly about the beautiful clothes they had once worn.

"Look at our sister," they said to each other. "She is so stupid and such a simpleton that she is perfectly satisfied with her miserable lot."

The good merchant did not agree with his daughters. He knew that Beauty stood out in company in a way that her sisters could not. He admired the virtue of his daughter, above all her patience. The sisters not only made her do all the housework, they also insulted her whenever they could.

The family had lived an entire year in seclusion when the merchant received a letter informing him that a ship containing his merchandise had just arrived safely in its home port. The news made the two elder sisters giddy with excitement, for they thought they would finally be able to leave the countryside where they were so bored. When they saw that their father was ready to leave, they begged him to bring back dresses, furs, laces, and all kinds of baubles. Beauty did not ask for anything, because she thought that all the money from the merchandise would not be enough to buy everything her sisters wanted.

"Don't you want me to buy anything for you?" asked her father.

"You are so kind to think of me," Beauty answered. "There are no roses growing here. Can you bring me one?"

It was not that Beauty was anxious to have a rose, but she did not want to do something that would make her sisters look bad. Her sisters would have said that she was asking for nothing to make herself look good.

The good man left home, but when he arrived at the port he found that there was a dispute going on about his merchandise. After much unpleasantness, he set off for home as impoverished as he had been on his departure. He had only thirty miles left to go and was already overjoyed at the prospect of seeing his children again when he had to cross a dense forest. He had no idea where he was. There was a fierce snowstorm, and the wind was so strong that it knocked him off his horse twice. When night fell, he felt sure that he was going to die of hunger or of the cold, or that he would be eaten by the wolves that he could hear howling all around. All of a sudden he saw a bright light at the end of a long row of trees. The bright light seemed very far away. He walked in its direction and realized that it was coming from an immense castle that was completely lit up. The merchant thanked God for sending help, and he hurried toward the castle. He was surprised that no one was in the courtyard. His horse went inside a large, open stable, where he found some hay and oats. The poor animal had nearly died of hunger and began eating voraciously. The merchant tied the horse up in the stable and walked toward the house, where not a soul was in sight. Once he entered the great hall, however, he found a warm fire and a table laden with food, with just a single place setting. Since the rain and snow had soaked him to the bone, he went over to the fire to dry off. He thought to himself: "The master of the house, or his servants, will not be offended by the liberties I am taking. No doubt someone will be back soon."

He waited a long time. Once the clock struck eleven and there was still no one in sight, he gave in to the pangs of hunger and, trembling with fear, he took a chicken and ate it all up in a few big bites. He also drank several glasses of wine and, feeling more daring, he left the great hall and crossed many large, magnificently furnished apartments. Finally he found a room with a good bed. Since it was past midnight and he was exhausted, he took it upon himself to close the door and go to bed.

When he awoke the next day, it was already ten in the morning. He was greatly surprised to find clean clothes in the place of the ones that had been completely soaked. "Surely," he thought to himself, "this palace belongs to some good fairy who has taken pity on me."

He looked out the window and saw that it was no longer snowing. Before his eyes a magnificent vista of gardens and flowers unfolded. He returned to the great hall where he had dined the night before and found a small table with a cup of hot chocolate on it. "Thank you, Madame Fairy," he said out loud, "for being so kind as to remember my breakfast."

After finishing his hot chocolate, the good man left to go find his horse. Passing beneath a magnificent arbor of roses, he remembered that Beauty had asked him for a rose, and he plucked one from a branch with many blossoms on it. At that very moment, he heard a loud noise and saw a beast coming toward him. It looked so dreadful that he nearly fainted.

"You are very ungrateful," said the beast in a terrible voice. "I saved your life by sheltering you in my castle, and now you repay me by stealing my roses, which I love more than anything else in the world. You will have to pay for your offense. I'm going to give you exactly a quarter of an hour to beg God's forgiveness."

The merchant fell to his knees and, hands clasped, pleaded with the beast: "My Liege, pardon me. I did not think I would be offending you by plucking a rose for my daughter, who asked me to bring her a flower or two."

"I am not called 'My Liege,'" said the monster. "My name is Beast. I don't like flattery, and I prefer that people say what they think. So don't try to move me with your compliments. But you said that you have some daughters. I am prepared to forgive you if one of your daughters consents to die in your place. Don't argue with me. Just go. If your daughters refuse to die for you, swear that you will return in three days."

The good man was not about to sacrifice one of his daughters to this hideous monster, but he thought: "At least I will have the pleasure of embracing them one last time."

He swore that he would return, and Beast told him that he could leave whenever he wanted. "But I don't want you to go empty-handed," he added. "Return to the room in which you slept. There you will find a large empty chest. You can fill it up with whatever you like, and I will have it delivered to your door."

The beast withdrew, and the good man thought to himself: "If I must die, at least I can console myself with the thought of leaving something for my poor children to live on."

The merchant returned to the room in which he had slept. He filled the great chest that Beast had described with the many gold pieces he found there. After he found his horse in the stable, he left the palace with sadness equal to the joy he had felt on entering it. His horse instinctively set out on one of the forest paths, and in just a few hours, the good man arrived at his cottage. His children rushed out to greet him, but instead of responding to their caresses, the merchant burst into tears as he gazed on them. In his hand, he was holding the branch of roses he had brought for Beauty. He gave it to her and said: "Beauty, take these flowers. They have cost your poor father dearly."

The merchant then told his children about the terrible events that had befallen him. Upon hearing his story, the two sisters uttered loud cries and said hurtful things to Beauty, who did not cry. "See what the pride of this little creature has brought down on us!" they said. "Why didn't she ask for fine clothes the way we did? No, she wanted to get all the attention. She's responsible for Father's death, and she's not even shedding a tear!"

"That would be quite pointless," Beauty replied. "Why should I shed tears about Father when he is not going to die? Since the monster is willing to accept one of his daughters, I am prepared to risk all his fury. I feel fortunate to be able to sacrifice myself for him, since I will have the pleasure of saving my father and proving my feelings of tenderness for him."

"No, sister," said her three brothers. "You won't die. We will find this monster, and we are prepared to die under his blows if we cannot slay him."

"Don't count on that, children," said the merchant. "The beast's power is so great that I don't have the least hope of killing him. I am moved by the goodness of Beauty's heart, but I refuse to risk her life. I'm old and don't have many years left. I will only lose a few years of my life, and I don't regret losing them for your sake, my dear children."

"Rest assured, Father," said Beauty, "that you will not go to that palace without me. You can't keep me from following you. I may be young, but I am not all that attached to life, and I would rather be devoured by that monster than die of the grief that your loss would cause me."

It was no use arguing with Beauty. She was determined to go to the palace. Her sisters were delighted, for the virtues of their younger sister had filled them with a good deal of envy. The merchant was so preoccupied by the sad prospect of losing his daughter that he forgot all about the chest he had filled with gold. But as soon as he repaired to his room to get some sleep, he was astonished to find it beside his bed. He decided not to tell his children that he had become rich, for his daughters would then want to return to town, and he was determined to die in the country. He did confide his secret to Beauty, who told him that several gentlemen had come during his absence and that two of them wanted to marry her sisters. Beauty begged her father to let them marry. She was so kind that she still loved her sisters with all her heart and forgave them for the cruel things they had done.

When Beauty left with her father, the two mean sisters rubbed their eyes with an onion in order to draw tears. But the brothers cried real tears, as did the merchant. Only Beauty did not cry at all, because she did not want to make everyone even sadder.

The horse took the road to the palace, and, when night fell, they could see that it was all lit up. The horse went on its own into the stable, and the good man walked with his daughter into the hall, where there was a magnificently set table with two place settings. The merchant did not have the stomach to eat, but Beauty, forcing herself to appear calm, sat down and served her father. "You see, Father," she said while forcing a laugh, "the beast wants to fatten me up before eating me, since he paid so dearly for me."

After dining, they heard a loud noise, and the merchant tearfully bid adieu to his poor daughter, for he knew it must be Beast. Beauty could not help but tremble at the sight of this horrible figure, but she tried as hard as she could to stay calm. The monster asked her if she had come of her own free will and, trembling, she replied that she had.

"You are very kind," said Beast, "and I am very grateful to you. As for you, my good man, get out of here by tomorrow morning and don't think of coming back here ever again. Goodbye, Beauty."

"Goodbye, Beast," she replied. Suddenly the monster vanished.

"Oh, my daughter!" cried the merchant, embracing Beauty. "I am half dead with fear. Trust me, you have to let me stay," he said.

"No, Father," Beauty said firmly. "You must go tomorrow morning and leave me to the mercy of heaven. Heaven may still take pity on me."

They both went to bed thinking that they would not be able to sleep all night long, but they had hardly climbed into their beds when their eyes closed. While she was sleeping, Beauty saw a woman who said to her: "I am pleased with your kind heart, Beauty. The good deed you have done in saving your father's life will not go unrewarded."

Upon awakening, Beauty recounted this dream to her father. While it comforted him a little, it did not keep him from crying out loud when he had to leave his dear daughter. After he left, Beauty sat down in the great hall and began to cry as well. But since she was courageous, she put herself in God's hands and resolved not to bemoan her fate during the short time she had left to live. Convinced that Beast was planning to devour her that very evening, she decided to walk around the grounds and to explore the castle while awaiting her fate. She could not help but admire the castle's beauty, and she was very surprised to find a door upon which was written: "Beauty's Room." She opened it hastily and was dazzled by the radiant beauty of that room. She was especially impressed by a huge bookcase, a harpsichord, and various music books. "Someone does not want me to get bored!" she said softly. Then she realized: "If I had only one hour left to live, no one would have made such a fuss about the room." This thought lifted her spirits.

She opened the bookcase and saw a book, on the cover of which was written in gold letters: "Your wish is our command. Here you are queen and mistress."

"Alas," she sighed, "I only wish to see my poor father again and to know what he's doing now."

She said this to herself, so you can imagine how surprised she was when she looked in a large mirror and saw her father arriving at his house with a dejected expression. Her sisters went out to meet him, and, despite the faces they made in order to look as if they were distressed, they were visibly happy to have lost their sister. A moment later, everything in the mirror vanished. Beauty could not help thinking that Beast was most obliging and that she had nothing to fear from him.

At noon, Beauty found the table set and, during her meal, she heard an excellent concert, even though she could not see a soul. That evening, as she was about to sit down at the table, she heard Beast making noises, and she could not keep herself from trembling.

"Beauty," said the monster, "will you let me watch you dine?"

"You are my master," said Beauty, trembling.

"No, you are the only mistress here," replied Beast. "If I bother you, order me to go, and I will leave at once. Tell me, do you find me very ugly?"

"Yes, I do," said Beauty. "I don't know how to lie. But I also think you are very kind."

"You are right," said the monster. "But in addition to being ugly, I also lack intelligence. I know very well that I am nothing but a beast."

"You can't be a beast," replied Beauty, "if you know that you lack intelligence. A fool never knows that he is stupid."

"Go ahead and eat, Beauty," said the monster, "and try not to be bored in your house, for everything here is yours, and I would be upset if you were not happy."

"You are very kind," said Beauty. "I swear to you that I am completely pleased with your good heart. When I think of it, you no longer seem ugly to me."

"Oh, of course," Beast replied. "I have a kind heart, but I am still a monster."

"There are certainly men more monstrous than you," said Beauty. "I like you better, even with your looks, than men who hide false, corrupt, and ungrateful hearts behind charming manners."

"If I were intelligent," said Beast, "I would pay you a great compliment to thank you. But I am so stupid that all I can say is that I am very much obliged."

Beauty ate with a hearty appetite. She no longer dreaded the monster, but she thought that she would die of fright when he said: "Beauty, would you be my wife?"

It took her a moment to reach the point of answering. She was afraid to provoke the monster by refusing him. Trembling, she said to him: "No, Beast."

At that moment, the poor monster meant to sigh deeply, but he made such a frightful whistling sound that it echoed throughout the palace. Beauty felt better soon, however, because Beast, turning to look at her from time to time, left the room and said adieu in a sad voice. Finding herself alone, Beauty felt great compassion for poor Beast. "Alas," she said, "it is too bad he is so ugly, for he is so kind."

Beauty spent three peaceful months at the castle. Every evening, Beast paid her a visit and, while she was dining, entertained her with good plain talk, though not with what the world would call wit. Each day Beauty discovered new good qualities in the monster. Once she began seeing him every day, she became accustomed to his ugliness, and, far from fearing his arrival, she often looked at her watch to see if it was nine o'clock yet. Beast never failed to appear at that hour. There was only one thing that still bothered Beauty. The monster, before leaving, always asked her if she wanted to be his wife, and he seemed deeply wounded when she refused.

One day she said to him: "You are making me feel upset, Beast. I would like to be able to marry you, but I am far too candid to allow you to believe that that could ever happen. I will always be your friend. Try to be satisfied with that."

"I will have to be," Beast replied. "I don't flatter myself, and I know that I'm horrible looking, but I love you very much. However, I am very happy that you want to stay here. Promise me that you will never leave."

Beauty blushed at these words. She had seen in her mirror that her father was sick at heart about having lost her. She had been hoping to see him again. "I can promise you that I will never leave you," she said to Beast. "But right now I am so longing to see my father again that I would die of grief if you were to deny me this wish."

"I would rather die myself than cause you pain," said Beast. "I will send you back to your father. Stay there, and your poor beast will die of grief."

"No," Beauty said, bursting into tears, "I love you too much to be the cause of your death. I promise to return in a week. You have let me see that my sisters are married and that my brothers have left to serve in the army. Father is living all alone. Let me stay with him for just a week."

"You will be there tomorrow morning," said Beast. "But don't forget your promise. All you have to do is put your ring on the table before going to sleep when you want to return. Goodbye, Beauty."

As was his habit, Beast sighed deeply after speaking, and Beauty went to bed feeling very sad to see him so dejected. The next morning, on waking up, she was in her father's house. She pulled a cord at the side of her bed and a bell summoned a servant, who uttered a loud cry upon seeing her. The good man of the house came running when he heard the cry, and he almost died of joy when he saw his beloved daughter. They held each other tight for over a quarter of an hour. After the first waves of excitement subsided, Beauty realized that she didn't have any clothes to wear. But the servant told her that she had just discovered in the room next door a huge trunk full of silk dresses embroidered with gold and encrusted with diamonds. Beauty thanked Beast for his thoughtfulness. She took the least ornate of the dresses and told the servant to lock up the others, for she wanted to make a present of them to her sisters. Hardly had she spoken these words when the chest disappeared. When her father told her that Beast wanted her to keep everything for herself, the dresses and the chest reappeared on the spot.

While Beauty was getting dressed, her two sisters learned about her arrival and hurried over to meet her with their husbands. Both sisters were very unhappy. The older one had married a remarkably handsome gentleman, but he was so enamored of his own good looks that he spent all day in front of a mirror. The other one had married a man of great wit, but he used it to infuriate everybody, first and foremost his wife. Beauty's sisters were so mortified that they felt ready to die when they saw her dressed like a princess and more beautiful than the day is bright. Beauty tried in vain to shower them with attention, but nothing could restrain their jealousy, which only increased when Beauty told them how happy she was. These two envious women walked down to the garden so that they could weep freely. They both asked themselves: "Why should this little beast enjoy more happiness than we do? Aren't we more likable than she is?"

"Dearest sister," the older one said, "I have an idea. Let's try to keep Beauty here for more than a week. Her stupid beast will get angry when he sees that she has broken her promise, and maybe he'll eat her up."

"You're right," the other one replied. "To make that work, we will have to lavish affection on her and act as if we are delighted to have her here."

Having made this decision, the two nasty creatures returned to Beauty's room and showed her so much affection that she nearly wept for joy. When the week had gone by, the two sisters started tearing out their hair and performed so well that Beauty promised to stay another four or five days. At the same time she felt guilty about the grief she was causing poor Beast, whom she loved with all her heart and missed seeing. On the tenth night she spent at her father's house, she dreamed that she was in the garden of the palace when she saw Beast lying in the grass, nearly dead and reproaching her for her ingratitude. Beauty woke up with a start and began crying. "Aren't I terrible," she said, "for causing grief to someone who has done so much to please me? Is it his fault that he's ugly and lacks intelligence? He is kind. That's worth more than anything else. Why haven't I wanted to marry him? I would be happier with him than my sisters are with their husbands. It is neither good looks nor great wit that makes a woman happy with her husband, but character, virtue, and kindness, and Beast has all those good qualities. I may not be in love with him, but I feel respect, friendship, and gratitude toward him. If I made him unhappy, my lack of appreciation would make me feel guilty for the rest of my life."

With these words, Beauty got up, wrote a few lines to her father to explain why she was leaving, put her ring on the table, and went back to bed. She had hardly gotten into bed when she fell sound asleep. And when she awoke in the morning, she was overjoyed to find herself in Beast's palace. She dressed up in magnificent clothes just to make him happy and spent the day feeling bored to death while waiting for the clock to strike nine. But the clock struck nine in vain. Beast was nowhere in sight.

Beauty feared that she might be responsible for his death. She ran into every room of the castle, crying out loud. She was in a state of despair. After having searched everywhere, she remembered her dream and ran into the garden, toward the canal where she had seen Beast in her sleep. She found poor Beast stretched out unconscious, and she was sure that he was dead. Feeling no revulsion at his looks, she threw herself on him and, realizing that his heart was still beating, she got some water from the canal and threw it on him. Beast opened his eyes and told Beauty: "You forgot your promise. The thought of having lost you made me decide to starve myself. But now I will die happy, for I have the pleasure of seeing you one more time."

"No, my dear Beast, you will not die," said Beauty. "You will live and become my husband. From this moment on, I give you my hand in marriage, and I swear that I belong only to you. Alas, I thought that I felt only friendship for you, but the grief I am feeling makes me realize that I cannot live without you."

Scarcely had Beauty uttered these words when the castle became radiant with light. Fireworks and music alike signaled a celebration. But these attractions did not engage her attention for long. She turned back to look at her dear Beast, whose perilous condition made her tremble with fear. How great was her surprise when she discovered that Beast had disappeared and that a young prince more beautiful than the day was bright was lying at her feet, thanking her for having broken a magic spell. Even though she was worried about the prince, she could not keep herself from asking about Beast. "You see him at your feet," the prince said. "An evil fairy condemned me to remain in that form until a beautiful girl would consent to marry me. She barred me from revealing my intelligence. You were the only person in the world kind enough to be touched by the goodness of my character. Even by offering you a crown, I still can't fully discharge the obligation I feel to you."

Pleasantly surprised, Beauty offered her hand to the handsome prince to help him get up. Together, they went to the castle, and Beauty nearly swooned with joy when she found her father and the entire family in the large hall. The beautiful lady who had appeared to her in a dream had transported them to the castle.

"Beauty," said the lady, who was a grand fairy, "come and receive the reward for your wise choice. You preferred virtue to looks and intelligence, and so you deserve to see those qualities united in a single person. You will become a noble queen, and I hope that sitting on a throne will not destroy your many virtues. As for you, my dear ladies," the fairy continued, speaking to Beauty's two sisters, "I know your hearts and all the malice that is in them. You will be turned into two statues, but you will keep your senses beneath the stone that envelops you. You will be transported to the door of your sister's palace, and I can think of no better punishment than being a witness to her happiness. You will not return to your former state until you recognize your faults. I fear that you may remain statues forever. You can correct pride, anger, gluttony, and laziness. But a miracle is needed to convert a heart filled with malice and envy."

The fairy waved her wand, and everyone there was transported to the great hall of the prince's realm, where the subjects were overjoyed to see him. The prince married Beauty, who lived with him for a long time in perfect happiness, for their marriage was founded on virtue.

EAST OF THE SUN AND WEST OF THE MOON

Norway

The zoologist Peter Christen Asbjørnsen and the parish priest Jørgen Moe joined forces in nineteenth-century Norway to collect folktales and create a rich cultural heritage. The two had been friends for over a decade when they published their first collection, Norske Folkeeventyr, *a work inspired by the Brothers Grimm and praised by them after its publication. Asbjørnsen and Moe conducted fieldwork in an effort to preserve regional folklore. They sought to create standard versions of folktales based on multiple regional variations. "East of the Sun and West of the Moon" shares many features with Apuleius's "Cupid and Psyche," as well as with Madame de Beaumont's "Beauty and the Beast." Its hard-luck heroine outdoes nearly every fairy-tale figure in her optimistic energy and opportunistic zeal.*

Once upon a time there was a poor farmer with so many children that he no longer had enough food for them, and barely enough to clothe them. They were all pretty children, but the loveliest was the youngest daughter, who was so beautiful that there was no end to her beauty.

One Thursday evening late in the fall, the weather was stormy, and it was dreadfully dark outside. Rain was pounding down on the roof, and the wind was blowing so fiercely that the cottage walls began to shake. The farmer and his children were all sitting around the fire, busy with one thing or another. All at once there were three taps on the window. The father went outside to find out what was going on. What should he see out there but a great big white bear!

"Good evening to you," said the white bear.

"Good evening to you too," the man replied.

"Will you let me have your youngest daughter? If you do, I will make you as rich as you are now poor," the bear said.

Well, the man thought it would not be a bad idea to be rich, but he thought he ought to talk things over with his daughter before making any agreements with the bear. He went back into the house and told everyone about the great white bear waiting outside and how the bear had promised to make him rich in exchange for the youngest daughter.

The girl said "No!" outright. Nothing could make her change her mind. So the farmer went out and told the white bear that he should come back next Thursday evening for an answer. In the meantime, he started talking with his daughter and kept on telling her how rich they would be and how well she herself would do. Finally, she agreed to the exchange. She washed and mended her tattered clothes and made herself up to look as smart as she could. It didn't take long for her to prepare for the trip, for she didn't have much to carry.

A week later the white bear came to fetch her. She climbed on his back with her little bundle, and off they went. After they had traveled a good stretch down the road, the white bear asked her, "Are you afraid?"

No, she wasn't.

"Hold on tight to my shaggy coat, and you won't have to be afraid," the bear said. After traveling a long, long time, they reached a mountain. The white bear knocked on a rocky slope, and a door opened. The two entered a castle in which there were many rooms, all lit up and sparkling with silver and gold. The table was already set, and everything was as grand as could be. The white bear gave the girl a silver bell. If she ever wanted anything, all she had to do was pick it up and ring, and she would have what she needed.

It was evening by the time the young woman had eaten, and she felt sleepy from her long journey and thought she would go to bed. And so she picked up the bell to ring it. As soon as it was in her hand, she found herself in a chamber with a bed that had beautiful white sheets, pillows and curtains of silk, all fringed with gold. Everything in the room was made either of gold or silver. After she went to bed and put out the light, a man appeared out of nowhere and lay down next to her. It was the white bear, and every night he cast off his pelt. But she never set eyes on him, because he always waited until she had put out the light. Before the sun rose, he was up and gone again.

The two lived happily for a while, but the girl soon turned silent and sorrowful. All day long she was by herself, and she was beginning to feel homesick for her father and mother, as well as her brothers and sisters. One day, when the white bear asked what was ailing her, she told him that she was very lonely and that she really wanted to go visit her father and mother and brothers and sisters. Not being able to see them made her sad.

"Well," said the bear, "perhaps we can find a cure for that. But you must promise me that you will not talk to your mother unless there are others around to listen. She will insist on taking you aside and going into a room to talk with her alone. If you do that, you will bring misfortune to us both."

One Sunday, not much later, the white bear came to see her and said that she could go that day to visit her father and mother. Off they went! She rode on his back, and they traveled far away. Finally they reached a grand house, where her brothers and sisters were outside running about and playing. Everything was so beautiful there. It was a joy to see.

"This is where your father and mother live now," the white bear said. "Don't forget what I said to you, otherwise you will make both of us unhappy."

No, heaven forbid, she would not forget.

When they reached the house, the white bear turned around and left.

The girl went in to see her father and mother, and there was no end to the joy they all felt. Her parents could not thank her enough for everything she had done for them. Now they had everything they could possibly want, and it was all just as fine as could be. They were eager to hear about how she was faring.

Well, she told them, living where she did was very comfortable.

She had everything she could ever want. I have no idea what else she said, but it's unlikely that she told anyone the full story. That evening, after they had eaten supper, everything happened just as the white bear had predicted. The girl's mother wanted to take her aside and talk with her alone in her bedroom. But the girl remembered what the white bear had told her, and she wouldn't go with her.

"What we have to talk about can keep," she said, and she put her mother off. But somehow or other, her mother managed to get her alone at last, and the girl had to tell her the whole story. She described how, every night, after she went to bed, a man came and lay down next to her as soon as she put out the light. She had never set eyes on him, because he was always gone before the sun rose. She felt very sad that she could not have a look at him, especially since she was by herself all day long, and things got really dreary and lonesome.

"On no!" her mother said. "You may be sleeping in the same bed as a troll! I'm going to give you some good advice on how you can get a look at him. Take this candle stub and hide it under your dress. Light it while he's sleeping, but just make sure that you don't drop any tallow on him."

Yes, the girl took the candle and hid it inside her dress. The next evening the white bear appeared and took her away. After they had traveled for a while, he asked whether things had happened as he had said they would.

She could not deny that they had.

"Be careful," he said. "If you take your mother's advice, you will bring misfortune down on both of us, and we will be done for."

"No, of course I won't!"

They returned home, and the girl went to bed, and everything happened as it had before. A man appeared and lay down next to her. But this time, in the middle of the night, after making sure that he was fast asleep, she climbed out of bed and lit the candle. She let the flame shine down on him and saw that he was the most handsome prince you could imagine. She felt so much love for him that she thought she could not go on living unless she could give him a kiss. And so she did, but when she kissed him, she let three drops of hot tallow drip onto his shirt. He woke up abruptly.

"What have you done?" he cried out. "Now you have brought misfortune down on both of us. If you had just waited a year, the spell would have been lifted. My stepmother bewitched me, and I have to live as a white bear by day and as a man by night. But now all the ties between us are severed. I have to leave you now and go find my stepmother. She lives in a castle east of the sun and west of the moon. A princess with a nose three ells long lives in the castle with her, and she is the one I must now wed."

The young woman wept and bemoaned her fate, but it was no use. He had to leave. She asked if she could accompany him. No, she could not. "Then tell me how to get there," she said. "Surely I can at least go and search for you." Yes, she could do that, but there was no road that led to the place where he was going. It lay east of the sun and west of the moon, and she would never be able to figure out how to get there.

The next morning, the girl woke up, and the prince had vanished, along with the castle. She was lying on a little patch of green in the midst of a dark forest. By her side was the bundle of tattered clothes she had brought with her from home.

After rubbing the sleep out of her eyes, she cried until she could weep no more. She decided to start her search, and she walked many, many days until she reached a steep cliff. An old woman was seated nearby, and she had a golden apple that she was tossing into the air. The girl asked her if she knew the way to the prince who was living with his stepmother in a castle east of the sun and west of the moon and who was to marry the princess with a nose three ells long.

"How do you know about him?" the old woman asked. "Maybe you are the girl destined for him." Yes, she was. "Well, well, so it's you then, is it?" said the old woman. "All I know is that he lives in a castle east of the sun and west of the moon and that you'll get there too late or never. But I'll lend you my horse, and you can ride it to my closest neighbor. Maybe she will be able to help you. And when you get there, just swat the horse under the left ear and tell it to go back home. You are also welcome to take this golden apple with you."

The girl climbed up on the horse and rode for a long, long time. She reached another cliff, and saw another old woman just sitting there. This one had a golden carding comb. The girl asked if she knew the way to the castle that was east of the sun and west of the moon. "You'll get there too late or never, but I'll lend you my horse, and you can ride it to my closest neighbor. Maybe she will be able to help you. And when you get there, just swat the horse under its left ear and tell it to trot back home." The old woman gave her the golden carding comb. She might find some use for it, she said.

The girl climbed up on the horse, and once again, she rode for a long, long stretch. Finally she reached another cliff, and sitting next to it was another old woman. This one was spinning with a golden spinning wheel. She asked her, too, if she knew how to find the prince and where the castle was that lay east of the sun and west of the moon. But it was just as before. "Perhaps you are the one destined for the prince," the old woman said. Yes, she was. But this woman didn't have any better idea of how to reach the castle. She knew it was east of the sun and west of the moon, but that was it. "And you'll get there too late or never. But I'll lend you my horse, and you can ride over to the east wind and ask him. He may know his way around those parts and can blow you over there. When you reach him, just swat the horse under the left ear, and it'll trot home on its own." The old woman gave her the golden spinning wheel. "Maybe you'll find some use for it," she said.

The girl rode many a long day before reaching the house of the east wind, but reach it she did. She asked the east wind to tell her the way to the prince who lived east of the sun and west of the moon. Yes, the east wind had often heard tell of the prince and the castle, but he didn't know the way there, for he had never blustered that far. "But if you want, I'll go with you to my brother the west wind. Maybe he knows, for he's much more powerful. If you climb on my back, I'll take you there." Yes, she climbed on his back, and off they went with a blast.

When they reached the house of the west wind, the east wind said that the girl he had brought with him was destined for the prince who lived in the castle east of the sun and west of the moon. She had set out to find him, and he had brought her this far and would be glad to know if the west wind knew how to get to the castle. "No," said the west wind. "I've never blown that far. But if you want, I'll go with you to our brother the south wind, for he's much more powerful than either of us, and he has blown far and wide. Maybe he'll be able to tell you. Climb on my back, and I'll take you to him." Yes, she climbed on his back, and they traveled to the south wind, and I think it didn't take them very long at all.

When they got there, the west wind asked if the south wind knew the way to the castle that lay east of the sun and west of the moon, for the girl with him was destined for the prince who lived there. "Is that so?" said the south wind. "Is she the one? Well, I've visited plenty of places in my time, but I have never yet sent blasts over there. If you want, I'll take you to my brother the north wind. He is the oldest and most powerful of us all. If he doesn't know where it is, you'll never find anyone in the world who will know. Climb on my back, and I'll take you over there." Yes, she climbed on his back, and off he went at a good clip.

They did not have to travel far. When they reached the house of the north wind, he was so fierce and cantankerous that he blew cold gusts at them from a long way off. "Blast you both, what do you want?" he roared from afar, and they both felt an icy shiver. "Well," said the south wind, "you don't need to bluster so loudly, for I am your brother, the south wind, and here is the girl who is destined for the prince who lives in the castle that lies east of the sun and west of the moon. She wants to know whether you were ever there and whether you can show her the way, for she so wants to find the prince."

"Yes, I know where it is," the north wind said. "Once I blew an aspen leaf over there, but afterward I was so exhausted that I couldn't blow a single gust for many a day. If you really want to go there and aren't afraid to come along with me, I'll take you on my back and try to send you over there." Yes, with all her heart she wanted to go and had to get there if it was at all possible. And she would not be afraid, no matter how wild the ride. "Very well, then," said the north wind. "But you will have to sleep here tonight, for we need an entire day if we are to get there at all."

Early the next morning the north wind woke her up. He pulled himself together, blustered around a bit, and made himself so stout and large that he looked terrifying. Off they went, high up in the air, as if they would not stop until they reached the end of the world.

Here on earth there was a terrible storm. Acres of forest and many houses were blown down. There were shipwrecks by the hundreds when the storm blew out to sea. The wind flew over the ocean with the girl—no one can imagine how fast the two traveled—and all the while they remained on the ocean. The north wind grew more and more weary. Soon he was so out of breath that he barely had another blast left in him. His wings drooped lower and lower until at last he sank so low that the tops of the waves splashed over his heels. "Are you afraid?" asked the north wind. No, she wasn't.

They were not very far from land by now, and the north wind had just enough strength left to toss her up on the shore under the windows of the castle that lay east of the sun and west of the moon. But he was so weak and exhausted that he had to stay there and rest for a number of days before returning home.

The next morning the girl sat down under the castle window and began playing with the golden apple. The first person she saw was the long-nosed princess who was to marry the prince. "What do you want for your golden apple, girl?" asked the long-nosed princess, as she opened up the window.

"It's not for sale, not for gold and not for money," said the girl.

"If it's not for sale for gold or for money, what is it that you want in return? You can name whatever you want," said the princess.

"Well, you can have it if I can spend the night in the room where the prince sleeps," said the girl whom the north wind had transported. Yes, that could be arranged. So the princess took the golden apple; but when the girl went up to the prince's bedroom that night, she found that he was fast asleep. She called out his name and shook him, and she wept and wailed, but she could not wake him up. The next morning, when the sun was rising, the princess with the long nose walked in and chased her out of the bedroom.

During the day, the girl sat under the castle window and began to card with her golden carding comb, and the same thing happened. The princess asked what she wanted for the comb. She said it wasn't for sale, not for gold and not for money, but if she were allowed to go to the prince and spend the night in his room, the princess could have it. When the girl went to his room, she found that he was fast asleep once again. No matter how loudly she called his name and shook him and cried and prayed she could not get him to respond. At the crack of dawn, the princess with the long nose came and chased her out of the bedroom again.

During the day, the girl sat down outside under the castle window and began to spin with her golden spinning wheel. The princess with the long nose wanted to have it too. She opened the window and asked what she wanted for it. The girl said, as she had said twice before, that it wasn't for sale, neither for gold nor for money, but if she could go to the prince who was there and stay in his room for the night, she would give it to her. Yes, she was welcome to do that. But now you must know that there were some good people who had been staying at the castle, and while they were sitting in their room, which was right next to the prince's, they heard a woman crying, praying, and shouting at the prince two nights running. They told the prince about it.

That evening the princess took a sleeping potion to the prince's room, but the prince only pretended to drink it. He threw it over his shoulder, for he had figured out what it was. When the girl came in, she found the prince wide awake, and then she told him the entire story of how she had found the castle. "Ah," said the prince, "you've come just in the nick of time, for tomorrow was to be our wedding day. But now I won't have to marry the long-nose. You are the one woman in the world

who could set me free. I'll tell the princess that I want to test my
bride to see if she's fit to be my wife. I'll ask her to wash the shirt
with the three wax stains on it. She'll try, for she doesn't know
that it was you who dropped the wax on the shirt and that the
person who stained the shirt is the only one who can wash it
clean, not the clever trolls who live in the castle. Then I'll tell her
that I must marry the person who can wash the shirt and make
it clean again, and I know that you can do that."

The two talked all night long about how much they loved
each other. The next day, when the wedding was about to take
place, the prince said, "First of all, I'd like to see what my bride
can do."

"Yes," said the stepmother, eager to please.

"Well," said the prince, "I have a fine shirt that I'd like to
wear to my wedding, but somehow or other it now has three
spots of wax on it. I have to have them washed out. I have vowed
to marry the woman who can do that. Anyone who can't is not
worth marrying."

Well, that was no great challenge, they said, and so they
agreed to the bargain. The princess with the long nose began to
scrub as hard as she could but the more she rubbed and scoured,
the larger the stains grew. "Ah!" said the old troll woman, her
mother, "you don't know how to scrub a shirt. Let me try it."
As soon as she touched the shirt, it was worse than before.
Even with all her rubbing and wringing and scrubbing, the
spots grew larger and darker, and the shirt became even more
dingy and ugly. Then all the other trolls began to help scrub,
but the longer they washed, the darker and uglier the shirt
became, until at last it was black all over as if it had been down
the chimney.

"Ah!" said the prince, "you are all worthless! You have no
idea how to wash a shirt. Why over there, outside, there's a
beggar girl. I'll bet that she knows how to wash better than the
whole lot of you. Come in, girl!" he shouted. She walked in.
"Can you wash this shirt and make it clean?" he asked.

"I'm not sure," she said, "but I think I can." Almost before
she had picked it up and dipped it in the water, it turned as white

as the driven snow, and whiter still. "Yes, you are the girl for me," said the prince.

At that, the old hag flew into such a rage that she burst into pieces on the spot, and the princess with the long nose did the same right after her, and the whole pack of trolls right after that. At least I haven't heard a word about them since.

As for the prince and the princess, they set free all the good people who had been carried off and locked up in the castle. They took all the silver and gold with them. And they fled as far as possible from the castle that lies east of the sun and west of the moon.

KING PIG

Italy

Contrary to the notion that stories about animal grooms revive memories of a time when animals were revered as deities or totemic beasts, this Italian tale invites us to feel gratitude that we were not born "brute beasts." The story appears in The Facetious Nights of Straparola, *a collection with a frame narrative set in Murano, Italy, with a group of Venetians, mainly women but also some men, telling stories to while away the time.*

Fair ladies, if we were to spend a thousand years giving thanks to our Creator for having made us in the form of humans and not of brute beasts, we could still not be grateful enough. This reflection calls to mind the story of one who was born a pig, but afterward became a comely youth. Nevertheless, to his dying day he was known to the people over whom he ruled as King Pig.

You must know, dear ladies, that Galeotto, King of Anglia, was a man highly blessed in worldly wealth, as well as in his wife, Ersilia, the daughter of Matthias, King of Hungary, a princess who, in virtue and beauty, outshone all the other ladies of the time. And Galeotto was a wise king, ruling his land so that no one ever complained about him. Although they had been married several years, the couple had no children, and for that reason were much aggrieved. While Ersilia was walking one day in her gardens she suddenly felt weary, and, catching sight of a spot covered with fresh green grass, she walked over to it and sat down. Overcome by fatigue and soothed by the sweet singing of the birds in the green foliage, she fell asleep.

While she was sleeping, it happened that three fairies who did not think much of humans walked by. When they beheld the sleeping queen, they stopped, and, gazing upon her beauty, took counsel together how they might bless her and yet at the same time also curse her. Together they agreed to a crafty plan, and the first cried out, "I command that no man shall be able to harm her, and that, the next time she lies with her husband, she will be with child and bear a son who shall not have his equal in all the world for beauty." Then the second said, "I command that no one shall ever have the power to offend her and that the prince who shall be born of her shall be gifted with every virtue under the sun." And the third said, "And I command that she shall be the wisest among women, but that the son whom she conceives shall be born in the skin of a pig, with a pig's ways and manners, and in this state he shall be constrained to remain until he shall have taken a woman to wife three times."

As soon as the three fairies had flown away, Ersilia woke up, and right away she stood up and returned to the palace, taking with her the flowers she had picked. Not many days passed before she knew herself to be with child, and when the time of her delivery arrived, she gave birth to a son with members like those of a pig and not of a human being. When tidings of this prodigy came to the ears of the king, he was greatly saddened. Bearing in mind how good and wise his queen was, he often felt moved to put this offspring of hers to death and cast it into the sea so that she might be spared the shame of having given birth to him. But when he debated in his mind and considered that this son, whatever he looked like, was of his own begetting, he put aside the cruel purpose which he had been harboring, and, seized with pity and grief, he made up his mind that the son should be brought up and nurtured like a rational being and not as a brute beast. The child, therefore, being nursed with the greatest care, would often be brought to the queen, and he would put his little snout and his little hooves in his mother's lap. Moved by natural affection, she would caress him by stroking his bristly back with her hand and embracing and kissing him as if he were a human child. Then he would wiggle his tail and give other signs to show that he was aware of his mother's affection.

As he grew older, the piglet began to speak like a human being and to wander about in the city, but whenever he saw any mud or dirt he would immediately wallow in it, after the manner of pigs, and then return home covered with filth. Then, when he approached the king and queen, he would rub himself against their beautiful garments, defiling them with all manner of dirt. But because he was their son, they endured it without complaint.

One day the pig came home covered in mud and filth, as was his wont, and he lay down on his mother's beautiful robe, and grunted, "Mother, I wish to get married." When the queen heard this, she replied, "Don't talk such foolishness. What maid would ever take you for a husband, and do you think that any nobleman or knight would give his daughter to someone as dirty and unsavory as you?" But the pig kept on grunting that he must have a wife of one sort or another. The queen, not knowing how to manage him in this matter, asked the king what they should do in this time of crisis: "Our son wishes to marry, but where can we find someone who would be willing to take him as a husband?" Every day the pig would return to his mother with the same demand: "I must have a wife, and I won't leave you in peace until you arrange a marriage with a certain young woman I saw today. I find her very attractive."

It happened that the young woman he had in mind was the daughter of a poor woman who had three girls, each one of them very lovely. When the queen heard this, she summoned the poor woman and her eldest daughter, and said, "Good mother, you are poor and burdened with children. If you will agree to what I propose, you will be rich. I have a son who is, as you see, in the form of a pig, and I would like him to marry your eldest daughter. Do not focus your thoughts too hard about him, but turn your attention to the king and me, and remember that your daughter will inherit this entire kingdom when the king and I are gone."

When the young girl heard what the queen had to say, she

was deeply upset and blushed for shame. She then said that she had no intention of accepting the queen's proposition. But the poor mother pleaded so urgently with her to give in that at last she yielded.

When the pig came home, all covered with dirt as usual, his mother said to him, "My son, we have found for you the wife you desire." And then she had the bride brought in, who by this time had been dressed up in regal attire. She presented the young woman to the pig prince. When he saw how lovely and desirable she was, he was filled with joy. All foul and dirty as he was, he leaped up and down around her, trying with all his might to show his affection by pawing and nuzzling her. But when she saw that he was soiling her beautiful dress, she shoved him aside. The pig asked, "Why are you pushing me away? Wasn't I the one who had these garments made for you?" She answered him with disdain, "No, neither you nor any one else in this kingdom of hogs has done that for me."

When it was time to retire, the young girl said to herself, "Whatever am I going to do with this foul beast? Tonight, while he is asleep, I will kill him."

The pig prince was not far off and heard those words, but said nothing. When the two retired to their chamber he climbed into the bed, stinking and dirty as he was, and defiled the sumptuous bed with his filthy hooves and snout. He lay down next to his wife, who did not take long to fall asleep. Then he struck her with his sharp hooves and drove them into her breast so that he killed her.

The next morning the queen went to visit her daughter-in-law, and to her great distress found that the pig had killed her. When the pig returned from wandering about in the city, he replied to the queen's bitter reproaches by telling her that he had only treated his wife as she was planning to treat him, and then he withdrew in a dark mood.

Not many days passed before the pig prince began to plead with the queen again, asking her to let him marry one of the other sisters. Even though the queen refused to listen to his request, he kept on insisting and threatened to destroy everything in sight if he were not allowed to remarry.

The queen learned about his threats, and she went to the king and told him everything. He said that it might be wiser to kill their ill-fated offspring before he made some real mischief in the city. But the queen still had tender maternal feelings for her child, and she loved him very dearly despite what he had done. She could not bear the thought of being separated from him. And so she summoned the poor woman to the palace again, this time with her second daughter. She talked with the child for a long time, pleading with her to marry her son. Finally, the girl agreed to take the pig prince for a husband. But her fate was no better than her sister's, for the bridegroom killed her, as he had killed his other bride, and then fled swiftly from the palace.

When he returned, as dirty as ever and smelling so foul that no one would go near him, the king and queen railed at him for having committed such an atrocity, but this time too he insisted that, had he not killed her, she would have killed him.

As before, not much time passed before the pig began to plead with his mother again to let him marry the youngest sister, who was more beautiful than either of the two others. When the queen refused his request, he became more insistent than ever. He began threatening the queen's own life—in terms violent and bloodthirsty—unless the young girl was given to him as a wife. The queen, when she heard his cruel and reprehensible words, was heartbroken. She felt that she was going to lose her mind. But putting all other considerations aside, she summoned the poor woman and her third daughter, who was named Meldina, and said the following to her: "Meldina, my child, I would be ever so pleased if you agreed to take the pig prince as your husband. Don't pay much mind to him, and just pay attention to his father and me. If you are patient and wise, you have a chance at becoming the happiest woman in the world."

Meldina turned to the queen with a grateful smile on her face and said that she was quite willing to do as she had asked. She thanked her humbly for seeing fit to choose her as a daughter-in-law. After all, she had nothing in the world, and it was a stroke of good fortune that a poor girl like her should become the daughter-in-law of a powerful sovereign. The queen, when she heard these kind, modest words, could not hold back tears of joy. But all the same she feared that Meldina might meet the same terrible fate as her sisters.

The new bride wore jewels and was dressed in regal fashion. She was waiting for the bridegroom. When the pig prince came in, he was dirtier and filthier than ever. What did she do but spread out the skirt of her gown and ask him to lie down by her side. The queen told her to push him away, but Meldina would not comply and said, "There are three wise maxims, gracious queen, which I remember having once heard. The first tells us that it is foolish to search for something that can't be found. The second tells us to believe only those things that bear the marks of sense and reason. The third tells us that you should hold on to and cherish any rare and precious treasures that come into your possession."

When the young woman had finished speaking, the pig prince, who had been wide awake and heard everything she said, got up and then kissed her on the face and neck and shoulders and chest with his tongue. She was not at all backward in returning his caresses, and soon he was fired with a warm love for her. When the time came to retire for the night, the bride went to bed and awaited her unseemly spouse. As soon as he climbed into bed, she raised the sheets and told him to come lie next to her and put his head upon the pillow. She covered him carefully with the blankets and drew the curtains so that he would not feel cold.

In the morning, the pig got up and ranged abroad to pasture, as was his wont. Not much later the queen entered the bride's chamber, expecting to find that she had met with the same fate as her sisters. But then she saw her lying in the bed, muddy as it was, looking entirely pleased and contented. And she thanked the Lord that her son had at last found a spouse who suited him.

A few days later, when the pig prince was talking casually with his wife, he decided to take her into his confidence. "Meldina, my beloved wife," he said, "if I can be completely sure that you can keep a secret, I will tell you one that I have, something

I have kept hidden for many years. I know that you are wise and discreet and that you love me truly. And because of that I want to share my secret with you."

"Your secret is safe with me," Meldina said, "for I promise never to reveal it to anyone without your consent."

Now that he was sure of his wife's discretion and fidelity, he stood up and shook off from his body the foul and dirty skin of a pig, and stood revealed as a handsome and well-proportioned young man. That night he slept soundly in the arms of his beloved wife. But he warned her to remain silent about the miracle she had witnessed, for the time had not yet come for complete liberation from his misery.

When he left the bed, he put the dirty pig's hide on again. I leave it to your imagination to consider how great was Meldina's joy when she discovered that, instead of a pig, she now had a handsome and gallant young prince as husband. Not much later, it turned out that she was with child, and, when the time came, she gave birth to a handsome and comely boy. The joy of the king and queen was unbounded, especially when they saw that the newborn child had the form of a human being and not that of a beast.

The burden of the strange and dark secret that her husband had shared with her weighed heavily on Meldina, and one day she went to her mother-in-law and said, "Gracious queen, when I married your son I believed that I had married a beast, but now I find that you have given me the comeliest, the worthiest, and the most gallant young man ever born as my husband. You must know that when he comes into my chamber to lie by my side, he casts off his dirty hide and leaves it on the ground and changes into a graceful, handsome youth. No one could ever believe this miracle unless they saw it with their own eyes."

When the queen heard those words she was sure that her daughter-in-law must be jesting, but Meldina insisted that what she said was true. And when the queen asked to witness with her own eyes the truth of this matter, Meldina replied, "Come to my chamber tonight, just as we are falling asleep. I will keep the door open, and you will discover that what I have told you is the truth."

That same night, when the time came, and everyone else had gone to sleep, the queen had some torches lit and went, accompanied by the king, to the chamber of her son. When she walked in, she saw the pig's skin lying on the floor in the corner of the room. Then she went over to the bedside and found Meldina lying in the arms of a handsome young man. When the king and queen set eyes on the two of them, their delight was very great, and the king ordered the pig's hide to be torn to shreds before anyone left the chamber, thus lifting the curse.* The king and queen nearly died from the shock and joy of finding that their son had become human.

And King Galeotto, when he saw that he had so fine a son and a grandchild as well, put aside his diadem and his royal robes and passed the crown on to his son, who was made king with great pomp. Ever afterward he was known as King Pig. To the great joy of the people in the land, the young king began his reign, and he lived long and happily with Meldina, his beloved wife.

---

*In this version of the story, Meldina's betrayal of the pig's confidence has no consequences, but in other variants, the heroine must undertake a perilous journey or carry out "impossible" tasks in order to redeem herself and be reunited with her husband. The phrase "thus lifting the curse" has been added by the editor.

THE FROG KING,
OR IRON HEINRICH

Germany

The Brothers Grimm made this story the first in their nineteenth-century collection. Some variant forms of the tale feature a princess who admits the frog to her chamber despite his revolting appearance, but most give us a princess who is perfectly capable of committing acts rivaling the cold-blooded violence of dashing a creature against a wall. Scottish and Gaelic versions of "The Frog King" show the princess beheading her suitor. A Polish variant replaces the frog with a snake and recounts in lavish detail the princess's act of tearing the creature in two. A more tame Lithuanian text requires the burning of the snake's skin before the prince is freed from his reptilian state. Acts committed in the heat of passion as much as acts of heartfelt compassion have the power to disenchant. Although the princess of "The Frog King, or Iron Heinrich" is self-absorbed, ungrateful, and cruel, in the end she does as well for herself as all of the modest, obedient, and charitable Beauties in other animal-groom tales.

In the olden days, when wishing could still help you, there lived a king whose daughters were all beautiful. But the youngest was so beautiful that even the sun, which had seen so much, was filled with wonder when it shone upon her face. There was a dark, vast forest near the king's castle, and in that forest, beneath an old linden tree, was a well. When the weather was really hot, the king's daughter would go out into the woods and sit down at the edge of the cool well. And if she was ever bored, she would just take out her golden ball, throw it up in the air, and catch it again. That was her favorite toy.

One day it happened that the golden ball didn't land in the princess's hands when she reached up to catch it, but fell down on the ground and rolled right into the water. The princess followed it with her eyes, but the ball was gone, and the well was so very deep that you couldn't see the bottom of it. She began to weep and cried louder and louder, unable to stop herself. While she was wailing, a voice called out to her: "What's going on, princess? Stones would be moved to pity if they could hear you."

She turned around to see where the voice was coming from and saw a frog, which had stuck its big old ugly head out of the water.

"Oh, it's you, you old splasher," she said. "I'm crying because my golden ball has fallen into the well."

"You can be quiet and stop crying," said the frog. "I can help you, but what will you give me if I fetch your toy?"

"Whatever you want, dear frog," she said. "My dresses, my pearls and jewels, even the golden crown I'm wearing."

The frog said, "I don't want your dresses, your pearls and jewels, or your golden crown. But if you promise to cherish me and let me be your companion and playmate, and let me sit beside you at the table and eat from your little golden plate, drink from your little cup, and sleep in your little bed, if you promise me that, I will crawl down into the well and bring back your golden ball."

"Oh, yes," she said. "I'll give you anything you want as long as you get my ball back." But to herself she thought, "What nonsense that stupid frog is talking! He's down there in the water croaking away with all the other frogs. How could anyone want him for a companion?"

Once the frog had her word, he dove down headfirst into the water. After a while he came paddling back up with the ball in his mouth and tossed it onto the grass. When the princess caught sight of her beautiful toy, she was overjoyed. She picked it up and ran off with it.

"Wait for me," the frog cried out. "Take me with you. I can't run the way you do."

He croaked as loudly as he could after her, but it was no use. She paid no attention, sped home, and quickly forgot about the poor frog, who crawled back down into the well.

The next day, after she had sat down for dinner with the king and all the other courtiers and was eating from her little golden plate, something came crawling up the marble staircase, splish, splash, splish, splash. When it reached the top of the stairs, it knocked at the door and called out: "Princess, youngest princess, let me in!"

She ran to the door to see who it was, and when she opened the door, the frog was waiting right there. Terrified, she slammed the door as fast as she could and went back to the table. The king could see that her heart was pounding with fear, and he said, "My child, why are you afraid? Was there a giant at the door coming to get you?"

"Oh, no," she replied. "It wasn't a giant, but it was a disgusting frog."

"What does a frog want from you?"

"Oh, father dear, yesterday when I was playing at the well, my golden ball fell into the water. And because I was crying so hard, the frog fetched it for me, and because he insisted, I promised that he could be my companion. I never thought that he would be able to leave the water. Now he's outside and wants to come in to see me." Just then there was a second knock at the door, and a voice called out:

> "Princess, youngest princess,
> Let me in.
> Did you forget
> Yesterday's promise
> Down by the chilly waters?
> Princess, youngest princess,
> Let me in."

Then the king said: "When you make a promise, you must keep it. Just go and let him in."

She went and opened the door. The frog hopped into the room and followed close on her heels until she reached her chair. Then he sat down and called out: "Lift me up beside you."

She hesitated, but the king ordered her to obey. Once the frog was up on the chair, he wanted to get on the table, and once he was up there he said, "Push your little golden plate closer to me so that we can eat together."

She did as he said, but it was obvious that she was not happy about it. The frog enjoyed his meal, but for her almost every little morsel stuck in her throat. Finally he said, "I've had enough to eat, and now I'm tired. Carry me up to your little room and prepare your little bed with the silken covers."

The princess began to cry, and was afraid of the clammy frog. She didn't dare touch him, and now he was going to sleep in her beautiful, clean bed. The king grew angry and said, "You shouldn't scorn someone who helped you when you needed it."

The princess picked up the frog with two fingers, carried him up to her room, and put him in a corner. While she was lying in bed, he came crawling over and said, "I'm tired and want to sleep as much as you do. Lift me up into your bed or I'll tell your father."

Then she grew really cross, picked him up, and threw him with all her might against the wall. "Now you'll get your rest, you disgusting frog!"

When he fell to the ground, he was no longer a frog but a prince with beautiful, sparkling eyes. At her father's bidding, he became her dear companion and husband. He told her that a wicked witch had cast a spell on him and that she alone could release him from the well. The next day they planned to set out together for his kingdom. They fell asleep, and, in the morning, after the sun had woken them, a coach drove up drawn by eight white horses in golden harnesses, with white ostrich plumes on their heads. At the back of the coach stood Faithful Heinrich, the servant of the young king. Faithful Heinrich had been so saddened by the transformation of his master into a frog that he had to have three hoops placed around his heart to keep it from bursting with pain and sorrow. Now the coach was there to take the young king back to his kingdom, and Faithful Heinrich lifted the two of them in and took his place in the back again. He was overjoyed by the transformation. When they had covered some distance, the prince heard a cracking noise behind him, as if something had broken. He turned around and called out:

> "Heinrich, the coach is falling apart!"
> "No, my lord, 'tis not the coach,
> But a hoop from round my heart,
> Which was in such pain,
> While you were down in the well,
> Living there as a frog."

Two more times the prince heard the cracking noise, and he was sure that the coach was falling apart. But it was only the sounds of the hoops breaking off from Faithful Heinrich's heart, for his master had been set free and was now happy.

THE SWAN MAIDENS

England

The folklorist Joseph Jacobs is often regarded as the British answer to the Brothers Grimm, and he hoped, in his Europa's Fairy Book, *to retell tales in such a way as "to bring out the original form from which all the variants are derived." Jacobs was convinced that, by studying variants of a tale type, he could "conjecture" the "original concatenation of incidents into plot" and produce a standard form. His story about swan maidens is remarkable in blending motifs from various tales to produce a story that retains the power of its core theme, the search for the lost wife.*

There was once a hunter who used often to spend the whole night stalking the deer or setting traps for game. Now it happened one night that he was watching in a clump of bushes near the lake for some wild ducks that he wished to trap. Suddenly he heard, high up in the air, a whirring of wings and thought the ducks were coming; and he strung his bow and got ready his arrows.

But instead of ducks there appeared seven maidens all clad in robes made of feathers, and they alighted on the banks of the lake, and taking off their robes plunged into the waters and bathed and sported in the lake. They were all beautiful, but of them all the youngest and smallest pleased most the hunter's eye, and he crept forward from the bushes and seized her dress of plumage and took it back with him into the bushes.

After the swan maidens had bathed and sported to their heart's delight, they came back to the bank wishing to put on their feather robes again; and the six eldest found theirs, but the youngest could not find hers. They searched and they searched until at last the dawn began to appear, and the six sisters called out to her, "We must away; 'tis the dawn; you meet your fate whatever it be." And with that they donned their robes and flew away, and away, and away.

When the hunter saw them fly away he came forward with the feather robe in his hand; and the swan maiden begged and begged that he would give her back her robe. He gave her his cloak but would not give her her robe, feeling that she would fly away. And he made her promise to marry him, and took her home, and hid her feather robe where she could not find it. So they were married and lived happily together and had two fine children, a boy and a girl, who grew up strong and beautiful; and their mother loved them with all her heart.

One day her little daughter was playing at hide-and-seek with her brother, and she went behind the wainscoting to hide herself, and found there a robe all made of feathers, and took it to her mother. As soon as she saw it she put it on and said to her daughter, "Tell father that if he wishes to see me again he must find me in the Land East o' the Sun and West o' the Moon"; and with that she flew away.

When the hunter came home next morning his little daughter told him what had happened and what her mother said. So he set out to find his wife in the Land East o' the Sun and West o' the Moon. And he wandered for many days until he came across an old man who had fallen on the ground, and he lifted him up and helped him to a seat and tended him until he felt better.

Then the old man asked him what he was doing and where he was going. And he told him all about the swan maidens and his wife, and he asked the old man if he had heard of the Land East o' the Sun and West o' the Moon.

And the old man said, "No, but I can ask."

Then he uttered a shrill whistle and soon all the plain in front of them was filled with all of the beasts of the world, for the old man was no less than the King of the Beasts.

And he called out to them, "Who is there here that knows

where is the Land East o' the Sun and West o' the Moon?" But none of the beasts knew.

Then the old man said to the hunter, "You must go seek my brother who is the King of the Birds," and told him how to find his brother.

And after a time he found the King of the Birds, and told him what he wanted. So the King of the Birds whistled loud and shrill, and soon the sky was darkened with all the birds of the air, who came around him. Then he asked, "Which of you knows where is the Land East o' the Sun and West o' the Moon?"

And none answered, and the King of the Birds said, "Then you must consult my brother the King of the Fishes," and he told him how to find him.

And the hunter went on, and he went on, and he went on, until he came to the King of the Fishes, and he told him what he wanted. And the King of the Fishes went to the shore of the sea and summoned all the fishes of the sea. And when they came around him he called out, "Which of you knows where is the Land East o' the Sun and West o' the Moon?"

And none of them answered, until at last a dolphin that had come late called out, "I have heard that at the top of the Crystal Mountain lies the Land East o' the Sun and West o' the Moon; but how to get there I know not save that it is near the Wild Forest."

So the hunter thanked the King of the Fishes and went to the Wild Forest. And as he got near there he found two men quarrelling, and as he came near they came toward him and asked him to settle their dispute.

"Now what is it?" said the hunter.

"Our father has just died and he has left but two things, this cap which, whenever you wear it, nobody can see you, and these shoes, which will carry you through the air to whatever place you will. Now I being the elder claim the right of choice, which of these two I shall have; and he declares that, as the younger, he has the right to the shoes. Which do you think is right?"

So the hunter thought and thought, and at last he said, "It is difficult to decide, but the best thing I can think of is for you to race from here to that tree yonder, and whoever gets back to me first I will hand him either the shoes or the cap, whichever he wishes."

So he took the shoes in one hand and the cap in the other, and waited until they had started off running toward the tree. And as soon as they had started running toward the tree he put on the shoes of swiftness and placed the invisible cap on his head and wished himself in the Land East o' the Sun and West o' the Moon. And he flew, and he flew, and he flew, over seven Bends, and seven Glens, and seven Mountain Moors, until at last he came to the Crystal Mountain. And on the top of that, as the dolphin had said, there was the Land East o' the Sun and West o' the Moon.

Now when he got there he took off his invisible cap and shoes of swiftness and asked who ruled over the Land; and he was told that there was a king who had seven daughters who dressed in swans' feathers and flew wherever they wished.

Then the hunter knew that he had come to the Land of his wife. And he went boldly to the king and said, "Hail, oh, king, I have come to seek my wife."

And the king said, "Who is she?"

And the hunter said, "Your youngest daughter." Then he told him how he had won her.

Then the king said, "If you can tell her from her sisters then I know that what you say is true." And he summoned his seven daughters to him, and there they all were, dressed in their robes of feathers and looking each like all the rest.

So the hunter said, "If I may take each of them by the hand I will surely know my wife"; for when she had dwelt with him she had sewn the little shifts and dresses of her children, and the forefinger of her right hand had the marks of the needle.

And when he had taken the hand of each of the swan maidens he soon found which was his wife and claimed her for his own. Then the king gave them great gifts and sent them by a sure way down the Crystal Mountain.

And after a while they reached home, and lived happily together ever afterward.

PRINCESS FROG

Russia

This Russian tale is unusual in tracing the source of an enchantment to a father, a paternal figure who is irritated by the wisdom of his daughter. Vasilisa has many skills, and, in addition to being wise, she can bake, weave, and dance, making her an expert in the domestic and the performing arts. In many tales about Vasilisa, Baba Yaga is her antagonist, but in this case the Russian witch, also known as the bony-legged one, is not the usual monstrous, child-devouring hag of Slavic folklore. Baba Yaga often poses a powerful threat to figures in fairy tales, but she can also, as is the case in this story, serve as helper and ally, providing whatever it is that a fairy-tale hero or heroine lacks.

A long time ago, in ancient times, there lived a tsar with the princess, his wife. They had three sons, all young and such brave fellows that no pen could describe them. The youngest was called Ivan Tsarevitch.

One day their father said to his sons, "My dear boys, I want each of you to take an arrow, draw your bow, and let your arrow fly. Wherever it falls, there you will find the bride for you."

The arrow of the eldest fell right near the house of a boyar, right in front of the quarters where the women were living. The arrow of the second son flew on the porch of a rich merchant, and right there on the porch was standing the merchant's daughter, a sweet girl. The youngest, the brave Ivan, had the bad luck of sending his arrow into a swamp, where it was caught by a croaking frog.

Ivan went straight to his father and asked, "How can I marry a frog? Is she my equal? She certainly cannot be!"

His father replied, "Never mind. You have to marry the frog, for that is your destiny."

The brothers married. The eldest wed a nobleman's child; the second, a merchant's beautiful daughter; and the youngest, Ivan, a croaking frog.

Some time passed and the tsar summoned his three sons and said, "Tell each of your wives to bake a loaf of bread by tomorrow morning."

Ivan returned home, and there was no smile on his face. Instead, his brow was furrowed.

"Croak! Croak! Ivan, my dear husband, why do you look so sad?" the frog asked gently. "Did anything disagreeable happen in the palace?"

"Disagreeable indeed," answered Ivan. "The tsar, my father, wants you to bake a loaf of white bread by tomorrow morning."

"Don't worry, Ivan. Go to bed. The morning hours are a better source of advice than the dark evening hours."

Ivan took his wife's advice and went to sleep. Then the frog threw off her frog skin and turned into a beautiful, sweet girl. Her name was Vasilisa. She stepped out onto the porch and called out, "Nurses and cooks, come to me at once and prepare a loaf of white bread for tomorrow morning, a loaf like the kind I used to eat at my royal father's palace."

Ivan woke up in the morning with the crowing cocks, and you know that the cocks and the chickens never sleep late.

The loaf was already made, and it was so fine that nobody could even describe it, for only in the land of the fairies can you find such marvelous loaves. It was decorated with pretty figures on the sides, with towns and fortresses on it, and the inside was as white as snow and as light as a feather.

Ivan's father was pleased and gave his son special thanks.

"Now there is another task I have," the tsar said with a smile. "Have each of your wives weave a rug for me by tomorrow."

Ivan returned home, and there was no smile on his face. Instead, his brow was furrowed.

"Croak! Croak! Dear Ivan, my husband and master, why are you so upset? Was your father not pleased?"

"How can I be anything but upset? The tsar, my father, has ordered a rug by tomorrow."

"Don't worry, Ivan. Go to bed and get some sleep. The morning hour will bring help."

Once again, the frog turned into Vasilisa, the wise maiden, and again she cried out, "Dear nurses and cooks, come to me for new work. Weave a silk rug like the one I used to sit upon in the palace of the king, my father."

Once said, quickly done. When the cocks began with their "cock-a-doodle-doo," Ivan woke up and lo and behold! There lay before him the most beautiful silk rug, a rug that no one could even begin to describe. Threads of silver and gold were woven in with bright-colored silk threads, and the rug was so beautiful that it was more for admiration than anything else.

The tsar was pleased and thanked his son Ivan. Then he issued a new order. This time he wanted to see the three wives of his handsome sons. He asked them to present their brides on the next day.

Ivan returned home with a furrowed brow, more furrowed even than before.

"Croak! Croak! Ivan, my dear husband and master, why do you look so sad? Did you hear some unpleasant news at the palace?"

"Unpleasant enough indeed! My father, the tsar, has ordered all three of us to present our wives to him. Now tell me, how do I dare go to him with you?"

"It's not really that bad, and it could be much worse," the frog answered, croaking softly. "You can go on ahead by yourself, and I will follow you. When you hear a loud noise, don't be afraid of the sound. Simply say, 'Here comes my miserable little frog in her miserable little box.'"

The two older brothers appeared with their wives, beautiful, bright, and cheerful women who were dressed in lovely dresses. Both of the happy bridegrooms made fun of Ivan.

"Why are you alone, brother?" they said to him as they burst out laughing. "Why didn't you bring your wife along with you? Didn't you have any rags to cover her? How could you have found such a beauty? We are willing to bet that you could not find another one like her in all the swamps around here." They could not stop laughing.

Suddenly, what a noise there was! The palace trembled, and the guests were all terrified. Ivan alone stayed quiet and said, "There is no danger at all. It's just my little frog arriving in her little box."

A golden carriage drawn by six splendid white horses pulled up to the red porch, and Vasilisa, beautiful beyond all description, gently reached for her husband's hand. He escorted her to the heavy oak tables, which were covered with snow-white linen and loaded with the wonderful dishes that are served only in the land of the fairies and nowhere else. The guests were all chatting in a lively way while they were eating.

Vasilisa drank some wine and then poured what was left in the goblet into her left sleeve. She ate some of the fried swan and threw the bones into her right sleeve. The wives of the two older brothers watched and did exactly what she did.

Once the long, hearty dinner was over, the guests began dancing and singing. The beautiful Vasilisa stepped out from the crowd, bright as a star, bowed to the tsar, bowed to the honorable guests, and then danced with her husband Ivan.

While dancing, Vasilisa waved her left sleeve and a pretty lake appeared right there in the hall and cooled the air. She waved her right sleeve and white swans swam on the water. The tsar, his guests, the servants, even the gray cat sitting in the corner were all astonished and filled with wonder as they watched the beautiful Vasilisa. The two sisters-in-law were filled with envy. When their turn came to dance, they also waved their left sleeves as Vasilisa had done, and oh, wonder! Wine was splashed all around. They waved their right sleeves and, instead of swans swimming, bones flew in the face of the tsar. The tsar grew angry and asked them to leave the palace.

In the meantime, Ivan looked for an opportunity to slip away unseen. He ran home, found the frog skin, and burned it in the fire.

When Vasilisa returned, she searched everywhere for the skin. She could not find it, and her beautiful face grew sad, and her bright eyes filled with tears.

She turned to Ivan and said, "Oh, dear husband, what have you done? I only had to wear that ugly frog skin for a little while longer. The moment was fast approaching when we could have lived happily together forever. Now I must say farewell. Search for me in a distant land to which no one has directions, at the palace of Kostshei the Deathless." Vasilisa turned into a white swan and flew out through the window.

Ivan wept bitter tears. Then he prayed and made the sign of the cross to the north, to the south, to the east, and to the west.

No one knows how long he was on the road, but one day he met an old man. He bowed, and the man said, "Good day, my brave fellow. Where are you going and what are you searching for?"

Ivan answered with the truth, revealing everything about his bad luck, without hiding anything.

"Why on earth did you burn the frog skin? It was wrong to do that. Now listen to me. Vasilisa was born wiser than her own father. He envied her wisdom and condemned her to live as a frog for three long years. I feel sorry for you and want to help you. Here is a magic ball. Take it, let it roll, and follow it without fear."

Ivan thanked the good old man and followed the ball, which became his new guide. The road stretched out endlessly. One day in a field of flowers he met a bear, a big Russian bear. Ivan took out his bow and arrows and was about to shoot the bear.

"Do not kill me, kind Ivan," the bear said. "Who knows? I may be able to help you one day." And Ivan did not shoot the bear.

A lovely white duck flew up in the sky over Ivan's head. Ivan drew his bow and was about to shoot it when the duck said, "Don't kill me, dear prince. I may be able to help you one day."

Ivan did as the duck had said and continued on his way. He saw in his path a hare, and was about to shoot when the gray hare said, "Don't kill me, brave prince. I may be able to show my gratitude sometime soon."

The prince did not shoot the hare and continued on his way.

He followed the rolling ball until he reached the deep blue sea. On the sand there lay a fish, and this big fish was dying.

"Oh, Ivan!" the fish pleaded. "Have mercy on me and put me back into the cool waters."

Ivan did as the fish asked and continued walking along the shore. He followed the ball, which was still rolling, and it led him to a hut, a mysterious little hut standing on tiny chicken feet.

"Izboushka! Izboushka!"—for that's the Russian name for small huts. "Izboushka, I want you to turn your door to me," Ivan cried, and lo! The tiny hut turned its front entrance to him. Ivan walked in and saw a witch, the ugliest witch he could imagine.

"Ho, Ivan! What brings you here?" the witch asked him.

"Oh, you old mischief-maker!" Ivan shouted. "Is this the way to greet a guest before he gets something to eat, something to drink, and some hot water to wash the dust off?"

Baba Yaga, the witch, gave Ivan plenty to eat and drink, along with some hot water to wash the dust off him. Ivan soon felt refreshed and became talkative, telling Baba Yaga the wonderful story of his marriage. He told her how he had lost his dear wife, and that all he wanted to do now was to find her.

"I've heard all about it," the witch replied. "Right now she is at the palace of Kostshei the Deathless, and I'm sure you know how terrifying he is. He watches her day and night, and no one has ever defeated him. The only way to kill him is with a magic needle. The needle is hidden in a hare, and the hare is in a large trunk, and the trunk is hidden in the branches of an old oak tree, and the oak tree is watched by Kostshei as closely as Vasilisa herself, which means closer than any treasure he owns."

Then the witch told Ivan where to find the oak tree and how. Ivan went there as fast as he could, but when he saw the oak tree he was discouraged, for he had no idea what to do and how to begin his work. Lo and behold! That old friend of his, the Russian bear, happened to come by just then, sized up the tree, uprooted it, and the trunk fell to the ground and broke in two. A hare jumped out of the trunk and began to run away, but another hare, Ivan's friend, went running after it, caught it, and tore it to pieces. From the hare there flew a duck, a gray one that soared up into the air until it was almost invisible. The beautiful white duck pursued it, struck it with its wings, and the gray duck dropped an egg, which fell into the deep sea. Ivan watched it all happening, and when the egg disappeared into the blue waters he could not stop himself from weeping. All of a sudden a big fish came swimming up, the same fish he had saved, with the egg in its mouth. How happy Ivan was when he had it in his hands. He broke it in two and found the needle inside, the magic needle on which everything depended.

At just that moment Kostshei lost his strength and his power. Ivan entered his vast domain and killed him with the magic needle. In one of the palaces he found his dear wife, the beautiful Vasilisa. He took her back home, and they lived happily ever after.

THE PERI WIFE

Hindu-Persian

This tale, from a Hindu-Persian source, features a Peri rather than an animal bride. In Persian mythology, Peris are winged sprites that occupy a border zone between good and evil spirits. Their radiant beauty comes in part from their association with fire. Depicted as half human and half avian, they are in some ways the aerial counterparts to mermaids.

The son of a merchant in the city of Hindustan was driven out of his father's house because of his undutiful conduct. He assumed the garb of a kalenderee or wandering dervish and left his native village. On the first day of his travels, overcome with fatigue before he could reach a place to rest, he turned off the high road and sat down under a tree near a pond. While he was sitting there, the sun began to set, and he caught sight of four doves flitting down from the branch of a tree at the edge of the pond. They removed their clothes and turned into women (for they were Peris), and they splashed around in the water.

The young man edged, unnoticed, over to the pond, took the garments they had been wearing, and then hid them in the hollow of a tree. He concealed himself behind the tree. When the Peris emerged from the water and discovered that their clothes were missing, they were distressed beyond measure. They ran in all directions looking for their clothes, but in vain. Finally they found the young man and realized that he must have their garments, and they pleaded with him, asking him to restore what he had taken. He would consent under one condition—that one of them would become his wife. The Peris insisted that a union like that was impossible, for their bodies were formed through fire, while mortals were made of clay and water. But he persisted and said he wanted to marry the youngest and most beautiful among them. The Peris finally had to give their consent. They tried to console their sister, who shed copious tears at the thought of parting from them and spending her days with a son of Adam. Once the others were given back their clothes, they took leave of her and flew away.

The young merchant took home his beautiful bride and gave her magnificent clothes. He hid the clothing she had worn in a secret place so that she would not be able to leave him. He made every effort to win her affection and at length he was successful.

> She placed her foot in the path of respect,
> And her head on the carpet of affection.

She bore him children, and gradually she began to enjoy the company of his female relatives and neighbors. All his concerns about her affection vanished, and he grew confident of her love and attachment to him.

Ten years later, the merchant was in financial straits, and he found it necessary to take a long voyage. He committed the Peri to the care of an aged matron, in whom he had the greatest trust and to whom he revealed the secret of his wife's true nature. He showed the matron where he had concealed the enchanted garments. He then placed the foot of departure in the stirrup of travel, and set out on his journey. The Peri, overwhelmed with sorrow, whether because of his absence or for some secret reason, talked endlessly about her feelings of remorse. The old woman tried to comfort her, assuring her that:

> The dark night of absence would soon come to an end,
> And the bright dawn of interview gleam from the horizon of
>   divine bounty.

One day, after bathing, the Peri was drying her amber-scented tresses with a corner of her veil, when the old woman

could not stop herself from expressing admiration for her dazzling beauty. "Ah, nurse," she replied, "you may admire my
charms, yet if you ever saw me in my native garb, you would
have the chance to discover what beauty and grace the Divine
Creator bestowed on Peris. We are among the most perfect
portraits on the tablets of existence. I want you to see for yourself the skills of the divine artist and admire the wonders of
creation. Bring me the robes that my husband hid away. I'll put
them on for just a moment and show you my true beauty, the
like of which no human eye but the Creator's has seen."

The simple woman agreed and fetched the robes for the Peri,
who put them on. Then, like a bird that had suddenly escaped
from its cage, she spread her wings, and crying Farewell, soared
up to the sky and was seen no more. When the merchant returned
from the voyage:

And found no signs of the rose of enjoyment on the tree of hope,
But the lamp of bliss lay extinguished in the chamber of joy.

He became as one Peri-stricken, a recluse in the cell of mad-
ness. Banished from the path of reason, he remained lost to all
the bounties of fortune and the useful purposes of life.

ANIMAL GROOMS

THE CONDOR AND
THE SHEPHERDESS

Bolivia

Using the pretext of a pourquoi *tale, or origins story, about how parrots came into being, "The Condor and the Shepherdess" gives us an emphatically unromantic pairing of woman and beast. It remains hauntingly enigmatic in its refusal to ennoble the condor as a totemic animal. Taking up the nature/culture divide, it creates a liminal space for the heroine, who tries to adjust to the condor colony and its carrion-eating habits. The contrast between condor and parrot, with the one a wild bird of prey, the other a tamed species that mimics human speech, adds much to the grotesque story of origins enacted in the tale's conclusion.*

A condor fell in love with a shepherdess, who had a brown face, black eyes, and a sweet countenance. Because he was unable to satisfy his passionate desires in the shape of a bird, the condor adopted the form of a handsome youth. To hide his scaly neck, he covered himself with a white handkerchief. Thus attired, he presented himself to the little shepherdess while she was tending her cattle.

"Lulu, what are you doing here?" he asked.

"I am grazing my lambs, singing, and using my slingshot to drive away the fox who wants to eat my sheep and the condor who is trying to snatch me away."

"Would you like me to accompany you and help you pursue the fox and frighten the condor?"

"No," she said to him, "companions spoil the young. I love my sheep, I adore my freedom in the wild, and I want to live alone, singing happily, oblivious to the sorrows of love."

"Then I will leave. Until tomorrow."

The following day the condor returned in the same disguise.

"Lulu, could we talk?" he said to the little shepherdess with the beautiful face and black eyes.

"We can talk," she replied. "Tell me where you are from."

"I have come here from the highest mountain, where terrifying thunder resounds. Its summit receives the first kisses of the rising sun and the final rays of the dying light. The snow shines like a diamond in that place, where solitude and silence prevail. Would you like to come with me? You will be the queen of the air. The sky, always clear and blue, will be the ceiling that covers our home. The flowers from the valley will send us their sweet scent to make our lives pleasant. Well, do you want to leave with me?"

"No, I do not want the hills you come from. I love my mother, who would cry on account of my absence. I love my fields, my sheep. Look at that lamb, so white and sweet—how much, how much it would suffer without me!"

"Well, Lulu, I won't pester you. I only ask that you lend me your broach so that I can scratch my back. I feel an itch."

The girl with the black eyes and coral lips gave him her broach, which he returned to her after using it.

The next day, the young man returned.

"Lulu, Lulu," he said, "your eyes have bewitched me. I cannot live without you. And because of that, I am here to see you. Let us leave this place."

"No, no, I cannot," she replied. "My mother would weep, my poor sheep would bleat for me and be inconsolable."

"You know," he replied, "the itch that I felt on my back is still there, and it feels worse than ever. I am begging you to scratch it. Your fingers, soft like the wool made from the alpaca, can put an end to this itching and cure me of it forever."

The unsuspecting girl climbed on his back when he bent over, and as soon as the wily suitor realized that she was on his back, he turned back into a condor, swiftly taking wing and carrying away his precious cargo.

They traversed the sky and, after a rapid flight, arrived at a grotto on a high mountain, where the mother of the condor lived. She was an ancient bird with discolored plumage. A number of condors dwelled in other grottos on the same mountain.

The arrival of the little shepherdess was celebrated with shrieks of joy accompanied by a loud flapping of wings. The mother, the old bird, received her with the greatest joy and lulled her to sleep beneath her huge wings, giving warmth to the little shepherdess who was shivering from the cold air at the top of the mountain.

The girl was happy to be with the young, affectionate condor, but he never brought her anything to eat.

"Listen to me," she told her suitor. "Your embraces nourish my soul, but the lack of food is weakening my body. Remember that I know how to eat and how to drink. I need fire. I need meat. I need the fruits of the earth. I'm hungry and I'm thirsty, my dear."

The condor took wing, broke into a deserted kitchen, stole some burning coals, and carried them off. With his beak, he opened a canal and a current of clear, crystalline water flowed out from it. From the fields and from the roads he gathered bits and pieces of meat from the carcasses of dead animals and presented them to the girl. He dug potatoes out of their patches and took them to her.

The meat smelled bad, and the potatoes were mushy, but the young girl, tormented by hunger, greedily devoured the bad food. She pined for bread, but her lover was not able to satisfy this desire.

While her grief-stricken mother wept in their abandoned home, the little shepherdess with the black eyes was consumed by nostalgia and wasting away from bad food. She grew weary of the amorous embraces of her winged lover. She began to grow thin as well. Feathers emerged from her body. She began laying eggs. And after she laid a great many eggs, she realized that she had turned into a hen. She was the wife of the condor, the queen of the skies, and her job was to breed chicks, which would take after their father and surge fearlessly across the skies.

The mother of the girl continued crying inconsolably in their home, abandoned by the runaway shepherdess.

A parrot living near the mother took pity on her and said,

"Don't cry, my dear woman. Your daughter is living on the great mountain as the mistress of the condor. If you let me eat the corn in your garden and use your leafy trees to rest my limbs and make my nest, I promise to bring the girl back to you."

The mother accepted the offer. She opened her garden of corn to him and let him nest in her trees.

The parrot flew over to the high mountain and, taking advantage of the condor's momentary distraction, picked up the young girl and flew her right back to her mother. The girl was emaciated and she smelled bad because of the terrible food she had been eating. Her eyes, black like a dark night, were all that remained of her former beauty. Her body, which bore silky feathers, gave her the appearance of an outcast human disguised as a bird. The mother took the girl in her arms, washed her body with the tears from her eyes, and then dressed her in her best clothes. She put the girl in her lap and gazed at her with infinite tenderness.

The condor, outraged and disconsolate after what the parrot had done to him, went out in search of the bird. He found him in the garden, stuffed with corn, flitting from tree to tree, carefree and happy.

The condor swooped down on the parrot and swallowed it whole with its big mouth. The parrot promptly came out the other end. The condor swallowed the parrot again and the parrot once again flew out from behind. The condor, furious because he was not able to destroy his hated adversary, took him between his sharp claws and tore him to pieces, which he ate one by one. Yet to his great surprise, a beautiful little parrot flew out from behind for every piece he ate.

The Amerindians say that this is how these attractive little birds came into being.

The grieving condor flew back to the mountain, dyed his feathers black as a sign of mourning, and wept bitter tears for his beloved shepherdess. His tears turned into black butterflies, which flew into the home of his beloved.

THE PARROT PRINCE

Chile

Combining features of "Cinderella" with "East of the Sun and West of the Moon," this story gives us a named heroine, one who becomes a commanding force in nature rather than allowing herself to become a prisoner of toxic family circumstances. Instead of weeping, she embarks on a mission. With many new twists (getting stepsisters drunk and learning to heal by listening to animals chatter), the tale challenges us to rethink how motifs are recycled and reinvented. The opening sentence emphasizes how stories are preserved and transmitted, while the final one points to the ephemeral nature of oral traditions. There is genius in creating a conclusion that invites listeners to be part of the project of conserving stories before they vanish, like breath in the wind.

There once lived a widowed gentleman who had a very beautiful daughter named Mariquita, and he loved her dearly, doted on her, and did whatever he could to make her happy. But Mariquita felt very lonely, and she wished that there were other girls in her house with whom she could play and have fun while her father went out and managed his business.

Well, in the neighboring house there was a widow with three young daughters, all older than Mariquita and quite ugly. This widow was always watching Mariquita, giving her sweets and all types of candies. The daughters treated her with affection and would say to her, "Tell your papa to marry our mama and then we will live together and play all day long." And they said this so often, and treated her so tenderly, that Mariquita came to believe that she would be the happiest girl in the land once the wedding took place. So she began to plead with her father, begging him at all hours of the day to marry the neighboring widow. Eventually, the man gave in to the girl's requests, but he did this only to please her. And thus a marriage ceremony was performed.

The wedding celebrations were barely over when things began to change completely for poor Mariquita. Instead of hugs, sweets, and candies, she received nothing from her stepmother and stepsisters but rude treatment, scolding, and beatings.

The poor girl felt responsible for what happened to her, so she endured everything in silence and said nothing to her father. And she would have continued to remain quiet about her suffering for who knows how long if the abuse had not become so excessive. One day, when the owner of the house was away, the daughters of the widow dragged Mariquita around by her hair. And when the girl complained about this to her stepmother, that evil woman, instead of reprimanding her daughters for their bad behavior, grabbed a stick and gave her several strong blows, saying to her, "Stop your complaining, you scamp. Who knows how many bad things you did before my little girls decided to punish you!" But the truth was that the three girls hated Mariquita. They envied her because she was beautiful, while they were ugly, and because she was the sole heiress to her father's wealth, while they were poor. And for these same reasons, the old woman could not stand her either.

When her father arrived home, Mariquita told him what had happened and revealed to him the suffering she had endured up to that point. She did not blame him for the situation, but begged him to let her live alone in a little house that her mother had bequeathed to her when she died. The father agreed to her request, since he saw no other way for peace to return to his family.

After so many days of suffering, a time of prosperity came to Mariquita. Her life passed by happily as she kept house and watched over a little garden with some trees whose shade invited her to rest.

One afternoon, while she was sweeping the patio, she heard

a voice, which spoke these words: "Mariquita, may I help you sweep?" Astonished, she looked around, but saw no one. Then she heard the voice again. "Don't be frightened, Mariquita, I'm speaking to you from the branches of the *peumo* tree." She looked up at the tree and saw a parrot dressed in brilliant feathers of the most beautiful colors.

"Hey, pretty little parrot," she said. "How can I come up to your perch?"

The parrot answered, "Would you like me to come down?"

"Yes, come down and stay with me. You will be my companion. I am so lonely! How I will watch over you! What delicious things I will give you to eat! Walnuts, chocolates, bread with wine, sweets. . . ."

"Right now I can't," the parrot replied. "I have to fly away, but I will return tonight. Open your window, and leave a basin of water, a hand towel, a comb, and a mirror there for me." And then he took flight.

As soon as it was dark, Mariquita opened the window and placed on the sill the objects that the parrot had requested. Full of impatience, she sat there, waiting for it to return. When midnight arrived, she heard the flapping of the parrot's wings and knew that it was approaching. She watched the parrot alight in the water and bathe happily. It left the basin and dried itself, then combed its feathers, admiring itself in the mirror. Finally, it leapt up, knelt down on its feet, and turned into the most handsome prince imaginable.

I will relate nothing of what the two said to each other, except that in the morning, upon departing, the prince promised to return to her every night and remain with her until dawn. He handed her a huge sack of money, then flew over to the bowl, and turned into a parrot again. He took flight and was lost in the skies.

The parrot fulfilled his promise and the visits were repeated night after night.

Mariquita felt happier than ever. The prince adored her. She wore costly silk dresses, and the most valuable jewels imaginable adorned her ears, her neck, and her arms.

One day, one of Mariquita's stepsisters passed by the house

and spotted her in the window. She went to tell her mother and sisters how beautifully dressed and bejeweled Mariquita was.

"Someone is giving her money," said the old woman, "because she doesn't have the wherewithal to buy things of such value." Turning to her oldest daughter, she added, "It would be good if you were to pay her a visit and spend the night there so that you could observe what happens and then come tell us what you saw."

The next day the oldest went to visit Mariquita and told her a thousand lies: that they regretted so much that she had left their house; that they missed her so much; that she had not been an ingrate; that her mother and her sisters were dying to see her again; and that she had come to see her to spend all day and all night with her. Mariquita, ever obliging, thanked her and showed her much affection. But fearing that her stepsister would see the prince arrive and hear the two of them talking, she plied her with one drink after another during dinner, and the girl, who was fond of drink, downed one glass after another. Before rising from the table, she was so drunk that a wagon could have rolled on top of her without her noticing it. Mariquita put her into a room next to hers and waited patiently for the prince.

The next day, the stepsister awoke not too early in the morning, after dreaming the previous night away and never realizing what had taken place so close to her. When she arrived back home, she told her mother and sisters how well Mariquita had arranged her household and how generously she had served her, which incited the envy of that evil trio all the more. The mother was annoyed with the girl because she had not seen what mattered, so she ordered the middle child, in her turn, to visit her stepsister, exhorting her not to fall asleep. But this girl fared no better than her older sister: she drank too much and returned home knowing as much as she knew before going out.

The youngest of the girls, who was also the most hideous, the most mean-spirited, and the most spiteful toward Mariquita, said to her mother, "I will go now, and I will find out everything there is to know."

And so it happened, indeed, because she only pretended to

drink, never slept, and passed the entire night near a candle, keeping an eye on the keyhole of the door that connected her bedroom with Mariquita's. She witnessed the arrival of the parrot, saw him bathe in the basin and then turn into the most beautiful prince. Finally, she watched as he sat down next to Mariquita, spoke to her affectionately, and caressed her. Rage was consuming the stepsister, who spent the entire night in the same position, with her eye glued to the keyhole, never blinking, never moving, no matter how uncomfortable the position was. She remained that way until the moment when, as the day brightened, the prince gave his lover a sack of money, said farewell with an affectionate kiss, dove into the basin, turned back into a parrot, and took flight.

Not much later, the jealous girl bid farewell to her stepsister, assuring her that she had had a wonderful day and night, and saying that, if it were not too much of a burden, she would gladly repeat the visit. Mariquita told her, in turn, that her presence had been a joy and that she should come to visit whenever she wished, assuring her that she would always be well received. The stepsister casually walked out of Mariquita's house with a smile on her face. When she was barely out of sight, she began to run home. Upon arrival, the furious girl shouted gleefully:

"Mama, look at how I beat them all! These stupid girls fell asleep and saw nothing, but I didn't fall asleep, and I saw everything, everything, everything!"

And speaking hastily, she recounted what she had witnessed.

Once her story was finished, the mother said, "Ah! We have them now! That hussy will not talk tonight with her famous prince. I will go and make sure of it."

Indeed, a little before midnight, the old woman, hiding herself in the shadows, reached the window where the prince entered, and without making the slightest noise, she put three sharp knives in the basin with their edges pointed upward. She then kept guard, watching everything from a distance.

At midnight, the parrot followed his usual ritual and landed in the basin, but this time the knives ripped into his body. He experienced pain so intense that he let out a shrill cry. And looking at Mariquita, who had hurried over to see what had happened, he spoke with a plaintive voice: "What have I done to you, ingrate, that you would mistreat me in this way? This is how you repay my affection? Today is the day that my enchantment was to end. With this betrayal, you have most likely lost me forever. Should you ever come to regret your actions and decide to search for me, you will need to wear out the soles of iron shoes in order to find me."

And so the parrot flew up into the sky, while tears ran down the face of the poor girl, who wasn't given the chance to say even one word. Only after she saw the knives in the water, reddened with the blood of the prince, did she understand what had happened.

The old woman saw and heard everything from the hiding place where she was spying on the two. Radiant with joy because of the success of her mission, she went back to her house to tell her daughters. All three of the girls celebrated their victory, but the one who took the greatest joy in the misfortune of Mariquita was the youngest.

Mariquita cried bitter tears for a good while, but she soon realized that searching for her beloved made better sense than weeping. She immediately ordered a pair of iron shoes to be made, which she put on as soon as they were delivered. Then she set out on her adventure. To move as quickly as possible, she packed nothing but a bundle of linen, some thread, a needle, a pair of sharp scissors, and a bottle for water. With this package for her prince, she walked for a long time through hills and plains, without stopping and resting, suffering a thousand hardships and miseries, until one day she became so tired that she simply could go no farther. She arrived at a mountain near a lagoon and lay down on a thicket in order to rest. Then she stretched her legs out to make herself comfortable and shouted, "Oh, joyous day!" for she realized that the soles of her iron shoes were completely worn out, so much so that her toes were sticking out of the fronts of both shoes—a clear sign, so she thought, that she would soon encounter her beloved.

It began to grow dark. Dead tired, Mariquita rested for a while with her eyelids closed, but she did not fall asleep, because she could hear the loud noise of fluttering wings, which stopped very close to her, causing her to open her eyes and pay attention. The next moment, she heard a renewed beating of wings and realized that three ducks were talking to each other. "Well, old friend, how are our plans going? And you, goddaughter, how are things?"

"We are fine, old friend. We have just arrived here from our house, where we left my idiot of a husband sleeping, and my two older daughters, who are no better than he is. Yes, the only worthy person in my life is your goddaughter, and for that reason I take her everywhere, since she is a witch just like us. And what news do you bring us of the parrot prince? Will he die soon?"

"He should be dead by now," said the goddaughter.

"He has no more than two or three days, old friend. The wounds made by the knives that you placed in the basin have begun to fester, and the doctors have not been able to find a remedy. And who could possibly find one? But let us speak quietly, old friend, and conceal ourselves, since the walls have ears and the bushes have eyes. Who could ever know that the prince would be able to heal in three days if someone plucked a feather from each of our right wings, dipped it in our blood, and placed one of the feathers over his wounds every day? Of course, in order for this to happen, someone would have to kill us first."

"They'll never be able to guess that, old friend, so dear to my soul! The Devil would never permit them to know such things!"

"Let's go to sleep, old friend. I'm very tired, because I woke up very early."

"Same for the two of us, old friend. We are going to rest. Tomorrow we'll continue our conversation."

Waddling around, the three ducks set themselves down between some reeds on the shores of the lagoon.

The talking ducks were actually three witches: the stepmother of Mariquita, the youngest daughter, and the girl's godmother. They met there every Saturday night, transformed into ducks, to discuss the news of the week.

Mariquita waited about an hour, then came out of hiding armed with her scissors, which were large and very sharp. She went over to where the ducks were sleeping. The three of them were situated some distance from each other. The first one that

Mariquita encountered was her stepmother. Taking her by the neck, she cut off her head with a single snip of the scissors. She placed some of the blood in the bottle that she had brought with her and plucked a feather from the right wing. She then went in search of the next duck, which she found right away, and it turned out to be her stepsister. Mariquita then did to her exactly what she had done to her stepmother. Finally, she performed the same operation on the stepsister's godmother. After this, Mariquita departed in haste for the city. Upon arrival, she swapped her clothing for what a man she met on the road was wearing. He gave her his clothes in exchange for all of the money she was carrying. Disguised as a man, she entered the city.

After walking for a while, she met a woman, who was moving very slowly because she seemed burdened by sorrows. Mariquita stopped the woman and asked her, "What is happening, sweet woman, that causes you to be so troubled?"

"Well, little boy, I will tell you what is happening," answered the old woman. "The prince, the son of the king our dear lord, is dying, and the doctors say that he is unlikely to survive beyond today."

"Oh, sweet woman! I am a doctor, and if I were allowed in the palace, I am sure that I could heal the ailing prince in three days."

"Really, little boy? I will take you to the palace. I raised the prince from when he was an infant, and I can enter the palace whenever I want."

And so the two of them made their way to the palace.

The little old woman was the first to speak with the king. He ordered the young doctor to be admitted to the prince's room, commanding everyone to leave the doctor alone with his patient.

When everyone had left, Mariquita could no longer hold back the bitter tears that flowed down her cheeks. The prince was unconscious, with his eyes closed, and his wounds gave off a repulsive odor. In tears, she took one of the feathers plucked from the wings of the ducks and, smearing it with the blood she had put into her bottle, she rubbed it gently against the prince's wounds.

Early the next day, the king went to see his son.

"How is he faring?" the king asked the fellow pretending to be a doctor.

"Much better, sir. Approach him and see for yourself: the worms have vanished and the wounds have formed a crust."

The doctor asked that the two be left alone until the following day, and the king withdrew most happily, filled with the hope that his son would survive.

As soon as the king departed, Mariquita took the second feather, dipped it into the blood of the witches, and rubbed it on the young man's wounds. At this point, the prince began to recover consciousness. His scabs came off, falling bit by bit from his body.

The next day the king returned and found his son in even better condition. Now he was able to speak. Naturally, the king left his room even happier than on the previous visit.

Soon after the king left the room, Mariquita took the third feather, covered it in the blood that remained in her bottle, and rubbed it over the body of the prince. At this point, the patient was fully recovered, and he asked to put on his clothes. He recognized Mariquita, and in the midst of her joy, she told him everything that had happened since the time he had been wounded, and how, through the conversation of the witches, she had discovered that her stepmother was responsible for placing the knives in the basin.

When Mariquita finished her story, the king entered, and words cannot describe the joy he experienced upon seeing his son standing on his feet, completely recovered. The prince told his father everything he had just found out from Mariquita and asked for permission to marry her, since they loved each other deeply, and he owed his life to her. The king happily consented, and the marriage was celebrated within a few days, amidst the great enthusiasm of everyone who lived in the kingdom.

And I can faithfully vouch for this, because I was present at the wedding, and I ate and drank so much there that I almost burst.

And with this my story ended, and the wind blew it out to sea.

NICHOLAS THE FISH

Colombia

A tale with a fascinating mélange of motifs, "Nicholas the Fish"
reminds us of how tropes can be reshuffled in kaleidoscopic
fashion to produce startlingly new and different narratives. The
story begins with the kind of foolish bargain familiar from tales
like "Jack and the Beanstalk" or "The Girl Without Hands."
Unique in its depiction of a sea monster, half human, half fish,
it takes many unexpected turns, with a heroine who struggles
to maintain her dignity despite what is imposed on her. The
mother of all animals seems to figure as an ancient deity whose
role is functionally equivalent to the devils and other folkloric
creatures from whose head a single strand of hair must be pulled
in order to restore order or win a reward. Her hair appears to
humans in the form of a meadow atop a mountain.

There was once a poor man who married a poor woman. Every
day the man would go fishing and return with enough fish to
sell and cover the day's expenses. The couple survived from one
day to the next on the fish caught by the husband. One day,
the man went fishing and wore himself out casting his net into
the water, yet he caught nothing, not even a single fish.

On the way home, the man passed by a well and heard a voice
say, "If you bring me the lovely thing that comes out to greet you
when you come home, I will give you all the fish you want."

The man thought to himself, "That must be the puppy I keep
at home. It always greets me by jumping up on me when I
return from fishing."

The voice repeated the offer three times, and the third time the man answered, "All right, I will bring it to you, but where should I bring it?"

"Right here," the voice replied.

Then the man cast his net and caught a load of fish. He walked home a very happy man that day. When he was about to arrive home, however, his little daughter came running out to greet him and hug him.

The man quickly realized exactly what this meant and said to her, "Oh! If you knew what just happened, you would not be hugging me."

He entered the house and his wife asked, "Why are you crying?"

"If you knew, you wouldn't ask," he responded.

The woman began to prepare the fish for dinner while the man remained silent. When the food was ready, he said, "My appetite has vanished."

"Why?" his wife asked.

"If you knew, you wouldn't ask."

"What happened? Tell me!"

The man began to weep, and then he told her, "Look, this is what happened. I was walking home empty-handed and a voice told me that if I handed over the precious thing that greeted me on my return, I would be given all the fish I wanted. And our little daughter came out to greet me!"

The woman said, "Well, you made a promise. Let the will of God be done."

The terms of the agreement gave the man three days. He dressed up his daughter and, on the third day, brought her to the well.

"Here is what you asked for," the man said. The voice then spoke, "Take her along the river until you find a house. Leave her there."

They found the house and entered it. It was a very well-arranged house, with nice chairs and tables inside. The man said, "My dear daughter, you must stay here without me." She consented happily, and he shut the door and went home. Night arrived, and it soon became apparent that the house was enchanted. When light was needed, candles were lit; when the girl wanted to eat, food appeared on the table; and when she was tired, a hammock was hung. Yet there was not a soul in sight.

When she wanted to rest, the lights went out, just like that. And when she woke up in the morning, the table was set. She saw food there, yet there was not a soul around.

Then, at night, after the lights went out, the voice of a man called out to her, "Come here and kill the louse that is bothering me."

So she walked over, found the man, and began to massage his head. After a little while, he said, "That's enough, go back to sleep." And so she did, for she was still just a little girl.

It was peaceful there in that house. One night the man returned and asked her again to rid him of the louse. While rubbing his head, she touched him a little lower and felt something strange, similar to wool, but in the darkness she was not able to see what it was.

One night the man said to her, "Tomorrow you can go see your family, and especially your father. A horse will be waiting for you at the door. But make sure that you do not let them touch you."

She agreed not to let herself be touched.

"Here, take some money for your father," the man said. She collected it and, in the morning, she left.

When she arrived home, her mother ran toward her to give her a hug, but the girl withdrew and said that she could not be touched.

"Come down from the horse," the parents said. But she responded, "I cannot come down now."

The parents were amazed to see her, for she was now a full-grown woman. She handed over the money and left them.

When she returned, she did not know who could have taken her horse and unsaddled it. Night arrived, and when the lights went out, the man returned. She went over to rub his head.

"Well, did you do as I asked?" he said.

"Yes, I didn't let them touch me."

"Good. On Sunday you're going to go back and do the same thing."

So she returned to her parents and carried out his orders perfectly. The man was very pleased.

However, when the man instructed the girl to visit her parents a third time, something different happened. She was rubbing his head, and she placed her hand on his body and felt something scaly. "This man is enchanted!" she thought. Then the man said, "Tomorrow you will go back to your house, but this time, you may not bring anything back from your house."

The girl agreed, and the next day she went home. This time, she got off the horse, entered the house, and let her mother and father hug her. The three of them ate and smoked and drank joyously. As the girl was preparing to leave, she said to her mother, "Mama, a man appears in my room every night and asks me to kill the lice on his head. There is something unusual about him. It might be a good idea for me to take a matchbox and a candle back with me."

And so the mother gave them to her. The girl placed the objects into her pocket and left. That night, when she was rubbing the man's head, she realized that her soothing touch had lulled him to sleep. Then she thought, "Now I'm finally going to see him." So she lit a match and saw that he was a fish from the waist down and a man from the waist up.

The man awoke from his feigned sleep and said, "Look at you, you scamp! Now I've caught you. I told you not to bring anything from home, but you went and brought back those candles!"

The girl was frightened. "Well," said the man, "the good time that you've had here is over. Now you will have to do some work. Tomorrow you will put on the workman's clothing that will be on the table, and you will have a sombrero, a machete, and sandals."

In the morning, the girl found the clothing and the man said to her, "Put on these clothes. It's time for you to go to the king and ask for work to make up for your failure to obey me." The girl dressed herself as a man, put on the sombrero, and left the house.

"Head toward the right," the man instructed her.

When she arrived before the king, she greeted him and noticed that he was still quite young. The king addressed her with affection, "Why are you here, young man?"

"I'm in need of work," she responded. "I'm here to see whether there might be some tasks here for me."

"Of course there are," the king replied. He knew all along that the laborer was not a man, for everything about her was feminine. She was given a room. The following day, the king set her a task.

"Look," he said, "this task will be difficult, because it will require you to walk a great distance. I need a strand of hair from the mother of all of the world's animals."

So, the girl set out without a clue as to where to go. After she had walked a good distance, she met a little old woman, who approached her and asked, "Where are you headed, young man?"

The girl answered, "I am walking in search of a strand of hair from the mother of all of the world's animals."

"That won't be difficult," the old woman replied. "Since you happen to be carrying food and water, could you spare some for my son and me? We're thirsty."

The girl divided up everything she had, giving food and water to them both. When they parted, the old woman pointed toward a mountain and said, "Walk to that mountain, and there you will find the mother of all animals. You will see a meadow. If its surface is covered with grass, step on it without fear and carefully pluck a strand of the hair. But if the meadow contains no grass, then do not step on it, for that means that the mother is awake."

When the girl reached the meadow, she found it covered with grass. She waded through the stalks and found a strand that she could pluck. She then wrapped it up, made it into a ball, and headed straight back to the king. She gave him the strand, and a joyous expression appeared on his face as he untangled it.

The strand was astonishingly long, and it seemed to be endless as it formed a huge pile before the king. The king then declared, "This youth has done an excellent job. How much should I pay you?"

"It's up to you to decide," she replied.

So he gave her thousands upon thousands of pesos, then said, "Now you can go work in a different part of the land."

Carrying the pesos, the girl set off. She encountered another old woman, actually the same one as before. Again she reported that she was lost and trying to find her way back home.

The little old woman said, "Don't be afraid! Take this wand and carry it home with you. Whenever you are lost, wave the wand and say, 'Wand, wand, by your power and by the power that God has given you, show me the way home.' It will guide you."

And so the girl departed. The wand sent her down the right path until she reached home at last. Her mother and father were thrilled to see her, even though she was dressed as a man, for they recognized the features of her face.

The mother asked, "Has our daughter turned into a man?"

The girl took off her clothing and put on one of her dresses. She was their daughter again, and now she would stay at home with them. With the money she had brought back home, the family established themselves as merchants, and their fortune grew. They opened up a shop and wanted for nothing from then on.

THE MUSKRAT HUSBAND

Alaska

This story was told in Cup'ik (a variety of Central Alaska Yupik Eskimo) by Thomas Moses in Chevak, Alaska. The year was 1978, and Anthony C. Woodbury recorded the tale. The Yupiks are a group of indigenous peoples living in Alaska and the Russian Far East. With a population of 24,000 in the 2001 U.S. census, the Yupik people form one of the largest Native American linguistic communities in the United States. This tale is known as a quliraq, *or story passed down by ancestors, and, like some stories of that type, it uses generic names for the characters. The tale is akin to many other narratives about animal bridegrooms, and the human wife suffers many of the same unutterable agonies of separation and loss. But the conclusion of this story, although traditional in a Yupik context, deviates sharply from that of "Beauty and the Beast."*

There was once a village
that lay
on the bank of a river.

This village
had a great hunter
and the great hunter
had a daughter.

Although many young men
asked to marry his daughter,

the great hunter did not permit her
to accept a husband.

There was one young man whom she wanted for a husband,
one of the young men of the village.
And this young man
tried to get her for his wife.
But though he asked to marry her, her father
would not let him,
this man
whom his daughter wanted for a husband.

So it was, and the girl decided in anger never to marry.
. . .
As time passed, even her father
tried to persuade her to accept a husband,
but she did not want to:
she still was angry that the man she wanted to marry
had been rejected by her father.

Well, life went on that way,
in that village there,
on the bank of the river.
. . .
One day,
the great hunter's daughter
went outside;
behind the village some boys were playing
at the bank of an oxbow lake,
noisily chasing something.
She went up to see what they were chasing,
and when she got there,
she saw it was a muskrat!

By that time
the muskrat was faltering,
and though it dove,

it never stayed underwater long;
it looked like it soon would die.

But then
she saved the muskrat by dispersing
the boys who were chasing it.
By the time she made them stop
the muskrat was exhausted; it was practically dead.
. . .
They [the boys] went home,
and she too went home
behind them.
And life went on as usual
for a few weeks.
. . .
Then one day,
while she was doing her chores,
the woman
saw
a man,
and his parka was made of muskrat!

He said to her
that out of gratitude he was coming to ask her to be his wife,
out of gratitude that she had saved him
as she did.

And the woman
accepted him,
because she was still without a husband.

Now, this man was a stranger,
an odd-looking sort of stranger.

Well, he married her, and they lived as husband and wife.

He always caught lots of game when he hunted;
he even caught lots of bearded seal.

. . .

But this man
warned his wife repeatedly,
never ever to take his clothes,
even when they were wet,
and put them by the fire pit
to dry in the heat.

And this was how it was to be,
even if he came home all wet.

. . .

Well, on one occasion
he was all wet when he came home,
and later on she dried his grass bootliners.

When the fireplace
was lit,
she dried them
in its heat.

Her husband was gone while she was doing this,
somewhere outside.

. . .

After a while he came back.
Well, when he got inside,
he saw his bootliners,
which had been dried in the heat.
"Ungh!" he sighed,
and he turned around quickly and ran out.

His wife
went out after him.

She saw as she followed him,
that he was running to the lake behind the village.

And she
chased him, running right behind him, because she still wanted
   him as her husband.

Now the lake they were going to
was where the boys had been chasing the muskrat,
and when her husband reached it, right away
he dove in.

When the woman
reached the lake herself, then
she too dove right in.

Both of them went underwater, and then came up together,
as muskrats!
   . . .
So, even though he had warned her,
she dried his bootliners in the heat.
By doing this, she made him turn back into a muskrat.

And this woman
also became a muskrat,
right there in the oxbow lake.

And now it is the end.

A BOARHOG FOR A HUSBAND

West Indies

In tales about Beauties and Beasts, the plot generally turns on a redemptive transformation from a beastly enchantment back to an authentic human self. But in this story about a boarhog, the animal is a master in the art of deception, turning himself into an attractive man. What also makes this tale unusual is the role of the Old Witch Boy, a cinderlad consigned to the hearth to carry out all the dirty work, a dark male double of the king's daughter, abject and most likely an illegitimate son, hidden away, yet also in the end heroic.

> *Scalambay, scalambay*
> *Scoops, scops, scalambay*
> *See my lover coming there*
> *Scoops, scops, scalambay.*

Once upon a time—it was a very good time—Massa King had an only daughter. And all the young fellows were constantly talking with each other about who was going to be able to marry her. They all came by to call on her, but none of them suited her. Each time one would come, her father would say "Now this is the one!" But she kept saying, "No, Daddy, this fellow here, I just don't like him," or "No, Mommy, this one really doesn't please me." But the last one to come along was a handsome young fellow, and she fell in love with him right away. And of course, when she fell in love, it was deep and wide—she just lost her head altogether. What she didn't know was that she'd actually chosen a boarhog who had changed himself into a human to go courting.

Now the Massa King had another child, a little Old Witch Boy who lived there and did all the nasty stuff around the palace. He was always dirty and smelly, you know, and no one liked to be around him, especially the King's beautiful daughter. One day after work the young fellow came in to visit his bride, and the Old Witch Boy whispered, "Daddy, Daddy, did you know that the fellow my sister is going to marry is a boarhog?" "What? You better shut your mouth and get back under the bed where you belong." (That's where they made the Old Witch Boy stay, you see, because he was so dirty.)

Now when they got married, they moved way up on the mountain up where they plant all those good things to put in the pot, roots like dasheen, tania, and all those provisions that hogs like to eat, too. One day, Massa King came up there and showed him a big piece of land he wanted his daughter and her husband to have for farming. The husband really liked that because he could raise lots of tanias—which is what boarhogs like to eat most.

So one day he went up to work, early early in the morning. Now there was this little house up by the land where he could go and change his clothes before he went to work. He went into one side of the little house, and he started singing:

> Scalambay, scalambay
> Scoops, scops, scalambay
> See my lover coming there
> Scoops, scops, scalambay.

And with each refrain he would take off one piece of clothing. And with every piece he took off he became more of a boarhog—first the head, then the feet, then the rest of the body.

> Scalambay, scalambay
> Scoops, scops, scalambay
> See my lover coming there
> Scoops, scops, scalambay.

Well, about noon, when he thought the time was coming for lunch to arrive in the field, he went back into the house and put back on his clothes, took off the boarhog suit and put back on the ordinary suit he came in. And as he got dressed he sang the same little song to change himself back into a handsome man.

> *Scalambay, scalambay*
> *Scoops, scops, scalambay*
> *See my lover coming there*
> *Scoops, scops, scalambay.*

After a while, the Old Witch Boy as usual came with the food, but this day he came early and saw what was going on, heard the singing, and saw the man changing. So he rushed home and told his father again, "Daddy, this fellow who married my sister up there really is a boarhog. It's true!" Massa King said "Boy, shut your mouth," and his sister said, "Get back underneath the bed, you scamp you."

The next day, the Old Witch Boy got up very early and went up the mountain and heard the song again:

> *Scalambay, scalambay*
> *Scoops, scops, scalambay*
> *See my lover coming there*
> *Scoops, scops, scalambay.*

All right, he thought, and he went down again and he told his father what he had seen and heard. He even sang the song. Now Massa King didn't know what to think. But he knew he was missing a lot of tanias from his other fields, so he loaded up his gun and went to see what was going on up there in his fields. Mr. Boarhog was up there changing and didn't know he was being watched, but he thought he heard something so he kind of stopped. The Old Witch Boy started to sing, and Mr. Boarhog couldn't do anything but join in with him. And so there they both were, singing:

> *Scalambay, scalambay*
> *Scoops, scops, scalambay*

See my lover coming there
Scoops, scops, scalambay.

And the man slowly changed into a boarhog. When the King saw this he couldn't believe his eyes. He took his gun and he let go, *pow*! And he killed Mr. Boarhog, and carried him down the mountain. The King's beautiful daughter couldn't believe what she saw and began to scream and cry, but Massa King told her what he had seen and what he had done, and then she had to believe it.

They cleaned Mr. Boarhog's body and had him quartered. And I was right there on the spot, and took one of the testicles and it gave me food for nearly a week!

THE MONKEY BRIDEGROOM

Japan

Japanese culture has a rich monkey lore, and in the Edo era, monkey worship was not uncommon. The monkey retained its power as a creature capable of warding off demons and diseases, and it was also seen as a patron of fertility, childbirth, and marriage. At the same time, monkeys were often portrayed as aggressive, malevolent trickster figures, and women were considered particularly vulnerable to their predations. The cherry blossoms on the tree, symbols of ephemeral beauty, add poignancy to the contrast between the lighthearted words of the girl and the pathos of the monkey's song.

In a certain place there lived an old man. One day he went out to dig up *gobo* [burdock] roots, but he couldn't dig out a single one. Just as he was wondering what to do, a monkey came along and called out, "Grandfather, grandfather, shall I help you pull up *gobo* roots?"

"Yes, please help me. If you will dig up some roots for me; I'll give you one of my daughters as your wife."

"Will you really do that!" the monkey cried. "Then I shall come to claim her in three days."

The old man, thinking that the monkey surely would never come to claim one of his daughters, agreed to all he said.

While they were talking, the monkey began pulling up *gobo* roots and soon had a large pile of them. "The monkey certainly has pulled up a lot of roots; perhaps he really intends to come for one of my daughters," the old man thought to himself, beginning to get a little worried.

Finally the monkey had pulled up every *gobo* root in the field. "Well," he said to the old man, "I shall surely come for your daughter." Then he scampered off.

The old man thought to himself: "He must really intend to come. Why did I ever tell him that I'd give him one of my daughters? What shall I do? What shall I do? I don't think that any of my girls will agree to become his wife. I must try to persuade one of them." The old man walked sadly home, talking to himself.

When he got home, he called his eldest daughter and, after telling her what had happened, said, "When the monkey comes in three days, will you go to be his bride?"

"What!" she cried. "Who would ever want to become a monkey's wife!" and she refused even to consider it.

The old man then called his second daughter and asked her the same thing.

"Why," she cried, "what a fool you are! Who would ever make a promise like that? I may be older than our youngest sister, but I'm not going to become that monkey's bride. I don't think anyone would do it," and so she refused completely.

"Since the other two have refused," the old man thought to himself, "I don't think that the youngest will agree either. However, I'll have to ask her; there's nothing else to do." He went to his youngest daughter and told her what he had promised and that the monkey would be coming in three days to get his bride. "Your sisters have both refused. Will you please go and be his bride?" His face paling, the old man made his request.

The girl thought for a while, then replied, "Yes, father, since you have promised, I will go."

Upon hearing this, the old man was overjoyed, crying, "Really! Will you really go?"

"I will go because of my duty to you," said the girl, "but you must give me three things to take with me."

"What things do you want?" he asked. "I will give you anything you request."

"Please give me a very heavy mortar, together with a heavy maul for pounding rice and one *to* [about 50 pounds] of rice."

"What!" he cried, "is that all you want! If so, you shall have them," and he soon brought them to her.

On the third day the monkey came as he had promised. The youngest daughter said to him: "I am to become your bride, but when we go back to the mountains, we will want to eat rice mochi, so let's take this mortar, maul, and bag of rice with us. You can carry it all on your back."

The monkey loaded everything on his back. It was very, very heavy, but since his bride had requested it, he did not want to refuse, and they set off up the mountain, the monkey carrying his heavy load.

It was just the beginning of April, and on both sides of the road the cherry trees were in full bloom. They traveled along until they came to a place where the road went close to the edge of a deep canyon. At the bottom of the canyon there was a river. At this point the branches of the cherry trees fell over into the canyon, making such a beautiful scene that the girl stopped, saying to the monkey, "Oh, such a lovely cherry tree. Won't you please climb up and get me a branch of those cherry blossoms."

Since this too was a request of his bride, the monkey agreed and began to climb up into one of the trees. "Please get some flowers from the topmost branch," the girl cried from below, so the monkey continued to climb higher and higher. "Isn't this about right?" he asked, but the girl urged him higher and higher until he had climbed up to where the branches were very small and weak.

The load on his back was very heavy, and the branch he was on was very small; suddenly it broke, and the monkey fell head-long into the canyon below, landing with a splash, *dossun*, in the river. As he sank from sight with the heavy mortar on his back, he sang this song:

> I do not regret my death,
> But oh, how sad for my poor bride.

And he soon disappeared from view.

The girl was very happy and returned to her home.

Naa, mosu mosu, komen dango. "Well, hallo, hallo, rice cakes."

TALE OF THE GIRL AND THE HYENA-MAN

Ghana

This tale was collected by a British colonial administrator in a region now known as Ghana. Angela Carter called the story the "best of all 'Mother knows best' stories." In it, the motif of a magical flight is invoked, with a girl who escapes a villain by changing herself into a tree, a body of water, and a stone. The traditional magical flight involves throwing obstacles (combs, needles, or whatever is at hand) in the path of a pursuer, but here the heroine becomes a shape-shifter, turning herself into the stumbling blocks. The story is ingeniously calculated to lure listeners into a conversation with its riddlelike ending.

A certain girl was given by her parents to a young man in marriage. She did not care for the youth, so she refused and said that she would choose a husband for herself. Shortly after, there came to the village a fine young man of great strength and beauty. The girl fell in love with him at first sight and told her parents that she had found the man she wished to marry, and as the latter was not unwilling the marriage soon took place.

Now it happened that the young man was not a man at all, but a hyena, for although as a rule women change into hyenas and men into hawks, the hyena can change itself into either man or woman as it may please.

During the first night the two newly married ones were sleeping together, the husband said: "Supposing that when we go to my town we chance to quarrel on the road what would you do?" The wife answered that she would change herself into a tree. The man said that he would be able to catch her even then. She said that if that was the case she would turn into a pool of water. "Oh! that would not trouble me," said the hyena-man, "I should catch you all the same." "Why, then I should turn into a stone," replied his spouse. "Still I should catch you," remarked the man.

Just at that moment the girl's mother shouted from her room, for she had heard the conversation: "Keep quiet, my daughter; is it thus that a woman tells all her secrets to her man?" So the girl said no more.

Next morning, when the day was breaking, the husband told his wife to rise up as he was returning to his home. He bade her make ready to accompany him a short way down the road to see him off. She did as he told her, and as soon as ever the couple were out of sight of the village the husband turned himself into a hyena and tried to catch the girl, who changed herself into a tree, then into a pool of water, then into a stone, but the hyena almost tore the tree down, nearly drank all the water and half swallowed the stone. Then the girl changed herself into that thing which the night before her mother had managed to stop her from betraying. The hyena looked and looked everywhere and at last fearing the villagers would come and kill him, made off.

At once the girl changed into her own proper form and ran back to the village. The story of her adventures was told to all, and that is why to this day women do not choose husbands for themselves and also that is why children have learned to obey their elders who are wiser than they.

THE STORY OF FIVE HEADS

South Africa

George McCall Theal emigrated from Canada to South Africa and became a teacher there. He worked as a journalist and in publishing for a time, but returned to teaching and became a leading historian of the British colonial era. "Kaffir" was a term used to refer to a non-Muslim African at the time Theal was documenting tales. Today it is considered a derogatory term for black Africans. "The Story of Five Heads" is akin to tales about kind and unkind girls, morality tales that show virtue and hard work rewarded, cruelty and laziness punished. By placing the emphasis on behavioral codes, the tale diminishes the element of fright generated by the prospect of marrying a chief with five heads.

Once there was a man with two daughters, and both had reached the age of marriage.

One day the man decided to cross the river to another village, where a great chief was living. The people there asked him for news, and he said that he had none. Then he asked for news about their village, and they told him that their chief was looking for a wife.

The man returned home and said to his two daughters, "Which of you wants to become the wife of a chief?"

The elder of the two, who was called Mapunzikazi, said, "I would be happy to marry him."

Her father replied, "The chief at the village I visited yesterday is looking for a wife, and you, my child, will go to him."

The man summoned all his friends to go with his daughter

to the village of the chief. But the girl refused to let them go with her. "I am the only one who is going to marry," she said.

Her father replied, "How can you talk that way? Isn't it customary for friends to accompany a girl when she decides to present herself as a bride? Don't be foolish, my child."

The girl replied, "I am going by myself to meet the chief and become his wife."

The man let his daughter do as she had resolved. She went alone to the village to present herself to the chief as a bride, and no bridal party accompanied her.

On the way to the village, Mapunzikazi met a mouse.

The mouse said, "Shall I show you the way?"

The girl replied, "Get out of my sight, as quick as can be."

The mouse replied, "If you act like this, you don't have a chance."

Then Mapunzikazi met a frog.

The frog asked, "Shall I show you the way?"

Mapunzikazi replied, "You are not good enough to speak to me, for I am going to be the wife of a chief."

The frog said, "Off with you! You will see soon enough what will happen to you."

The girl began to grow tired, and she stopped by a tree to rest. A boy who was herding goats nearby walked over to her. He was very hungry.

The boy asked, "Where are you going?"

Mapunzikazi replied with anger in her voice, "How dare you speak to me? Get away as fast as you can."

The boy said, "I am very hungry. Can't you give me some of your food?"

"Go away," she replied.

The boy said, "You will never get back home if you act like this."

Mapunzikazi continued walking, and this time she met an old woman sitting next to a large rock.

The old woman said, "Let me give you some advice. You are going to see some trees that start laughing at you. Don't laugh back. You will find a big bag of thick milk. Don't take a sip from the bag. You will meet a man carrying his head under one arm. Don't let him give you any water."

Mapunzikazi replied, "You ugly old hag. How dare you try to give me advice!"

The girl kept on walking. She reached a place where she saw many trees, and they began laughing at her. She laughed back at them. She saw a bag filled with thick milk, and she took a sip. She met a man carrying his head under his arm, and she took water to drink from him.

Mapunzikazi reached the river near the chief's village. She saw a girl there dipping water out of the river. The girl said, "My sister, where are you going?"

Mapunzikazi replied, "How dare you call me sister! I am going to be the wife of the chief."

The girl drawing the water was the sister of the chief. She said, "Wait! Let me give you some advice. Don't enter the village from this side."

Mapunzikazi did not listen to her and kept on walking. She reached the chief's village. The people asked her where she had come from and why she was there.

She replied, "I have come to marry the chief."

They said, "This is the first time that a bride has arrived without a retinue."

Then they said, "The chief is not at home. You must start preparing a meal for him so that he will have something to eat when he returns home."

They gave her some millet to grind. She ground it very coarse, and then she made some bread that was not very tasty.

In the evening, she could hear that the wind was blowing hard outside, and that meant that the chief was coming home. He was a huge snake with five heads and large eyes. Mapunzikazi was frightened when she saw him. He sat down right near the door and told her to bring him some food. She brought him the bread she had made. Makanda Mahlanu, also known as Five Heads, did not like the bread at all. He said, "You are not going to be a wife of mine." And he struck her with his tail and killed her.

Not much later, the sister of Mapunzikazi told her father, "I would like to become the wife of a chief."

Her father replied, "That is fine, my daughter. It is right that you would want to be a bride."

The man summoned his friends, and a great retinue prepared to accompany the bride. The girl's name was Mapunzanyana.

On the way, they met a mouse. The mouse said, "Do you want me to show you the road?"

Mapunzanyana answered, "I would be very grateful for directions."

Then the mouse pointed the way to the village.

The girl came to a valley, where she saw an old woman standing near a tree.

The old woman said to her, "You are going to reach a place where two paths branch off from the main road. You must take the narrower one, because if you take the wider one, you will not have much luck."

Mapunzanyana replied, "I will take the narrow path, little mother." And she went on her way.

Then Mapunzanyana met a rabbit.

The rabbit said, "The chief's village is not far from here. You will meet a girl by the river, and you must speak politely to her. She will give you millet to grind. You must grind it as well as you can. When you see your husband, don't be afraid."

Mapunzanyana said, "I will do as you say."

Near the river, she met the chief's sister carrying water.

The chief's sister asked, "Where are you going?"

Mapunzanyana replied, "I have reached the end of my journey."

The chief's sister said, "Why have you come here?"

Mapunzanyana replied, "I am with a bridal party."

The chief's sister said, "I see. But won't you be afraid when you see your husband?"

Mapunzanyana replied, "I will not be afraid."

The chief's sister pointed her in the direction of the hut where she would be staying. The bridal party was given food. The mother of the chief took some millet and gave it to the bride, saying, "You must prepare some food for your husband. He is not here now, but he will return in the evening."

That evening she heard the wind blowing hard, so hard that

it made the hut shake. The poles of the tent collapsed, but she did not run away. Then she saw the chief Makanda Mahlanu walking toward her. He asked her for food. Mapunzanyana took the bread she had made and gave it to him. He was very pleased with the food and said, "You shall be my wife." He gave her beautiful jewels and ornaments.

Afterward Makanda Mahlanu turned into a man, and Mapunzanyana remained the wife he loved the best.

THE GOLDEN CRAB

Greece

Andrew Lang included this story in his celebrated multivolume, color-coded series of fairy-tale anthologies. This Greek tale from The Yellow Fairy Book *rounds up many different themes— a fisherman's lucky catch, a groom test set by a king, a disobedient bride, and the transformation of brothers into birds. The prince's double transformation into eagle and crab signals a blending of three domains—land, sea, and air—so that what seems like a punishment is also a territorial claim from a cursed figure destined to become a ruler.*

Once upon a time there lived a fisherman who had a wife and three children. Every morning he would go fishing, and any fish he caught were sold to the king. One day, among the fish in his net was a golden crab. When he returned home he put all the fish together into one big bowl, but he kept the crab separate because it was shining so brightly. He put the crab up on a high shelf in the cupboard. While his wife was cleaning the fish, she tucked up her dress so that her feet were visible. Suddenly she heard a voice, and it said:

> "Let down your dress, let it down.
> Everyone can see those feet peeping out."

The startled woman turned around and saw a little creature up there, the Golden Crab.

"What! You can talk, can you, you ridiculous crab?" she said, for she was irritated by the crab's remarks. Then she picked the crab up and placed him on a dish.

The fisherman came home, and just as the two were sitting down to dinner, they heard the crab's little voice saying, "Give me some of your supper." They were taken by surprise, but they gave him something to eat. When the old man went to take the plate from which the crab had eaten, he discovered that it was covered with gold coins. The same thing happened every day, and he soon grew very fond of the crab.

One day the crab said to the fisherman's wife, "Go tell the king that I wish to marry his younger daughter."

The old woman went and put the matter before the king, who laughed at the notion of his daughter marrying a crab, but did not dismiss the idea out of hand. He was a wise monarch, and he knew that there was a good chance that the crab could be a prince in disguise. He told the fisherman's wife, "Go tell the crab that I will give him my daughter if he can build a wall in front of my castle by tomorrow. It has to be much higher than the tower of my castle, and all the flowers on earth have to be growing around it, and in full blossom."

The fisherman's wife went home and gave the crab the message from the king. The crab handed her a golden switch and said, "Go strike this switch three times on the ground, in the place the king showed you, and tomorrow morning the wall will be there." And that's what the woman did, and then she returned home.

The next morning, when the king woke up, what do you think he saw? The wall was standing right before his eyes, exactly as he had described it.

The old woman went back to the king and said, "Your Majesty's orders have been carried out."

"That is all well and good," the king said, "but I can't give my daughter's hand in marriage until three fountains are built in front of my palace. The first must spray gold; the second silver; and the third diamonds."

The old woman hit the ground with the switch three times, and the next morning the three fountains were there right in front of the palace. Now the king gave his consent, and the wedding was set for the very next day.

The crab said to the old fisherman, "Take this switch and beat it against the side of the mountain over there. A dark man will come out and ask you what you want. Tell him this: 'Your master, the king, has sent me to tell you that you must sew a garment that is as golden as the sun.' Tell him also to give you royal robes of gold fit for a queen, with precious stones that look like flowers in a meadow. Bring those both to me, and don't forget to bring back a golden cushion for good measure."

The old man hurried off to carry out the orders. Once he had brought back the precious robes, the crab put the golden garment on and then crawled on to the golden cushion. That's how the fisherman carried him over to the castle, and there the crab presented the other garment to his bride. The ceremony took place, and when the two were finally alone together, the crab revealed his identity to his young wife. He told her how he was the son of the most powerful king in the world. He was under a spell, which meant that he was a crab in the daytime and a man at night. He could also change himself into an eagle whenever he wanted. No sooner had he said this than his body began to shake and he turned into a handsome young man. The next morning he had to creep back into the crab shell. The same thing happened every day.

The royal family was perplexed by the princess's affection for the crab and her attentive manner to the creature. They had a hunch that there was something they didn't know, but no matter how hard they tried to snoop around, they could not figure out what was going on.

A year went by, and the princess had a son, whom she called Benjamin. Her mother was mystified, and finally she told the king that he should ask his daughter whether she would like another husband instead of the crab. But when the daughter was asked, she replied:

"I am married to a crab, and I want no one else."

Then the king said, "I am going to hold a tournament in your honor and invite every prince in the world to attend. If any one of them there pleases you, you shall marry him."

The princess told all of this to the crab, who said to her, "Take this switch and hit the garden gate with it. A dark man will come out and ask, 'Why have you summoned me, and what do you want from me?' Answer him this way: 'Your master, the king, dispatched me to ask you for his golden armor, his steed, and the silver apple.' Then bring them all to me."

The princess did as he told her, and she brought him what he had requested.

The next evening the prince dressed for the tournament. Before he left, he said to his wife, "Just make sure you do not reveal who I am when you see me at the tournament. If you do, things will go badly. Watch it all from the castle window with your sisters. I'll ride by and throw you the silver apple. Take it in your hand, but if your sisters ask who I am, just say that you don't know." He kissed her, repeated the words of warning, and left.

The princess stood at the window with her sisters and watched the tournament. Her husband rode by and threw the apple up to her. She caught it and took it to her room. Her husband returned from the tournament. The princess's father was surprised that she did not seem to care for any one of the princes. And so he decided to hold a second tournament.

The crab gave his wife the same instructions as before, only this time the apple she received from the dark man was made of gold. Before the prince left for the tournament, he said to his wife, "I know that you are going to betray me today."

But she swore that she would not reveal who he was. He repeated the warning once more and then left.

In the evening, while the princess was standing at the window with her mother and sisters, the prince galloped past on his steed and tossed the golden apple over to her.

Then her mother threw a fit, boxed her ears, and shouted, "Don't you feel anything at all, even for that prince, you fool?"

The princess recovered from her shock and shot back, "That is the crab himself!"

Her mother was now even angrier, for she had not been told sooner that he was at the tournament. She ran straight into her daughter's room where the crab shell still was, grabbed it, and threw it into the fire. Then the poor princess wept bitter tears, but it did her no good. Her husband did not return.

Now we must leave the princess and turn our attention to others in the story. One day an old man dipped a crust of bread he was going to eat into a stream. Suddenly a dog jumped out of the water, snatched the bread from his hand, and ran off. The old man ran after him, but the dog found a door, pushed it open, and ran in, the old man following him. The old man was not able to overtake the dog, but he found himself at the top of a staircase, which he walked down. He saw before him a stately palace, and, entering, he found in a large hall a table set for twelve people. He hid himself in the hall behind a picture so that he could see what was happening. At noon he heard a roar so loud that he was trembling with fear. When he finally had the courage to look out from behind the picture, he saw twelve eagles flying around outside. He grew even more fearful. The eagles flew right into the basin of a fountain and began to bathe in it. Suddenly they were changed into twelve handsome youths. Now they went into the hall and sat down at the table. One of them picked up a goblet filled with wine, and said, "To my father!" And another said, "To my mother!" and so the toasts continued. Then one of them said, "To my dearest wife! May she live long and well! But a curse on the cruel mother who burned my golden shell!"

The young man began to weep as he spoke. Then the young men rose up from the table, went back to the great stone fountain, turned themselves into eagles again, and flew away.

The old man left as well, waited for daylight, and went back home. Not much later he learned that the princess was ill and that the only thing that made her feel better was having stories told to her. He therefore went to the royal castle, obtained an audience with the princess, and told her about the strange things he had seen in the underground palace. No sooner had he finished than the princess asked him whether he could find the way back to that palace.

"Yes," he replied. "Of course I can."

She asked him to guide her over there at once. The old man did so, and when they came to the palace he showed her the hiding place behind the picture and advised her to keep quiet. He hid behind the picture as well. Before long, the eagles came flying and turned themselves into young men. Instantly the princess recognized her husband among the others and tried to emerge from her hiding place, but the old man held her back. The youths seated themselves at the table; and now the prince said again, after he had picked up a glass of wine, "Here's to the health of my dear wife. May she live long and well. But a curse on the cruel mother who burned my golden shell!"

The princess could restrain herself no longer. She ran out from behind the picture and threw her arms around her husband. He recognized her right away and said, "Do you remember how I told you that you were going to betray me? Now you can see that I spoke the truth. But those bad times are behind us. Now listen to me: I must remain in my enchanted state for three months. Will you stay here with me until that time is over?"

The princess stayed with him and said to the old man, "Go back to the castle and tell my parents that I am staying here." The princess's parents were at first vexed when they heard the news from the old man. But it was not long before the three months of the enchantment were over, and the prince finally was no longer an eagle. He and his wife returned home together. And then they lived happily, and we who are listening to the story are happier still.

THE GIRL WHO
MARRIED A DOG

Native American

*As often happens with Native American tales, our expectations
are reversed; in this case with a father who runs off with his
offspring. The Pleiades are usually referred to as a constellation
of Seven Sisters, and, in this story, boy pups move into their
role. Wearing out seven pairs of moccasins seems less arduous
than the iron shoes found in stories like "The Parrot Prince."*

A chief had a fine looking daughter. She had a great many
admirers. At night she was visited by a young man, but she did
not know who he was. She worried about this and determined
to discover him. She put red paint near her bed. When he
crawled on her bed, she put her hand into the paint. When they
embraced, she left red marks on his back.

The next day she told her father to call all the young men to
a dance in front of his tent. They all came, and the whole village turned out to see them. She watched all that came, looking
for the red marks she had made. As she turned about, she
caught sight of one of her father's dogs with red marks on his
back. This made her so unhappy and she went straight into her
tent. This broke up the dance.

The next day she went into the woods near the camp, taking
the dog on a string. She hit him. He finally broke loose. She
was very unhappy, and several months later she bore seven
pups. She told her mother to kill them, but her mother was
kind toward them and made a little shelter for them. They
began to grow, and sometimes at night the old dog came to

them. After a time, the woman began to take an interest in them and sometimes played with them. When they were big enough to run, the old dog came and took them away.

When the woman went to see them in the morning, they were gone. She saw the large dog's tracks, and several little ones, and followed them at a distance. She was sad and cried. She returned to her mother and said, "Mother, make me seven pairs of moccasins. I am going to follow the little ones, searching for them." Her mother made seven pairs of moccasins, and the woman started out, tracking them all the way. Finally, in the distance, she saw a tent. The youngest one came to her and said, "Mother, father wants you to go back. We are going home. You cannot come." She said, "No! Wherever you go, I go." She took the little one and carried him to the tent. She entered and saw a young man, who took no notice of her. He gave her a little meat and drink, which did not grow less no matter how much she ate. She tied the little pup to her belt with a string. Next morning, she was left alone and the tent had vanished. She followed the tracks and again came upon them. Four times this happened in the same way. But the fourth time the tracks stopped.

She looked up into the sky. There she saw her seven pups. They had become seven stars, the Pleiades.

THE SNAKE PRINCE

India

Andrew Lang published this story in The Olive Fairy Book *and attributed the narrative to a Major Campbell, most likely a British colonial administrator who recorded the tale in Feroshepore (or Firozpur) in Punjab, India. Secrets are the consuming idea in many "Beauty and the Beast" tales, and "The Snake Prince," with its animal groom redeemed and then re-enchanted, is no exception. In place of the arduous redemptive journeys undertaken by women, this story offers a model of courageous fortitude.*

Once upon a time there lived by herself, in a city, an old woman who was desperately poor. One day she found that she had nothing but a handful of flour left in the house, and no money to buy more and no hope of earning any. Carrying her little brass pot, very sadly she made her way down to the river to bathe and to obtain some water, thinking afterward to come home and to make herself an unleavened cake of what flour she had left. After that she did not know what was to become of her.

While she was bathing she left her little brass pot on the riverbank covered with a cloth, to keep the inside nice and clean. But when she came up from the river and took the cloth off to fill the pot with water, she saw inside it the glittering folds of a deadly snake. At once she popped the cloth back into the mouth of the pot and held it there; and then she said to herself, "Ah, kind death! I will take you home, and there I will shake you out of my pot and you can bite me and I will die, and then all my troubles will be ended."

With these sad thoughts in her mind the poor old woman hurried home, pressing the cloth carefully to the mouth of the pot. When she reached home, she shut all the doors and windows, removed the cloth, and turned the pot upside down on her hearthstone. What was her surprise to find that, instead of the deadly snake she had expected to see fall out, there fell out with a rattle and a clang a most magnificent necklace of flashing jewels!

For a few minutes she could hardly think or speak, but just stood there gaping. And then, with trembling hands, she picked the necklace up, and folding it in the corner of her veil, she hurried off to the king's hall where he held public audiences.

"A petition, O king!" she said. "A petition for your ears alone!" And when her plea had been granted, and she found herself alone with the king, she shook out her veil at his feet, and out fell in glittering coils the splendid necklace. As soon as the king saw it, he was filled with amazement and delight, and the more he looked at it the more he felt that he must possess it at once. So he gave the old woman five hundred silver pieces for it, and put it straightaway into his pocket. Away she went full of happiness, for the money the king had given her was enough to keep her for the rest of her life.

As soon as he could finish up his royal duties, the king hurried off and showed the prize to his wife. She was as pleased as he was, if not more so. Once they had finished admiring the wonderful necklace, they locked it up in the great chest where the queen's jewelry was kept, the key to which the king always wore around his neck.

A short while later, a neighboring king sent a message to say that a most lovely girl baby had been born to him, and he invited his neighbors to come to a great feast in honor of the occasion. The queen told her husband that of course they must be present at the banquet, and she would wear the new necklace that he had given her. They had only a short time to prepare for the journey, and at the last moment the king went to the jewel chest to take the necklace out for his wife to wear, but the necklace was gone and in its place was a chubby little boy baby, crowing and shouting. The king was so astonished that he nearly fell over, but soon he found his voice, and called for his wife so loudly that she came running, thinking that some-one must have stolen the necklace.

"Look! Just look!" cried the king, "Haven't we always longed for a son? And now heaven has sent us one!"

"What are you talking about?" cried the queen. "Are you mad?"

"Mad? No, I hope not," shouted the king, dancing in excite-ment around the open chest. "Come here, and take a look! Look what we now have instead of that necklace!"

Just then the baby boy crowed with joy, as though he would like to jump up and dance with the king. The queen let out a cry of surprise and ran up and looked into the chest.

"Oh!" she gasped, as she looked at the baby, "what a darling child! Where could he have come from?"

"I'm sure I don't know," the king said. "All I know is that we locked a necklace up in the chest, and when I unlocked it just now there was no necklace, but a baby, and as fine a baby as ever was seen."

By this time the queen had the baby in her arms. "Oh, the blessed child!" she cried. "He is a fairer ornament for a queen than any necklace that ever was wrought. Write to our neigh-bor," she added, "and tell him that we cannot attend his feast, for we are holding a feast of our own, and a baby of our own! Oh, happy day!"

So the visit was abandoned, and, in honor of the new baby, the bells of the city, and its guns, and its trumpets, and its people, rich and poor, hardly had a moment's rest for a week. There was such a ringing, and banging, and blaring, and such fireworks, and feasting, and rejoicing, and merry-making as had never been seen before.

A few years went by. The king's baby boy and his neighbor's baby girl grew and flourished, and the kings arranged that the two would marry as soon as they were old enough. And so, after much signing of papers and agreements, and wagging of wise heads, and stroking of gray beards, the compact was made, and signed, and sealed, and lay waiting for its fulfill-ment. And this too came to pass, for, as soon as the prince and princess reached the age of eighteen, the kings agreed that it was time for the wedding. The young prince traveled to the neighboring kingdom for his bride, and there they were married with great rejoicing.

I should now tell you that the old woman who had sold the king the necklace had been summoned by him to serve as nurse to the young prince. Although she loved her charge dearly and was a most faithful servant, she could not help talking just a little, and so, by and by, it began to be rumored that there was some kind of magic mixed in with the young prince's birth. And the rumors reached the ears of the parents of the princess. Now that she was going to be the wife of the prince, her mother (who was curious, as many other people are) said to her daughter on the eve of the ceremony, "Remember that the first thing you must do is to learn about the prince's story. And in order to do that, you must not speak a word to him no matter what he says until he asks you why you are silent. Then you must ask him for the truth about his magic birth, and until he tells you, you must not speak to him again."

The princess promised to follow her mother's advice.

When the two were married, the prince spoke to his bride, but she did not answer him. He could not imagine what was the matter, for she would not utter a word, not even about her old home. Finally he asked why she would not speak, and then she said, "Tell me the secret about your birth."

The prince was very sad and disappointed. Although she pressed him hard, he refused to say anything and just told her, "If I tell you, you will regret that you ever asked me."

For several months they lived together, and it was not a happy time for the one or the other, as it might have been. A secret is a secret, and it lay between them like a cloud between the sun and the earth, making what could have been fair, dull and sad.

At length the prince could bear it no longer. One day he told his wife, "At midnight I will reveal my secret if you still want to know it, but you will regret it all your life." The princess was overjoyed that she had succeeded at last and paid no attention to his warning.

That night, a little before midnight, the prince ordered horses to be ready for the princess and himself. He placed her on one, and he mounted the other, and the two rode together down to the river to the place where the old woman had first found the snake in her brass pot. The prince drew the reins in right there and said mournfully, "Do you still insist on knowing my secret?" The princess answered, "Yes." "If I tell you," the prince replied, "remember that you will regret it all your life." But the princess only replied, "Tell me!"

"Then," said the prince, "know that I am the son of the king of a distant country, but by enchantment I was turned into a snake."

The word "snake" had hardly left his lips when he disappeared, and the princess heard a rustle and saw a ripple on the water. In the faint moonlight she caught sight of a snake swimming into the river. Soon it disappeared and she was left alone. In vain she waited with a heart beating fast for something to happen, and for the prince to return to her. Nothing happened and no one came. Only the breezes sighed through the trees on the riverbank, and the night birds cried, and a jackal howled in the distance, and the river flowed black and silent beneath her.

In the morning they found her, weeping and disheveled, on the riverbank. They could not learn anything from her or from anyone else about what had happened to her husband. At her bidding, they built a little house of black stone on the riverbank. And there she dwelt in mourning, with a few servants and guards to watch over her.

A long, long time passed, and still the princess was living in mourning and would see no one. She never left the house on the riverbank or the garden that surrounded it. One morning, when she woke up, she found a track of fresh mud left on the carpet. She sent for the guards, who kept watch outside the house day and night, and asked them who had entered her room while she was sleeping. They declared that no one could possibly have entered, for they kept such careful watch that not even a bird could fly in without their knowing it. And none of them could explain the track of mud. The next morning, the princess found another stain made by wet mud, and she questioned everyone carefully. But no one could explain how the mud got there. The third night the princess was determined to stay awake. Afraid that she might fall asleep, she cut her finger with a penknife and rubbed salt into the wound so that the pain would keep her from sleeping. And so she lay awake, and at midnight she saw a snake come wriggling along the ground with some mud from the river in its mouth. When it reached her bed, it reared up its head and then let the mud drop on her covers. The princess was frightened, but tried to control her fear, and called out, "Who are you, and what are you doing here?"

The snake replied, "I am the prince, your husband, and I have come to visit you."

Then the princess began to weep, and the snake continued, "Alas! Didn't I tell you that if I told you my secret you would regret it? And don't you regret it now?"

"Oh, indeed!" cried the poor princess, "I have regretted it and shall continue to regret it all my life! Is there nothing I can do?"

And the snake replied, "Yes, there is one thing you can do, if you dare."

"Just tell me what it is," said the princess. "I will do whatever you ask!"

"Then on a certain night," the snake replied, "you must put a large bowl of milk and sugar in each of the four corners of this room. All the snakes in the river will come out to drink the milk, and the one that leads the way will be the queen of the snakes. You must stand in her way at the door, and say: 'Oh, Queen of Snakes, Queen of Snakes, give me back my husband!' and perhaps she will do it. But if you become frightened and fail to stop her, you will never see me again." And he glided away.

On the night designated by the snake, the princess put four large bowls of milk and sugar into each corner of the room, and stood in the doorway waiting. At midnight there was a great hissing and rustling coming from the direction of the river, and before long the ground appeared to be alive with the horrible writhing forms of snakes. Their eyes glittered, and their forked tongues quivered as they turned in the direction of the princess's house. Leading them was a huge, repulsive scaly creature at the head of the dreadful procession. The guards were so terrified that they all ran off, but the princess stayed in

the doorway, as white as death, with her hands clasped tightly
together for fear that she might scream or faint and thus fail to
do her part.

As the snakes drew closer and saw her in the way, they raised
their horrifying heads and swayed them back and forth and
looked at her with wicked beady eyes, while their breath seemed
to poison the very air. Still the princess stood her ground, and,
when the leader of the snake procession was within a few feet
of her, she cried out: "Oh, Queen of Snakes, Queen of Snakes,
give me back my husband!" Then the entire rustling, writhing
crowd of snakes seemed to whisper to one another, "Her husband? Her husband?" But the queen of snakes edged forward
until her head was almost in the princess's face, and her little
eyes seemed to flash fire. And still the princess stayed in the
doorway and would not move, but cried again: "Oh, Queen of
Snakes, Queen of Snakes, give me back my husband!" Then the
queen of snakes replied, "Tomorrow you shall have him back—
tomorrow!"

When the princess heard these words and knew that she had
succeeded, she staggered away from the door, sank down on
her bed, and fainted. As if in a dream, she could see that her
room was full of snakes, all jostling and squabbling over the
bowls of milk until they were done. And then they went away.

In the morning the princess was up early and took off the
mourning dress, which she had worn for five whole years, and
put on beautiful, cheerful clothes. And she swept the house,
cleaned it, and decorated it with garlands and nosegays of
sweet flowers and ferns. She prepared it as though she were
preparing for her wedding. And when night fell, she lit up the
woods and gardens with lanterns, set a table as if for a feast,
and lit a thousand wax candles in the house. Then she waited
for her husband, not knowing in what form he would appear.
At midnight the prince came marching up from the river, laughing, but with tears in his eyes. And she ran over to meet him
and threw herself in his arms, crying and laughing too.

And so the prince returned home, and the next day the two
went back to the palace. The old king wept with joy to see
them. And the bells, so long silent, were set a-ringing again,

and the guns firing, and the trumpets blaring, and there was fresh feasting and rejoicing.

And the old woman who had been the prince's nurse became nurse to the prince's children—at least that's what they called her, for she was far too old to do anything for them but love them. Yet she believed she was useful, and she was happy beyond compare. And happy, indeed, were the prince and princess, who in due time became king and queen, and lived and ruled long and prosperously.

THE SMALL-TOOTH DOG

England

The British folklorist Sidney O. Addy collected this story for his Household Tales. *In the introduction to his anthology, he explained that he had "either written the tales down from dictation" or had used a "written copy" given to him. This version of "Beauty and the Beast" includes a wonderful inventory of magical objects and, like many other folktales, it emphasizes the damaging effects of name-calling and the redemptive power of words that ennoble and elevate.*

Once upon a time, there was a merchant who traveled about the world a great deal. On one of his journeys thieves attacked him, and they would have taken both his life and his money if a large dog had not come to his rescue and driven the thieves away. When the dog had driven the thieves away he took the merchant to his house, which was a very handsome one, and he dressed his wounds and nursed him until he was well.

As soon as he was able to travel the merchant began his journey home, but before starting he told the dog how grateful he was for his kindness, and asked him what reward he could offer in return, and he said he would not refuse to give him the most precious thing that he had.

And so the merchant said to the dog, "Will you accept a fish that I have that can speak twelve languages?"

"No," said the dog, "I will not."

"Or a goose that lays golden eggs?"

"No," said the dog, "I will not."

"Or a mirror in which you can see what anybody is thinking about?"

"No," said the dog, "I will not."

"Then what will you have?" said the merchant.

"I will have none of such presents," said the dog, "but let me fetch your daughter, and take her to my house."

When the merchant heard this he was grieved, but what he had promised had to be done, so he said to the dog, "You can come and fetch my daughter after I have been at home for a week."

So at the end of the week the dog came to the merchant's house to fetch his daughter, but when he got there he stayed outside the door, and would not go in. But the merchant's daughter did as her father told her, and came out of the house dressed for a journey and ready to go with the dog.

When the dog saw her he looked pleased, and said, "Jump on my back, and I will take you away to my house." So she mounted on the dog's back, and away they went at a great pace until they reached the dog's house, which was many miles off.

But after she had been a month at the dog's house she began to mope and cry.

"What are you crying for?" said the dog.

"Because I want to go back to my father," she said.

The dog said, "If you will promise me that you will not stay at home more than three days I will take you there. But first of all," said he, "what do you call me?"

"A great, foul, small-tooth dog," said she.

"Then," said he, "I will not let you go."

But she cried so pitifully that he promised again to take her home. "But before we start," said he, "tell me what you call me."

"Oh!" said she, "your name is Sweet-as-a-honeycomb."

"Jump on my back," said he, "and I'll take you home." So he trotted away with her on his back for forty miles, when they came to a stile.

"And what do you call me?" said he, before they got over the stile.

Thinking that she was safe on her way, the girl said, "A great, foul, small-tooth dog." But when she said this, he did not jump over the stile, but turned right round about at once, and galloped back to his own house with the girl on his back.

Another week went by, and again the girl wept so bitterly that the dog promised to take her to her father's house. So the girl got on the dog's back again, and they reached the first stile as before, and then the dog stopped and said, "And what do you call me?"

"Sweet-as-a-honeycomb," she replied.

So the dog leaped over the stile, and they went on for twenty miles until they came to another stile.

"And what do you call me?" said the dog, with a wag of his tail.

She was thinking more of her own father and her own home than of the dog, so she answered, "A great, foul, small-tooth dog."

Then the dog was in a great rage, and he turned right round about and galloped back to his own house as before. After she had cried for another week, the dog promised again to take her back to her father's house. So she mounted upon his back once more, and when they got to the first stile, the dog said, "And what do you call me?"

"Sweet-as-a-honeycomb," she said.

So the dog jumped over the stile, and away they went—for now the girl made up her mind to say the most loving things she could think of—until they reached her father's house.

When they got to the door of the merchant's house, the dog said, "And what do you call me?"

Just at that moment the girl forgot the loving things that she meant to say, and began, "A great . . ." but the dog began to turn, and she got fast hold of the door-latch, and was going to say "foul," when she saw how grieved the dog looked and remembered how good and patient he had been with her, so she said, "Sweeter-than-a-honeycomb."

When she had said this she thought the dog would have been content and have galloped away, but instead of that he suddenly stood up on his hind legs, and with his fore legs he pulled off his dog's head, and tossed it high in the air. His hairy coat dropped off, and there stood the handsomest young man in the world, with the finest and smallest teeth you ever saw.

Of course they were married, and lived together happily.

THE QUEEN OF THE PIGEONS

South Africa

Ethel McPherson, who collected South African fairy tales, relied on print sources compiled by British and French missionaries in Africa for her child-friendly version of a Zulu tale. McPherson felt sure that the pigeons in the story were symbolic horsemen, who "fly" through the air. Humor, charm, romance, and poetry: these were features McPherson saw as "characteristic" of African lore. And yet this particular tale turns on the tragedy of separation and loss, as well as on the use of trickery and deceit to find a way back home.

Once there was a beautiful young woman who was as fair as a star. She was the delight of the village, and her mother loved her more than anything in the world.

One day when the men of the village had left for the hunt and the women were working in the fields, the maiden, leaving her young companions in the kraal, went out on to the veld to gather some soft grass. She sat down to do her work when, suddenly, a flock of gray wood pigeons came flying out from the west and began to hover over her. Struck by her beauty, they lifted her up from the ground and carried her off across the fields where the women were doing their hoeing. Weeping and wailing, she called out, "Mother, help me, the pigeon-folk are taking me away!"

Her mother looked up from her work, and, seeing her child up above her, she stretched out her arms and tried to reach her, but the pigeons flew up over her head, and then they swooped down again until the girl was almost in her grasp. Then the birds quickly flew up again, mocking her, and off they went into the distance.

The birds traveled in the direction of the setting sun, and the mother, in tears, followed the pigeons, begging them to bring back her child. But they paid no attention to her. When darkness fell, they perched in a tree and stayed there all night, keeping the girl with them. The mother, exhausted from the long journey chasing after them, lay down beneath the tree and slept so deeply that at dawn she did not hear the rustling of the gray wings as the birds started taking flight. She did not wake up until the sun was high in the heavens.

When she realized that the pigeons had left, taking her child with them, she returned to the village to tell everyone about the great calamity that had befallen her. The pigeons, in the meantime, reached their own land, feeling proud of the captive they had brought back with them.

Now when the king of the pigeons set eyes on the beautiful maiden, he longed to make her his wife, and he soon married her. She became the queen. And for years she lived among the pigeon-folk and bore her husband three sons. But she was unable to forget her own people, and her heart longed to see them. Years passed by, and her sons grew to be fine young men, tall and straight. One day, when the king was making preparations for a hunting expedition with his warriors, he told the queen that he was planning to take his sons along. The queen gave her consent, but before they left she took them aside and told them that they should leave the hunt and return to the village. She told them to pretend that they had been injured or to say that they were not feeling well and then ask their father if they could miss the hunt. Then they would be able to return to the village and leave with her for her native land.

When the king left the village with his expedition, the queen was all alone with her husband's mother, who was deeply suspicious of her daughter-in-law. She feared that this stranger-wife was up to no good.

Meanwhile, before the huntsmen had gone very far, the youngest of the king's sons stumbled down to the ground and asked his father if he could return to the kraal. The king, suspecting nothing, sent the boy back home.

A little later, the second boy complained that he was ill and asked his father if he could return home. And the third said that he felt a throbbing pain in his head and wanted to go back home.

Once all three had reached the kraal, the queen gathered her possessions together and set out with her sons. She was sure that no one had seen her, but the king's mother knew exactly what was happening, and she rushed to the outskirts of the village and cried out with a shrill voice, "*Yi! Yi!* The queen has run away and has taken her sons with her."

One of the hunters had ears as keen as a hare's, and he heard her voice. "Hark!" he cried out, "I just heard someone shouting that the queen has run away and taken the king's children with her."

The others in the party were enraged and said, "Hold your tongue. You will bring misfortune to the king's children." Because men hate the bearers of bad tidings, they killed him and continued on their way.

Meanwhile the evil omen sounded again across the veld, and this time it was heard by another one of the hunters, who told the others to listen. "I hear a voice," he said. "And it is shouting out that the queen has run away with her children." They, too, believed that he meant to harm the young princes, and they killed him as well.

The shrill voice was heard a third time, and a third hunter told everyone to stop and listen. He too would have been slain, but he said, "You have already killed two of the king's men because they paid attention to the warning. I can hear it now too, but don't kill me. Let me return to the village to determine whether this is true or not."

They paid heed to his words and took him before the king, who listened to his tale and then said, "Let the man go back to the kraal and bring back tidings of the queen and my sons."

The hunter returned to the village as fast as he could, and when he discovered that the queen had left, taking her sons with her, he returned to the king and told him what had happened.

The king of the pigeons summoned his vast army, and in all quarters of the heavens you could hear the whirring of gray wings. There were so many birds in the sky that the face of the sun disappeared and the sky grew dark. When all the birds had assembled, the king told his warriors about how the queen had run away with his children. To save his good name and his honor, they had to bring her back home.

After the king had spoken, there was a stirring of angry wings like the sound of a stormy sea beating upon the shores, and, with the king leading the charge, the pigeon army swept southward in pursuit of the truant queen.

Meanwhile the queen had reached a deep sea, the farther shore of which could be dimly seen against the sky. Standing at a place where the waves broke at her feet, she cried, "Sea, Sea, divide and make a path in the waters so that I may cross with my children."

At the sound of her voice, the waters parted, and the queen and her children walked on dry land and reached the farther shore in safety. Then the waters rolled back with a crash of thunder, just when the army of pigeons reached the edge of the waters.

The pigeons could see the queen and her sons on the opposite shore, and they wondered how she had managed to cross, especially since the sea was so vast that their wings could not possibly bear them to the other shore.

When she saw the pigeons on the other side of the sea, the queen began to think about how she could fool them, and she braided a long rope from grass and flung it across the waters, shouting, "Fly up on this rope, and I will pull you across."

The pigeons flew up onto the rope as fast as they could, and the queen began looking around for a sharp stone. While the pigeons and the hunters were on the rope, she severed it, and the king and his whole army sank into the sea. The waters closed over them, and no one was left to tell the tale of their destruction.

The queen returned with her sons to her own people, and her homecoming was celebrated with dancing and singing and much rejoicing.

ANIMAL BRIDES

THE GRATEFUL CRANE

Japan

Into the most humdrum of laboring lives comes a sudden burst of beauty. In this darkly intense drama, pathos mingles with sensuality as Musai's tender act of kindness is rewarded with a graceful bride, lovely beyond his wildest imagination. In Asian cultures, cranes are omens of good fortune, happiness, and longevity, and they are said to have a life span of a thousand years. "The Crane Wife," as the story is also called, became one of the most widely known folktales in Japan, rivaled only by "Momotaro, the Peach Boy." It migrated into new media in Japanese culture during the era following World War II. The bride in this tale is not at all reluctant and willingly makes her home with humans, despite the pain she suffers as a supportive wife and the unbidden voyeuristic gaze to which she is subjected.

"Fighting sparrows are not afraid of man," as the old proverb says. Yet it was not a sparrow but a crane that fell down to earth one day. It landed near the feet of Musai, a farmer's boy, as he waded in the rice-fields, working from dawn to dusk.

The farmer's boy was accustomed to seeing cranes, for these long-legged birds stride right into the furrows made by ploughs on dry land. The birds are not at all afraid, for who would think of harming the white-breasted creatures that everyone calls Honorable Lord Crane? The graceful birds seem to love being near men working in the rice paddies, where the seeds from which the rice plants grow are sown under four inches of water. The crane is so elegant in all its movements that many a young woman who moves gracefully will hear people referring to her as the "bird that rises up from the water without muddying the stream."

Musai hurried to the grassy bank at the edge of the rice paddy as fast as he could move through the muddy waters to see what was wrong with the crane. He threw his hoe down when he saw the crane lying on the grass, with an arrow in its back. Drops of red blood were spattered on its white plumage. The bird was not at all frightened when Musai edged closer. Instead, it bent its neck down, as if to make it easier for the farmer's boy to help.

Musai pulled the arrow out as gently as possible and helped the bird rise by pushing back the undergrowth so that nothing would be in the way of the broad white pinions. After making a few feeble attempts to fly, the bird spread its wings, rose up from the ground, and, after flying in circles around its benefactor as if to thank him, soared off toward the mountains.

Musai returned to work, hoping that his labor would yield a new crop at harvesting time. He had to work every day, for he had a widowed mother to support. His one joy was to return home and take a hot bath after working long hours in the muddy rice paddies. His mother always made sure that it was ready for him. Once he finished the bath and put on a fresh kimono, he would rest up before supper and was ready for a quiet evening with his neighbors.

Autumn was on its way, and one day, returning home before sunset, Musai saw a beautiful girl sitting next to his mother. Even though he was covered with mud from the fields where he had been knee-deep in the mire, the young woman welcomed him with the graciousness of a princess.

Unprepared to return the warm greeting and embarrassed by his unwashed state, Musai took off the kerchief covering his head, drew in his breath, and, bowing to his mother, asked, "Who is this young woman and how did she come here?"

"My son," his mother replied. "You have become a man, but you still do not have a wife. Your reputation for obedience, filial respect, fidelity, and politeness is well known. For that reason, this fair lady is ready to be your wife. I was unable to reply to her request without your consent. What do you think?"

The young farmer was flattered, but he thought hard before speaking. "The young woman appears to be well bred and is most likely of noble birth. If I were to marry her, how could she endure the poverty we live in? Will she be patient when she goes hungry? It may be that the promise of love and happiness will last for just a while, and then we will separate. All that will remain is gloom mixed with sorrow."

As the days passed by, he saw how kindly the woman treated his mother. She was patient, undemanding, and respectful. Soon all his fears were driven away, like clouds by the wind. And the young man and woman were married.

When harvest time came, the rice ears turned out to be nothing but husks and shells. They had failed to ripen, and the crop was a total failure. With taxes unpaid and no food in the house, famine threated them. By winter, they were in dire straits.

The patient wife then cheered up her husband by revealing the powers she had. "If you can build me a spinning room, I will make a cloth that has never been seen before in these parts. But I can't weave out in the open, and I can't make my fine pattern of red and white in the cloth unless I am completely alone in a quiet place. Build me that room, and the money you need will flow in."

The mother was skeptical about her daughter-in-law's project, and even Musai doubted she could succeed. Still, he went to work on making the room. He built a separate hut, using beams and thatching. He put mats on the floor and finished the windows with latticed paper. And finally he put a smooth layer of clay on the walls, to make sure the place was sealed off from the world. There, day after day, secluded from everyone, the sweet wife worked alone and unseen. Her husband and his mother waited patiently for a week, when the little woman rejoined the family circle. In her hands she was carrying a roll of woven fabric, white with a satin sheen, as lustrous and pure as fresh snow. Here and there a crimson thread could be seen in the fabric, and it only strengthened the purity of the otherwise completely white cloth. The wonderful fabric was made up of just white threads and red.

"What shall we call it?" the astonished husband asked.

"It has no name, for there is nothing on earth like it," the fair weaver replied.

"But it has to have a name. I shall take it to the *Daimio*. He will not buy it if he does not know what it is called."

"Then," said his wife, "tell him that it is called 'White Crane's cloth.'"

The fine fabric quickly passed into the hands of the lord of the castle, who sent it as a gift to the Empress in Kioto. Everyone was astonished by its sheen, and the Empress asked that the weaver be richly rewarded. The farmer husband soon had a thousand coins in his bag, and he hurried home to spread the shiny coins at his mother's feet and to thank the wife who had brought him so much wealth. A feast was held, and for many weeks the family lived in prosperity on the money earned from the cloth.

A second time the harvest failed, and Musai asked his wife if she would be willing to weave another "White Crane's cloth." She cheerfully agreed, but told him to let her weave in private and not to look in on her until she was finished weaving the cloth.

But alas for human curiosity and the prying spirit! Not content with having been rescued from starvation by a wife who served him like a slave, Musai crept up to the paper partition, touched his tongue to the latticed pane, and poked his finger quietly through it, making a hole to which he glued his eye as he looked into the room.

What a sight! There was no woman weaving there, but a noble white crane, the same crane he had seen in the rice paddy, from whose back he had pulled the hunter's arrow. Bending over the spinning wheel, the bird pulled the silky thread right from her own breast. By twisting and twining it, she turned it into the finest thread ever beheld by human eyes. From time to time, she pressed drops of red blood from her heart to dye a few strands, and so the weaving continued. The fabric was nearly finished.

Musai was so enthralled that he did not move. Suddenly, his mother called him, and he cried out in response, "Yes, I'm coming."

The startled crane looked up and saw the eye in the wall.

Throwing down thread and web she rushed angrily to the door, let out a shrill cry, and flew out the window. Like a white speck against the blue hills, she could be seen for a moment, and then she disappeared.

Son and mother were once again faced with poverty and loneliness. Musai spent the rest of his days splashing barelegged in the rice paddies.

THE PIQUED BUFFALO-WIFE

Native American

Clark Wissler and D. C. Duvall collected this story in 1909 from an unnamed member of the Blackfoot tribe of Native Americans. Suggesting that the lines demarcating animals from humans are fluid, the tale also reinforces the binary that keeps the two apart by showing the challenges of crossing the line and of shape-shifting. In this particular tale, we find many odd gender reversals, with a male mortal taking "advantage" of a female beast and a husband losing his wife through an act of disobedience.

Once a young man went out and came to a buffalo-cow fast in the mire. He took advantage of her situation. After a time she gave birth to a boy. When he could run about, this boy would go into the Indian camps and join in the games of the children, but would always mysteriously disappear in the evening. One day this boy told his mother that he intended to search among the camps for his father. Not long after this he was playing with the children in the camps as usual, and went into the lodge of a head man in company with a boy of the family. He told this head man that his father lived somewhere in the camp, and that he was anxious to find him. The head man took pity on the boy, and sent out a messenger to call into his lodge all the old men in the camp. When these were all assembled and standing around the lodge, the head man requested the boy to pick out his father. The boy looked them over, and then told the head man that his father was not among them. Then the head man sent out a messenger to call in all the men next in age; but, when these were assembled, the boy said that his father was not among them. Again the head man sent out the messenger to call in all the men of the next rank in age. When they were assembled, the boy looked them over as before, and announced that his father was not among them. So once again the head man sent out his messenger to call in all the young unmarried men of the camp. As they were coming into the head man's lodge, the boy ran to one of them, and, embracing him, said, "Here is my father."

After a time the boy told his father that he wished to take him to see his mother. The boy said, "When we come near her, she will run at you and hook four times, but you are to stand perfectly still." The next day the boy and his father started out on their journey. As they were going along they saw a buffalo-cow, which immediately ran at them as the boy had predicted. The man stood perfectly still, and at the fourth time, as the cow was running forward to hook at him, she became a woman. Then she went home with her husband and child. One day shortly after their return, she warned her husband that whatever he might do he must never strike at her with fire. They lived together happily for many years. She was a remarkably good woman. One evening when the husband had invited some guests, and the woman expressed a dislike to prepare food for them, he became very angry, and, catching up a stick from the fire, struck at her. As he did so, the woman and her child vanished, and the people saw a buffalo cow and calf running from the camp.

Now the husband was very sorry and mourned for his wife and child. After a time he went out to search for them. In order that he might approach the buffalo without being discovered, he rubbed himself with filth from a buffalo-wallow. In the course of time he came to a place where some buffalo were dancing. He could hear them from a distance. As he was approaching, he met his son, who was now, as before, a buffalo-calf. The father explained to the boy that he was mourning for him and his mother and that he had come to take them home. The calf-boy explained that this would be very difficult, for his father would be required to pass through an ordeal. The calf-boy explained to him that, when he arrived among the buffalo and inquired for his wife and son, the chief of the buffalo would order that he select his child from among all the buffalo-calves in the herd. Now the calf-boy wished to assist his father, and told him that he would know his child by a sign, because, when the calves appeared before him, his own child would hold up its tail. Then the man proceeded until he came to the place where the buffalo were dancing. Immediately he was taken before the chief of the buffalo-herd. The chief required that he first prove his relationship to the child by picking him out from among all the other calves of the herd. The man agreed to this and the calves were brought up. He readily picked out his own child by the sign.

The chief of the buffalo, however, was not satisfied with this proof, and said that the father could not have the child until he identified him four times. While the preparations were being made for another test, the calf-boy came to his father and explained that he would be known this time by closing one eye. When the time arrived, the calves were brought as before, and the chief of the buffalo directed the father to identify his child, which he did by the sign. Before the next trial the calf-boy explained to his father that the sign would be one ear hanging down. Accordingly, when the calves were brought up for the father to choose, he again identified his child. Now, before the last trial, the boy came again to his father and notified him that the sign by which he was to be known was dancing and holding up one leg. Now the calf-boy had a chum among the buffalo-calves, and when the calves were called up before the chief so that the father might select his child, the chum saw the calf-boy beginning to dance holding up one leg, and he thought to himself, "He is doing some fancy dancing." So he, also, danced in the same way. Now the father observed that there were two calves giving the sign, and realized that he must make a guess. He did so, but the guess was wrong. Immediately the herd rushed upon the man and trampled him into the dust. Then they all ran away except the calf-boy, his mother, and an old bull.

These three mourned together for the fate of the unfortunate man. After a time the old bull requested that they examine the ground to see if they could find a piece of bone. After long and careful search they succeeded in finding one small piece that had not been trampled by the buffalo. The bull took this piece, made a sweat-house, and finally restored the man to life. When the man was restored, the bull explained to him that he and his family would receive some power, some head-dresses, some songs, and some crooked sticks, such as he had seen the buffalo carry in the dance at the time when he attempted to pick out his son.

The calf-boy and his mother then became human beings, and returned with the man. It was this man who started the Bull and the Horn Societies, and it was his wife who started the Matoki.

THE TURTLE AND
THE CHICKPEA

Greece

*Collected in 1885 in Greece, this tale reminds us of the deep
and enduring connection between beauty and the domestic
arts, with a turtle that transforms into a woman of unmatched
looks and equally impressive cooking skills. The enigmatically
named Chickpea, who rides a rooster as his mount, is another
reminder that cuisine and elements of agrarian life constantly
infiltrate fairy-tale worlds.*

Once upon a time there was a fisherman, a widower who had
no children at all.

He went one day to fish and caught nothing, but there was a
turtle caught up in his nets; so he said, "Such is my luck; so I'll
take it home," and he took it and kept it in his house.

But where his house had once been full of rubbish, the day
after he took home the turtle, he found the house cleaned and
shining like crystal, and the poor fisherman wondered who
could have done it. One day he took some fish home, and at
midday he went to light a bit of a fire to cook the fish and he
saw that the fish were no longer on the spit.

"That cat has never taken the fish till now! How can she
have taken them?" But in a corner of the room he saw steamed
fish in the kettle, fried fish on one plate and baked on another.
He saw that the house had again been cleaned and swept, and
he was amazed.

"Who can have done it, I wonder?"

So the next day he kept watch and he saw come out of the turtle's shell a maiden whose beauty had no match in the world.

When she came out, he seized her and said, "Is it you, then, who keeps my house, unbeknown to me?"

And he broke the turtle shell, and the maiden stayed. He crowned her in holy matrimony and made her his wife.

The King of that place was unmarried; so he gave all the girls a veil to embroider, and whoever embroidered the best would be his wife. He also gave one to the fisherman's wife, for he thought she was his daughter. And without knowing why she was to embroider it, she sat down and embroidered on it the sea with fish and with ships. Other girls also embroidered, as the King had ordered that these girls were to go on the same day and each show her veil. So each took her veil, and the fisherman's wife went, too.

When the King saw her, he was astounded at her beauty. He looked, too, at the veil she had embroidered, and it was the best of all. He said that he would wed with her, but she answered that she was married to a fisherman.

"But why did you embroider the veil?" asked the King.

"Because I did not know why you had ordered the veils to be embroidered. I embroidered it for your pleasure."

"Bid your husband come here," the King said to her.

"As you will, Lord King," she said, and went home and told her husband, "The King has bidden you go to him."

The poor fisherman went and said to the King, "What is your will, Lord King?"

"The wife that you have is not for you. So either you provide a meal of fish to feed all my army till they have their fill or I shall take your wife away from you."

"It is well, Lord King," answered the fisherman, and went home and told his wife, "Alas, wife, that veil has brought us misfortune. The King has ordered me to feed all his army with fish for one day, or he will take you for himself; he says you are not the wife for me."

"Let the King sleep on it," said his wife. "And you, husband, go to the place where you fished me up and call to my mother to give you the little fish kettle."

So the fisherman went to the sea, and called, "Lady mother of the sea, come, for I have need of thee."

A woman came out from the midst of the sea, and said to him, "Welcome, son-in-law, and greetings. What is your wish?"

"Your daughter sent me to you for the little fish kettle."

"It is well, son-in-law," she said, and went down and brought him a fish kettle big enough for only one plate of food.

She gave it to her son-in-law, and he went and said to his wife, "Why, cook in this, and it won't be enough for me, let alone the King's army."

"Never you fear, husband, this kettle can suffice for ten times the King's army; only go and invite the King and his army to come tomorrow to our table."

So the fisherman got up and went to the King and said to him, "Tomorrow, Lord King, be so good as to come, and the meal will be ready."

So the next day the King summoned his army and they went and sat down in a wide place. He brought three servants to bear the dishes.

The king's servants went forward, and the fisherman said to them: "Ask the King what dish he would like first?"

They went and asked the king and he ordered them to bring him fish soup to begin with. The fisherman's wife put the ladle in the fish kettle and brought out all the bread they needed. Then, again from the kettle, she took out as many bowls of soup as there were men in the King's army.

When the soup had been eaten, the King ordered steamed fish. The fisherman's wife again put in the ladle and brought out steamed fish. Then the King ordered, in turn, fish with onions, fried fish, baked fish, and fish done in all kinds of ways. And all these dishes came out of the fish kettle, until the King's army had had their fill and got up and went about their business, and the fisherman saved his wife.

When several days had gone by, the King again summoned the fisherman, and said to him, "That woman is not the wife for you. Either you feed all my army with grapes tomorrow, or I shall take your wife away from you." (It was the month of January.)

"It is well, Lord King," said the fisherman, and he went complaining home, and said to his wife, "The King has set his eye on you, wife, and is doing all he can to take you away from me. Now he's ordered me to feed all his army with grapes. Where can we find grapes at this time of year?"

"Never you fear, husband, I shall never be the King's wife, but I shall make a King of you. Go now to my mother, and ask her for a pannikin of grapes."

The fisherman went to the sea, and called, "Lady mother of the sea, come, for I have need of thee."

The Sea came forth, and said to him, "Greetings, son-in-law, greetings, indeed. What is your wish?"

"Your daughter sent me to you for a pannikin of grapes."

"At once, son-in-law," said the Sea, and went and brought him a pannikin of grapes.

It had in it barely an *oka* of grapes, and he took it to his wife and said, "These grapes are hardly enough for me."

"Never you fear, this is a wonder-working pannikin, so go to the King and tell him to come with his army and eat his fill of grapes."

The fisherman went and said to the King, "The grapes are ready; so be so good as to come with your army."

The next day, the King summoned his army and they went and sat down in the same wide place, and the King's servant went to the fisherman's house and bore the grapes back in platefuls; the fisherman's wife took them out of the pannikin and it never emptied itself until the army had eaten its fill and the King took them away with him.

The fisherman went home, and said to his wife, "I saved you again today, wife. But we shall see what else our King (may he live for ever) will think up."

"Never you fear, husband, I'm here, never fear."

After several days had gone by, the king summoned the fisherman, and said "That woman is not suited to you: she is the wife for me. So now I want you to bring me a man two hands' span tall, with a beard three hands' span long."

"As you will, Lord King (may you live for ever)," he replied, and went.

He went to his wife, and said, "Now we're up against it, wife. The King wants us to bring him a man two hands' span tall, with a beard three hands' span long."

"Never you fear, husband. That, too, will be done. I have a brother of that like. Go to my mother and ask her to send back with you my brother, Chickpea, so that he may rock our child in the cradle."

The fisherman went to the sea, and called, "Lady mother of the sea, come, for I have need of thee."

The Sea came forth, and he said to her, "Your daughter sent me for you to send her Chickpea, so he may rock our child in the cradle."

"It is well, son-in-law," said the Sea, and called, "Chickpea, go to your sister and rock her child."

"It is well, I'm coming; just let me feed the chickens."

When he had fed his chickens, he mounted a cockerel and came out of the midst of the sea. The fisherman saw that he was two hands' span in height and had a beard three hands' span long that fell to the ground.

The fisherman went on ahead and after him Chickpea on the cockerel, and they went to the house.

"What is your will with me, sister?"

"Go to the King for him to see you, then put his eyes out, and make your brother-in-law king."

"It is well, sister," answered Chickpea.

The fisherman went in first, and after him Chickpea, before the King.

"What is your will, Lord King?" asked Chickpea.

"I called you so I might see you," said the King.

"And now have you seen me?" he asked him.

"I have," said the King.

Then Chickpea said, "Leap, cockerel, and put out the King's eyes."

The cockerel leapt and put out the King's eyes, and from the pain of the pecking, the King died.

Then said Chickpea to the King's Council of Twelve, "Will you make my brother-in-law King, or shall I set my cockerel on you?"

"We'll make him King," said the Council.

And they put the fisherman on the King's throne and brought his wife to be Queen, and they are reigning to this day; they have Chickpea on his cockerel as their knight, and he rides up and down in the palace.

THE FROG MAIDEN

Myanmar

The series of three tests in this story from the country known today as Myanmar reminds us of the values endorsed in fairy tales. A golden deer embodies wealth in all its gleaming solidity; the dish of rice and meat reminds us that there is nothing better than a full stomach; and the radiant beauty of the princess offers the promise of an ennobling transformation.

An old couple was childless, and the husband and the wife longed for a child. So when the wife found that she was with child, they were overjoyed; but to their great disappointment, the wife gave birth not to a human child, but to a little she-frog. However, as the little frog spoke and behaved as a human child, not only the parents but also the neighbors came to love her and called her affectionately "Little Miss Frog."

Some years later the woman died, and the man decided to marry again. The woman he chose was a widow with two ugly daughters and they were very jealous of Little Miss Frog's popularity with the neighbors. All three took a delight in ill-treating Little Miss Frog.

One day the youngest of the king's four sons announced that he would perform the hair-washing ceremony on a certain date and he invited all young ladies to join in the ceremony, as he would choose at the end of the ceremony one of them to be his princess.

On the morning of the appointed day the two ugly sisters dressed themselves in fine raiment, and with great hopes of being chosen by the Prince they started for the palace. Little

Miss Frog ran after them, and pleaded, "Sisters, please let me come with you."

The sisters laughed and said mockingly, "What, the little frog wants to come? The invitation is to young ladies and not to young frogs." Little Miss Frog walked along with them toward the palace, pleading for permission to come. But the sisters were adamant, and so at the palace gates she was left behind. However, she spoke so sweetly to the guards that they allowed her to go in. Little Miss Frog found hundreds of young ladies gathered round the pool full of lilies in the palace grounds; and she took her place among them and waited for the Prince.

The Prince now appeared, and washed his hair in the pool. The ladies also let down their hair and joined in the ceremony. At the end of the ceremony, the Prince declared that as the ladies were all beautiful, he did not know whom to choose and so he would throw a posy of jasmines into the air; and the lady on whose head the posy fell would be his princess. The Prince then threw the posy into the air, and all the ladies present looked up expectantly. The posy, however, fell on Little Miss Frog's head, to the great annoyance of the ladies, especially the two step-sisters. The Prince also was disappointed, but he felt that he should keep his word. So Little Miss Frog was married to the Prince, and she became Little Princess Frog.

Some time later, the old king called his four sons to him and said, "My sons, I am now too old to rule the country, and I want to retire to the forest and become a hermit. So I must appoint one of you as my successor. As I love you all alike, I will give you a task to perform, and he who performs it successfully shall be king in my place. The task is, bring me a golden deer at sunrise on the seventh day from now."

The Youngest Prince went home to Little Princess Frog and told her about the task. "What, only a golden deer!" exclaimed Princess Frog. "Eat as usual, my Prince, and on the appointed day I will give you the golden deer." So the Youngest Prince stayed at home, while the three elder princes went into the forest in search of the deer. On the seventh day before sunrise, Little Princess Frog woke up her husband and said, "Go to the palace, Prince, and here is your golden deer." The young Prince looked, then rubbed his eyes, and looked again. There was no mistake about it; the deer which Little Princess Frog was holding by a lead was really of pure gold. So he went to the palace, and to the great annoyance of the elder princes who brought ordinary deers, he was declared to be the heir by the king. The elder princes, however, pleaded for a second chance, and the king reluctantly agreed. "Then perform this second task," said the king. "On the seventh day from now at sunrise, you must bring me the rice that never becomes stale, and the meat that is ever fresh."

The Youngest Prince went home and told Princess Frog about the new task. "Don't you worry, sweet Prince," said Princess Frog. "Eat as usual, sleep as usual, and on the appointed day I will give you the rice and meat." So the Youngest Prince stayed at home, while the three elder princes went in search of the rice and meat. On the seventh day at sunrise, Little Princess Frog woke up her husband and said, "My Lord, go to the palace now, and here is your rice and meat." The Youngest Prince took the rice and meat, and went to the palace, and to the great annoyance of the elder princes who brought only well-cooked rice and meat, he was again declared to be the heir. But the two elder princes again pleaded for one more chance, and the king said, "This is positively the last task. On the seventh day from now at sunrise, bring me the most beautiful woman on this earth."

"Ho, ho!" said the three elder princes to themselves in great joy. "Our wives are very beautiful, and we will bring them. One of us is sure to be declared heir, and our good-for-nothing brother will be nowhere this time." The Youngest Prince overheard their remark, and felt sad, for his wife was a frog and ugly. When he reached home, he said to his wife, "Dear Princess, I must go and look for the most beautiful woman on this earth. My brothers will bring their wives, for they are really beautiful, but I will find someone who is more beautiful."

"Don't you fret, my Prince," replied Princess Frog. "Eat as usual, sleep as usual, and you can take me to the palace on the appointed day; surely I shall be declared to be the most beautiful woman."

The Youngest Prince looked at the Princess in surprise; but

he did not want to hurt her feelings, and he said gently, "All right, Princess, I will take you with me on the appointed day."

On the seventh day at dawn, Little Princess Frog woke up the Prince and said, "My Lord, I must make myself beautiful. So please wait outside and call me when it is nearly time to go." The Prince left the room as requested. After some moments, the Prince shouted from outside, "Princess, it is time for us to go."

"Please wait, my Lord," replied the Princess, "I am just powdering my face."

After some moments the Prince shouted, "Princess, we must go now."

"All right, my Lord," replied the Princess, "please open the door for me."

The Prince thought to himself, "Perhaps, just as she was able to obtain the golden deer and the wonderful rice and meat, she is able to make herself beautiful," and he expectantly opened the door, but he was disappointed to see Little Princess Frog still a frog and as ugly as ever. However, so as not to hurt her feelings, the Prince said nothing and took her along to the palace. When the Prince entered the audience chamber with his Frog Princess the three elder princes with their wives were already there. The king looked at the Prince in surprise and said, "Where is your beautiful maiden?"

"I will answer for the prince, my king," said the Frog Princess. "I am his beautiful maiden." She then took off her frog skin and stood a beautiful maiden dressed in silk and satin. The king declared her to be the most beautiful maiden in the world, and selected the Prince as his successor on the throne. The Prince asked his Princess never to put on the ugly frog skin again, and the Frog Princess, to accede to his request, threw the skin into the fire.

CHONGUITA

Philippines

This tale was told by Pilar Ejercito, a woman living in the province of Laguna in the Philippines. Her aunt had told her the story when she was a little girl. It is not easy to commiserate uncritically with Don Juan, the son who marries Chonguita, even if he is inexplicably obliging when told to marry a monkey. The Philippines were named after Philip II, king of Spain, and the names in this tale reflect three centuries of colonial rule.

There once lived a king who had three sons. They were called Pedro, Diego, and Juan. One day the king ordered the three young gentlemen to set out and seek their fortunes. The brothers each took a different direction, but before they separated, they agreed to meet later at a certain place in the forest.

After walking for many days, Don Juan met an old man on the road. The old man gave Don Juan some bread and told him to walk to a palace that was about a mile away. "When you enter the gate," he said, "you must divide the bread I have given you among the monkeys guarding the gate to the palace. Otherwise you won't be able to pass through the gate."

Don Juan took the bread. When he reached the palace, he did exactly as the old man had said. When he walked through the gate, he saw a big monkey. Frightened by the sight of the animal, Don Juan was about to run away when the animal called out to him and said, "Don Juan, I know that you came here to make your fortune. Right now my daughter Chonguita is willing to marry you." The archbishop of the monkeys was summoned, and Don Juan and Chonguita were married without delay.

A few days later Don Juan asked his wife for permission to go to the place where he and his brothers had agreed to meet. When Chonguita's mother heard that Don Juan was going away, she said, "If you are going away, take Chonguita with you." Don Juan was ashamed to take Chonguita because she was a monkey, but he was forced to take her, and the two set off on the road. When Don Juan met his two brothers and their beautiful wives at the appointed place, he could not get out a word. Don Diego noticed that his brother looked gloomy and asked, "What is the matter with you? Where is your wife, Don Juan?"

Don Juan sadly replied, "Here she is."

"Where?" asked Don Pedro.

"Right behind me," replied Don Juan.

When Don Pedro and Don Diego saw the monkey, they were startled. "Oh!" exclaimed Don Pedro, "What happened to you? Have you lost your mind?"

Don Juan was at a loss for words. Finally he managed to say, "Let's all go back home! Our father must be waiting for us!" With that, Don Juan turned around and began walking home. Don Pedro and Don Diego, together with their wives, followed Don Juan. Chonguita walked by her husband's side.

The king learned that his three sons had returned, and he rushed down the stairs to meet them. When he discovered that one of his sons had married a monkey, he fainted. But once he recovered his senses, he thought to himself: "This may be a stroke of bad luck, but it is God's will. I must take the news calmly and be patient." The king gave each of the couples a house to live in.

The more the king thought about it, the more disgraceful his son's marriage seemed. One day, he called his three sons together and said to them, "Tell your wives that I want each one of them to make a coat for me and to embroider it. The one who fails to finish the task in three days will be put to death." The king had issued this order with the hope that Chonguita would be put to death. He was sure she would not be able to make a coat for him. But his hopes were dashed. On the third day, the three daughters-in-law presented him with the coats they had made. The one embroidered by Chonguita was the prettiest of the three.

The king was still anxious to get rid of the monkey-wife. He ordered his daughters-in-law to embroider a cap for him in the next two days, under penalty of death if they failed. The caps were all finished right on time.

Finally he was at a loss for ideas, but he came up with the following plan. He summoned his three daughters-in-law and said, "Each of you will draw pictures on the walls of my chamber. Whoever draws the prettiest within the next three days—her husband will succeed me on the throne." At the end of the three days the pictures were finished. When the king went to inspect them, he found that Chonguita's was by far the prettiest, and so Don Juan was crowned king.

A feast was held in the palace to celebrate the new king. In the midst of the festivities, Don Juan became furious with his wife for insisting that he dance with her, and he hurled her against the wall. The hall suddenly turned dark after this brutal act took place. But then it grew bright again, and there was Chonguita, transformed into a beautiful woman.

URASHIMA TARO

Japan

Urashima Taro is the Japanese Rip Van Winkle, and the oldest known variant of his story can be found in an eighth-century volume called the Nihongi. *The Crane and Turtle Dance is a traditional dance performed in the region around Ise, where the oldest Shinto shrine can be found.*

Long ago a man named Urashima Taro lived at Kitamae Oshima. He lived with his mother, who was nearly eighty years old. He was a fisherman and was still unmarried. One day his mother said to him, "Urashima, Urashima, while I still have my health, won't you please take a bride."

"I am as yet unable to earn a living. Even if I took a bride, I could not support her; while you are still living, I shall continue fishing and go on living like this," he said.

The days and months passed, and the mother became eighty years old. Urashima was forty. It was autumn, and the north wind blew day after day so that it was impossible to go out to fish. Since he could catch no fish, he could make no money, and it began to appear that he would be unable even to get food for his mother. "Ah, if we could only have good weather tomorrow," he thought, as he lay around with nothing to do.

Suddenly the sky began to clear. Urashima Taro jumped up, climbed onto his raft, and set out to fish. He fished until it began to get light in the east, but he could not catch a single fish. He was greatly troubled, but as the sun rose higher in the sky, a large fish finally struck the hook. Quickly he hauled in the line and found that he had caught a turtle. The turtle clung to the edge of the raft and made no move to go away.

"I thought maybe you were a sea bream, but you are only a turtle. Since you're here, no other fish will take the hook. Here, I'll take you off the hook; now please go away somewhere," said Urashima, throwing the turtle back into the sea.

Urashima lighted his pipe and smoked as he continued fishing, but he caught nothing. He was greatly troubled, but just before noon it again felt as if a large fish had struck the hook. He hauled it in, and it was the turtle again. "No matter how much I ask him to go away, the turtle keeps coming back and the fish won't bite. I'm having very bad luck," he said and again chased the turtle away. Since he could not return home with nothing at all, he patiently kept fishing until mid-afternoon, when again something struck the hook. Thinking that surely this time it must be a fish, he hauled in the line and saw that it was the turtle again; so again he chased it away. It kept on like this until the sun began to set, and he had not caught a single fish. Soon the sun sank from sight, and he started home, wondering what to say to his mother.

He was paddling the raft along when he noticed a seagoing ship in the distance. For some reason or other it was coming toward him. Urashima steered his boat to starboard, and the ship did the same; he steered to port, and the seagoing ship also steered to port. Finally the ship came alongside Urashima's boat. The captain called out, "Urashima, please come on board this ship; we have come to you from the princess of Ryugu [the dragon kingdom at the bottom of the sea]."

"If I went to the dragon kingdom, my mother would be all alone, so I cannot go."

"We will see that your mother is well taken care of; please come on board our ship," urged the captain, and so Urashima, without further thought, boarded the ship.

As soon as Urashima was on board, the ship sank into the water and went to the world at the bottom of the sea. When Urashima arrived, he saw that there was a beautiful palace there; the princess came and, saying that he surely must be hungry, gave him a feast. "Please stay two or three days and enjoy yourself," she said. "Then you can return home."

Urashima saw that the princess and many other beautiful young girls were there; he was given new kimonos, and in this way days and months passed without his noticing, until three years had gone by. Urashima felt that he must return home. When he asked the princess if he might go, she gave him a three-tiered jewel box. "In case of necessity, you may open the box," she said. Then Urashima was put on board the seagoing ship, and they landed at a place similar to this one here, which looks like a mountain's nose.

Urashima went to his village and looked around, but even the face of the mountain had changed; the trees on the hills had died or disappeared. "How could all this have happened in only three years?" he thought to himself as he went to where his house was. There in a thatched house was an old man working with straw. Urashima entered the house, greeted the old man, and inquired about himself, asking, "Do you know a man by the name of Urashima?"

The old man replied, "There was a story that in my grandfather's time a man named Urashima went to the dragon kingdom at the bottom of the sea, but no matter how long his relatives waited, he never returned."

"What became of that man's mother?" asked Urashima and was told that she had died long, long ago.

Urashima went to see the remains of his own house. Only the stone wash basin and the garden steppingstones remained; other than that, there was nothing. Lost in reverie, he opened the lid of the box; in the first box there was a crane's feather. He opened the next box, and a puff of white smoke came from it; at this Urashima was turned into an old man. In the third box there was a mirror. He looked in the mirror and saw to his surprise that he had become an old man.

While he was looking in the mirror, the crane's feather from the first box attached itself to his back. He flew up into the sky and circled around his mother's grave. When he did this, the princess from the sea, who had turned herself into a turtle, came up on the beach to see him.

It is said that this is the origin of the Crane and Turtle Dance at Ise.

OISIN IN TIR NA N-OG

Ireland

Oisin (also spelled Ossian) was the legendary great poet of Ireland and a warrior figure in Irish mythology. His name means "young deer" or "fawn." Tir na n-Og is "the land of the young," and, in this tale, it is paradoxically beset by anxieties about succession. Some versions of this tale have an ending that resembles the one in "Urashima Taro," the Japanese Rip Van Winkle tale.

There was a king in Tir na n-Og, and he had long held the throne and crown against all comers. And the law of the kingdom was that every seventh year the champions and best men of the country should run for the office of king.

Once in seven years they all met at the front of the palace and ran to the top of a hill two miles distant. On the top of that hill was a chair, and the man who sat down first in the chair was the king of Tir na n-Og for the next seven years. After he had ruled for ages, the king began to grow anxious. He was afraid that someone might sit on the chair before him and take the crown off his head. So he called up his Druid one day and asked, "How long shall I keep the chair to rule this land, and will any man sit on it before me and take the crown off my head?"

"You will keep the chair and the crown forever," said the Druid, "unless your own son-in-law takes them from you."

The king had no sons and but one daughter, the finest woman in Tir na n-Og; and the like of her could not be found in Erin or any kingdom in the world. When the king heard the words of the Druid, he said, "I'll have no son-in-law, for I'll put the daughter in a way no man will marry her."

Then he took a rod of Druidic spells, and calling the daughter up before him, he struck her with the rod, and put a pig's head on her in place of her own.

Then he sent the daughter away to her own place in the castle, and turning to the Druid said, "There is no man that will marry her now."

When the Druid saw the face that was on the princess with the pig's head that the father gave her, he grew very sorry that he had given such information to the king; and some time after he went to see the princess.

"Must I be like this forever?" she asked the Druid.

"You must," he said, "until you marry one of the sons of Fin MacCumhail in Erin. If you marry one of Fin's sons, you'll be freed from the blot that is on you now, and you will have back your own head and countenance."

When she heard this she grew impatient and could not rest until she left Tir na n-Og and reached Erin. When she made inquiries, she learned that Fin and the Fenians of Erin were at that time living on Knock an Ar, and she made her way to the place without delay and lived there for a while. And when she saw Oisin, he pleased her. When she found out that he was a son of Fin MacCumhail, she kept trying to find ways to spend time with him. And it was usual for the Fenians in those days to hunt in the hills and mountains and in the woods of Erin. When one of them went he always took five or six men with him to bring home the game.

One day Oisin set out with his men and dogs for the woods. He went so deep into the woods and killed so much game that when it was hauled into one place, the men were so tired, weak, and hungry that they couldn't carry it. They went back home and left him to shift for himself with the three dogs, Bran, Sciolán, and Buglén.

Now the daughter of the king of Tir na n-Og, who was herself the Queen of Youth, followed closely in the hunt all that day, and when the men left Oisin she came up to him. As he stood there, looking at the great pile of game, he said, "I am very sorry to leave behind anything that I've had the trouble of killing." She looked at him and said, "Tie up a bundle for me, and I'll carry it to lighten the load off you."

Oisin gave her a bundle of the game to carry, and took the remainder himself. The evening was very warm and the game heavy, and after they had gone some distance, Oisin said, "Let us rest a while."

Both threw down their burdens and leaned against a great stone that was by the roadside. The woman was flushed and out of breath. She loosened her dress to cool herself. Then Oisin looked at her and saw her beautiful form and her white bosom.

"Oh, then," said he, "it's a pity you have the pig's head on you, for I have never seen such an appearance on a woman in all my life before."

"Well," she said, "my father is the king of Tir na n-Og, and I was the finest woman in his kingdom and the most beautiful of all until he put me under a Druidic spell and gave me the pig's head that's on me now in place of my own. And the Druid of Tir na n-Og came to me afterward and told me that if one of the sons of Fin MacCumhail would marry me, the pig's head would vanish, and I should get back my face in the same form as it was before my father struck me with the Druid's wand. When I heard this I never stopped till I came to Erin, where I found your father and picked you out among the sons of Fin MacCumhail, and followed you to see would you marry me and set me free."

"If that is the state you are in, and if marriage with me will free you from the spell, I'll not leave the pig's head on you long."

So they got married without delay, not waiting to take home the game or to lift it from the ground. That moment the pig's head was gone, and the king's daughter had the same face and beauty that she had before her father struck her with the Druidic wand.

"Now," said the Queen of Youth to Oisin, "I cannot stay here long, and unless you come with me to Tir na n-Og we must part."

"Oh," said Oisin, "wherever you go I'll go, and wherever you turn I'll follow."

Then she turned around, and Oisin went with her, not going

back to Knock an Ar to see his father or his son. That very day they set out for Tir na n-Og and never stopped till they came to her father's castle. And when they arrived, there was a welcome before them, for the king thought his daughter was lost.

That same year there was to be a choice of a king, and when the appointed day came at the end of the seventh year, all the great men and the champions, and the king himself, met together at the front of the castle to run and see who should be first in the chair on the hill. But before a man of them was halfway to the hill, Oisin was sitting above in the chair before them.

After that time no one stood up to run for the office against Oisin, and he spent many happy years as king in Tir na n-Og.

THE DOG BRIDE

India

In this tale recorded in the eastern part of India, the narrative circuits are fully loaded to produce both comedy and tragedy. Like the kind and unkind girls in the tale type of that name, the two young men in the story follow similar paths but end with sharply contrasting destinies, in this case without any kind of lesson about the wages of virtue and vice.

Once upon a time there lived a young man whose job it was to herd buffaloes. One day, as he was watching his animals graze, he noticed that a dog would appear every day at high noon and make its way over to a ravine with some pools of water. His curiosity was aroused, and he wondered who owned the dog and what it was doing in that ravine. He decided to start paying attention to the animal. One day when it appeared, he hid in a place where he could watch the dog. It got into the water, shed its dog skin, and out stepped a beautiful maiden. She bathed in the waters, and when she was finished, she put the skin back on and became a dog. Off she went to the village. The shepherd followed her and saw her enter a house. He asked about the owner of the house, and, once he found out his name, he went back to his work.

That year the shepherd's father and mother decided that it was time for him to marry. They began looking around for a suitable wife. But he announced that he had already made up his mind. He had decided to marry a dog, and he would never have a human wife.

Everyone laughed out loud when they heard what he had

said. But he would not change his mind. Finally everyone began to believe that he must have the soul of a dog in him and that it was best to let him have his way. His mother and father asked whether he had any particular dog in mind for his bride. He gave them the name of the man into whose house he had tracked the dog that had bathed in the area of the ravines. The dog's master found it hilarious that anyone would want to marry his dog, but he was happy to accept a bride price from the family for her. The day was set for the wedding, and they began building a booth for the ceremony. The bridegroom's party went to the bride's house, and the wedding went off without a hitch. The bride was escorted back to her husband's house.

Every night, after her husband fell asleep, the bride would remove her dog's skin and leave the house. After her husband discovered what she was doing, he pretended the next night to go to sleep and kept an eye on her. Just as she was about to leave the room, he jumped up and grabbed her. He seized the dog skin and threw it into the fire, where it burned to ashes. The bride kept her human shape, but she was of more than human beauty. Everyone in the village found out what happened, and they congratulated the shepherd for having the wisdom to marry a dog.

Now the shepherd had a friend named Jitu, and when Jitu saw what a prize his friend had won, he decided that he could not do better than to marry a dog. His relatives did not object, and a bride was chosen. The wedding celebrations began, but when they were putting vermilion on the bride's forehead, she began to growl. Still, they dragged her to the bridegroom's home and anointed her with oil and turmeric. But when the bride's party set off for home, the dog broke loose and started running back to them. Everyone shouted at Jitu, telling him to run after his bride and bring her back. But she growled at him and then bit him so that he had to give up. Everyone laughed so hard at him that he was too ashamed to say a word. Two or three days later he hanged himself.

THE SWAN MAIDEN

Sweden

With its precise geographical designation, this story aims to present itself as legend rather than fairy tale. The earth-weighted wife, in this instance, does not need to think twice before seizing the opportunity set before her by her husband. That the hero is a hunter is one of many pungent ingredients in this tale about a swan maiden, captured and forced into domestic servitude. The allegorical elements pointing to the power relationships in domestic arrangements could hardly have escaped listeners.

A young peasant, in the parish of Mellby, who often amused himself with hunting, saw one day three swans flying toward him, which settled down upon the strand of a sound nearby.

Approaching the place, he was astonished at seeing the three swans divest themselves of their feathery attire, which they threw into the grass, and three maidens of dazzling beauty step forth and spring into the water.

After sporting in the waves awhile they returned to the land, where they resumed their former garb and shape and flew away in the same direction from which they came.

One of them, the youngest and fairest, had, in the meantime, so smitten the young hunter that neither night nor day could he tear his thoughts from the bright image.

His mother, noticing that something was wrong with her son, and that the chase, which had formerly been his favorite pleasure, had lost its attractions, asked him finally the cause of his melancholy, whereupon he related to her what he had seen, and declared that there was no longer any happiness in this life for him if he could not possess the fair swan maiden.

"Nothing is easier," said the mother. "Go at sunset next Thursday evening to the place where you last saw her. When the three swans come, give attention to where your chosen one lays her feathery garb, take it and hasten away."

The young man listened to his mother's instructions, and, betaking himself, the following Thursday evening, to a convenient hiding place near the sound, he waited, with impatience, the coming of the swans. The sun was just sinking behind the trees when the young man's ears were greeted by a whizzing in the air, and the three swans settled down upon the beach, as on their former visit.

As soon as they had removed their swan attire they were again transformed into the most beautiful maidens, and, springing out upon the white sand, they were soon enjoying themselves in the water.

From his hiding place the young hunter had taken careful note of where his enchantress had laid her swan feathers. Stealing softly forth, he took them and returned to his place of concealment in the surrounding foliage.

Soon thereafter two of the swans were heard to fly away, but the third, in search of her clothes, discovered the young man, before whom, believing him responsible for their disappearance, she fell upon her knees and prayed that her swan attire might be returned to her. The hunter was, however, unwilling to yield the beautiful prize, and, casting a cloak around her shoulders, carried her home.

Preparations were soon made for a magnificent wedding, which took place in due form, and the young couple dwelt lovingly and contentedly together.

One Thursday evening, seven years later, the hunter related to her how he had sought and won her. He brought forth and showed her, also, the white swan feathers of her former days. No sooner were they placed in her hands than she was transformed once more into a swan, and instantly took flight through the open window. In breathless astonishment, the man stared wildly after his rapidly vanishing wife, and before a year and a day had passed, he was laid, with his longings and sorrows, in his allotted place in the village church-yard.

THE HUNTER AND THE TORTOISE

Ghana

This story, a variant of the widely known "Talking Skull," was collected in Accra, Ghana, in the early part of the twentieth century. It has a softly confrontational speaker, one whose beautiful voice teaches harsh lessons about loose talk. Readers will notice the kinship with folktales about selkies, mermaids, swan maidens, and all those animal brides who leave their natural habitat to live with a human and move from nature to culture. Doomed and divided, they have conflicted allegiances to their two habitats and families.

A village hunter had one day gone farther afield than usual. Coming to a part of the forest with which he was unacquainted, he was astonished to hear a voice singing. He listened; this was the song:

> *"It is man who forces himself on things,*
> *Not things, which force themselves on him."*

The singing was accompanied by sweet music—which entirely charmed the hunter's heart.

When the little song was finished, the hunter peeped through the branches to see who the singer could be. Imagine his amazement when he found it was none other than a tortoise, with a tiny harp slung in front of her. Never had he seen such a marvelous thing.

Time after time he returned to the same place in order to listen to this wonderful creature. At last he persuaded her to let him carry her back to his hut that he might enjoy her singing daily in comfort. This she permitted, only on the understanding that she sang to him alone.

The hunter did not rest long content with this arrangement, however. Soon he began to wish that he could show off this wonderful tortoise to the entire world, and thereby thought he would gain great honor. He told the secret, first to one, then to another, until finally it reached the ears of the chief himself. The hunter was commanded to come and tell his tale before the Assembly. When, however, he described the tortoise and how it could sing and play the harp, the people shouted in scorn. They refused to believe him.

At last he said, "If I do not speak truth, I give you leave to kill me. Tomorrow I will bring the tortoise to this place and you may all hear her. If she cannot do as I say, I am willing to die." "Good," replied the people, "and if the tortoise can do as you say, we give you leave to punish us in any way you choose."

The matter being then settled, the hunter returned home, well pleased with the prospect. As soon as the morrow dawned, he carried tortoise and harp down to the Assembly Place—where a table had been placed ready for her. Everyone gathered round to listen. But no song came. The people were very patient, and quite willing to give both tortoise and hunter a chance. Hours went by, and, to the hunter's dismay and shame, the tortoise remained mute. He tried every means in his power to coax her to sing, but in vain. The people at first whispered, then spoke outright, in scorn of the boaster and his claims.

Night came on and brought with it the hunter's doom. As the last ray of the setting sun faded, he was beheaded. The instant this happened the tortoise spoke. The people looked at one another in troubled wonder: "Our brother spoke truth, then, and we have killed him." The tortoise, however, went on to explain. "He brought his punishment on himself. I led a happy life in the forest, singing my little song. He was not content to come and listen to me. He had to tell my secret (which did not at all concern him) to the entire world. Had he not tried to make a show of me this would never have happened."

> "It is man who forces himself on things,
>   Not things that force themselves on him."

THE PEASANT AND ZEMYNE

Lithuania

In Lithuania, the name Zemyne means "earth." The snake in this story, associated with mobility, fertility, and metamorphosis, bears a strong resemblance to Ishtar, Astarte, and other ancient goddesses. In her animal form she is an ambiguous creature, able to kill but also to heal. Successfully assimilating her to the human sphere becomes an impossible challenge.

Zemyne is a snake with a single eye. Whoever she bites will die immediately. She may only be seen in summer, and then only at either noon or midnight. The blood of Zemyne is black, but it can cure every illness. Whoever bathes in the black blood of Zemyne is protected against all magic.

God has granted Zemyne dominion in the realm beneath the ground. The metals belong to her. "If I had two eyes instead of one," Zemyne once said, "I would kill enough people to cover the walls of my home with their skulls."

Some say Zemyne was once a lovely young girl who refused the advances of a wicked magician. Upon his curse, she assumed her present form. Whoever wishes to rescue her must beat her until her skin falls off. Then, he must burn the skin immediately.

A young peasant habitually killed all the snakes which he found in the garden, forest, and field. One day he was cutting the grass in a meadow, when he suddenly heard a loud hiss. He became aware of a movement in the grass behind him. Looking around, he recognized Zemyne.

Seeing his chance, the peasant pinned the head of Zemyne firmly against the earth with the blade of his sickle. Then he grabbed a knotted branch with his free hand and pounded the snake furiously, until the skin of Zemyne broke open. All of a sudden, a beautiful maiden was standing before him. Beside her sparkled a many-colored dress.

The maiden immediately reached for the dress, but the peasant was faster. He grabbed the garment, placed it beneath his arm and led the maiden to his home. There he gave her food and new clothes.

The young people were married and lived happily together for many years. Their joy increased still more as the wife presented her husband with many children.

But one day the wife found a chest containing the many-colored dress. She put it on, changed immediately back into a snake and killed her husband and children with her poisonous kiss. Leaving the farmstead, she took up her old residence in the meadow by the forest.

PUDDOCKY

Germany

Combining elements of "Rapunzel" with stories about a young man and his animal bride, this tale, which was collected from a German-speaking informant, is closely related to Madame d'Aulnoy's "The White Cat."

There was once upon a time a poor woman who had one little daughter called "Parsley." She was so called because she liked eating parsley better than any other food, indeed she would hardly eat anything else. Her poor mother hadn't enough money always to be buying parsley for her, but the child was so beautiful that she could refuse her nothing, and so she went every night to the garden of an old witch who lived near and stole great branches of the coveted vegetable, in order to satisfy her daughter.

This remarkable taste of the fair Parsley soon became known, and the theft was discovered. The witch called the girl's mother to her, and proposed that she should let her daughter come and live with her, and then she could eat as much parsley as she liked. The mother was quite pleased with this suggestion, and so the beautiful Parsley took up her abode with the old witch.

One day three princes, whom their father had sent abroad to travel, came to the town where Parsley lived and perceived the beautiful girl combing and plaiting her long black hair at the window. In one moment they all fell hopelessly in love with her, and longed ardently to have the girl for their wife; but hardly had they with one breath expressed their desire than, mad with jealousy, they drew their swords and all three set upon each other. The struggle was so violent and the noise so loud that the old witch heard it, and said at once, "Of course Parsley is at the bottom of all this."

And when she had convinced herself that this was so, she stepped forward, and, full of wrath over the quarrels and feuds Parsley's beauty gave rise to, she cursed the girl and said, "I wish you were an ugly toad, sitting under a bridge at the other end of the world."

Hardly were the words out of her mouth when Parsley was changed into a toad and vanished from sight. The princes, now that the cause of their dispute was removed, put up their swords, kissed each other affectionately, and returned to their father.

The king was growing old and feeble, and wished to yield his scepter and crown in favor of one of his sons, but he couldn't make up his mind which of the three he should appoint as his successor. He determined that fate should decide for him. So he called his three children to him and said, "My dear sons, I am growing old, and am weary of reigning, but I can't make up my mind to which of you three I should yield my crown, for I love you all equally. At the same time I would like the best and cleverest of you to rule over my people. I have, therefore, determined to set you three tasks to do, and the one that performs them best shall be my heir. The first thing I shall ask you to do is to bring me a piece of linen a hundred yards long, so fine that it will go through a gold ring." The sons bowed low, and, promising to do their best, they started on their journey without further delay.

The two elder brothers took many servants and carriages with them, but the youngest set out quite alone. In a short time they came to three crossroads; two of them were gay and crowded, but the third was dark and lonely.

The two elder brothers chose the more frequented ways, but the youngest, bidding them farewell, set out on the dreary road.

Wherever linen was to be bought, there the two elder brothers hastened. They loaded their carriages with bales of the finest linen they could find and then returned home.

The youngest brother, on the other hand, went on his weary way for many days, and nowhere did he come across any linen that would have done. So he journeyed on, and his spirits sank with every step. At last he came to a bridge which stretched over a deep river flowing through a flat and marshy land. Before crossing the bridge he sat down on the banks of the stream and sighed dismally over his sad fate. Suddenly a misshapen toad crawled out of the swamp, and, sitting down opposite him, asked: "What's the matter with you, my dear prince?"

The prince answered impatiently, "There's not much good my telling you, Puddocky, for you couldn't help me if I did."

"Don't be too sure of that," replied the toad; "tell me your trouble and we'll see."

Then the prince became most confidential and told the little creature why he had been sent out of his father's kingdom.

"Prince, I will certainly help you," said the toad, and, crawling back into her swamp, she returned dragging after her a piece of linen not bigger than a finger, which she lay before the Prince, saying, "Take this home, and you'll see it will help you."

The prince had no wish to take such an insignificant bundle with him; but he didn't like to hurt Puddocky's feelings by refusing it, so he took up the little packet, put it in his pocket, and bade the little toad farewell. Puddocky watched the prince till he was out of sight and then crept back into the water.

The farther the prince went the more he noticed that the pocket in which the little roll of linen lay became heavier, and in proportion his heart grew lighter. And so, greatly comforted, he returned to the Court of his father, and arrived home just at the same time as his brothers with their caravans. The king was delighted to see them all again, and at once drew the ring from his finger and the trial began. In all the wagonloads there was not one piece of linen the tenth part of which would go through the ring, and the two elder brothers, who had at first sneered at their youngest brother for returning with no baggage, began to feel rather small. But what were their feelings when he drew a bale of linen out of his pocket which in fineness, softness, and purity of color was unsurpassable! The threads were hardly visible, and it went through the ring without the smallest difficulty, at the same time measuring a hundred yards quite correctly.

The father embraced his fortunate son, and commanded the rest of the linen to be thrown into the water; then, turning to his children he said, "Now, dear princes, prepare yourselves for the second task. You must bring me back a little dog that will go comfortably into a walnut shell."

The sons were all in despair over this demand, but as they each wished to win the crown, they determined to do their best, and after a very few days set out on their travels again.

At the crossroads they separated once more. The youngest went by himself along his lonely way, but this time he felt much more cheerful. Hardly had he sat down under the bridge and heaved a sigh, than Puddocky came out; and, sitting down opposite him, asked, "What's wrong with you now, dear prince?"

The prince, who this time never doubted the little toad's power to help him, told her his difficulty at once. "Prince, I will help you," said the toad again, and crawled back into her swamp as fast as her short little legs would carry her. She returned, dragging a hazelnut behind her, which she laid at the prince's feet and said, "Take this nut home with you and tell your father to crack it very carefully, and you'll see then what will happen." The Prince thanked her heartily and went on his way in the best of spirits, while the little puddock crept slowly back into the water.

When the prince got home he found his brothers had just arrived with great wagonloads of little dogs of all sorts. The king had a walnut shell ready, and the trial began; but not one of the dogs the two eldest sons had brought with them would in the least fit into the shell. When they had tried all their little dogs, the youngest son handed his father the hazelnut, with a modest bow, and begged him to crack it carefully. Hardly had the old king done so than a lovely tiny dog sprang out of the nutshell, and ran about on the king's hand, wagging its tail and barking lustily at all the other little dogs. The joy of the Court was great. The father again embraced his fortunate son, commanded the rest of the small dogs to be thrown into the water and drowned, and once more addressed his sons. "The two most difficult tasks have been performed. Now listen to the third and last: whoever brings the fairest wife home with him shall be my heir."

This demand seemed so easy and agreeable and the reward was so great, that the princes lost no time in setting forth on their travels. At the crossroads the two elder brothers debated if they should go the same way as the youngest, but when they saw how dreary and deserted it looked they made up their minds that it would be impossible to find what they sought in those wilds, and so they stuck to their former paths.

The youngest was very depressed this time and said to himself, "Anything else Puddocky could have helped me in, but this task is quite beyond her power. How could she ever find a beautiful wife for me? Her swamps are wide and empty, and no human beings dwell there; only frogs and toads and other creatures of that sort." However, he sat down as usual under the bridge, and this time he sighed from the bottom of his heart.

In a few minutes the toad stood in front of him and asked, "What's the matter with you now, my dear prince?"

"Oh, Puddocky, this time you can't help me, for the task is beyond even your power," replied the prince.

"Still," answered the toad, "you may as well tell me your difficulty, for who knows but I mayn't be able to help you this time also."

The prince then told her the task they had been set to do. "I'll help you right enough, my dear prince," said the little toad; "just you go home, and I'll soon follow you." With these words, Puddocky, with a spring quite unlike her usual slow movements, jumped into the water and disappeared.

The prince rose up and went sadly on his way, for he didn't believe it possible that the little toad could really help him in his present difficulty. He had hardly gone a few steps when he heard a sound behind him, and, looking round, he saw a carriage made of cardboard, drawn by six big rats, coming toward him. Two hedgehogs rode in front as outriders, and on the box sat a fat mouse as coachman, and behind stood two little frogs as footmen. In the carriage itself sat Puddocky, who kissed her hand to the prince out of the window as she passed by.

Sunk deep in thought over the fickleness of fortune that had granted him two of his wishes and now seemed about to deny him the last and best, the prince hardly noticed the absurd equipage, and still less did he feel inclined to laugh at its comic appearance.

The carriage drove on in front of him for some time and then turned a corner. But what was his joy and surprise when suddenly, round the same corner, but coming toward him, there appeared a beautiful coach drawn by six splendid horses, with outriders, coachmen, footmen and other servants all in the most gorgeous liveries, and seated in the carriage was the most beautiful woman the prince had ever seen, and in whom he at once recognized the beautiful Parsley, for whom his heart had formerly burned. The carriage stopped when it reached him, and the footmen sprang down and opened the door for him. He got in and sat down beside the beautiful Parsley, and thanked her heartily for her help, and told her how much he loved her.

And so he arrived at his father's capital, at the same moment as his brothers who had returned with many carriageloads of beautiful women. But when they were all led before the king, the whole Court with one consent awarded the prize of beauty to the fair Parsley.

The old king was delighted, and embraced his thrice-fortunate son and his new daughter-in-law tenderly, and appointed them as his successors to the throne. But he commanded the other women to be thrown into the water and drowned, like the bales of linen and the little dogs. The prince married Puddocky and reigned long and happily with her, and if they aren't dead I suppose they are living still.

THE MAN WHO
MARRIED A BEAR

Native American

Collected by the American anthropologist Herbert J. Spinden, this story was described to him as a "true tale of recent times, and not a myth." Asotin Creek flows into the Snake River near Lewiston, Idaho. The Grande Ronde River is located in northeastern Oregon and flows into the Snake River.

A man named Five-Times-Surrounded-in-War (Pákatamápaütx) lived with his father at Asotin, and in the spring of the year the youth would go away from home and lose himself till fall. He would tell no one where he had been. Now, he really was accustomed to go up the Little Salmon (Hune'he) branch of the Grande Ronde River to fish for salmon. It was the second year that he went there that this thing happened.

A bear girl lived just below the forks of Asotin Creek, and from that place she used to go over onto the Little Salmon, where Five-Times-Surrounded-in-War had a camp made of boughs. One day, after fishing, he was lying in his camp not quite asleep. He heard the noise of someone walking in the woods. He heard the noise of walking go all around the camp. The grizzly-bear girl was afraid to go near the man, and soon she went away and left him. Next morning he tried to track her; and while he could see the tracks in the grass, he could not tell what it was that made them.

Next day the youth hunted deer in order to have dried meat for the winter; and that evening the grizzly-bear girl, dressed up as a human being, came into his camp. Five-Times-Surrounded-in-War had just finished his supper when he heard the footfalls, and, looking out into the forest, he saw a fine girl come into the open. He wondered if this person was what he had heard the night before.

He asked the girl to tell him what she wanted, and she came and sat down beside him. The youth was bashful and could not talk to her, although she was a pretty girl. Then he said, "Where are you camping?" And she told him that three days before she had come from the forks of Asotin Creek.

"I came to see you, and to find out whether or not you would marry me."

Now, Five-Times-Surrounded-in-War did not know of anyone who lived above the mouth of Asotin Creek, and for that reason he told the girl he would take home his meat and salmon and return in ten days. So the girl went back to the forks of Asotin Creek, and the youth to the mouth of the stream with his meat. Then they returned and met; and the youth fell deeply in love with the girl, and married her.

So they lived in his camp until she said to him, "Now we will go to my home."

And when they arrived, he saw that she had a fine supply of winter food—dried salmon, dried meat, camas, *kaus*, *sanitx*, serviceberries, and huckleberries. But what most surprised him was that they went into a hole in the ground, because then he knew she must be a bear.

It grew late in the fall, and they had to stay in the cave, for the girl could not go out. In the dead of winter they were still in the cave when the snow began to settle and harden. One night, near midnight, when both were asleep in their beds, the grizzly-bear girl dreamed, and roared out in her sleep.

She told her husband to build a fire and make a light. Then the grizzly-bear girl sang a song, and blood came running from her mouth. She said, "This blood you see coming from my mouth is not my blood. It is the blood of men. Down at the mouth of Asotin Creek the hunters are making ready for a bear hunt. They have observed this cave, and five hunters are coming here to see if a bear is in it." The grizzly-bear girl in her sleep knew that the hunters were making ready.

Next morning the five hunters went up to that place, and

that same morning the grizzly-bear girl donned a different dress from what she usually wore, a dress that was painted red. She told her husband, "Soon after the sun leaves the earth, these hunters will be here, and then I will do my killing."

They arrived, and Five-Times-Surrounded-in-War heard them talking. He heard them say that something must be living in the cave. When the first hunter came to the door of the cave, the grizzly-bear girl rushed out and killed him. Then the four other hunters went home and told the news, and ten hunters made ready to come up and kill the bear. They camped close by for the night.

About midnight the grizzly-bear girl had another dream. She sang a song, and told her husband, "I will leave you as soon as the sun is up. This blood you see coming out of my mouth is my own blood. The hunters are close by, and will soon be here."

Soon the youth could hear the hunters talking. Then they took a pole and hung an empty garment near the mouth of the cave, and the bear rushed out at this decoy. When she turned to go back, they fired, and killed her.

The youth in the cave heard the hunters say, "Watch out! There must be another one in the cave."

So he decided he would go out; and when he came into the light, the hunters recognized him. He went home with them and told the story.

This was the year before the French trappers came, and Five-Times-Surrounded-in-War went away with them. In a year he returned, and after that he disappeared.

Sources

ZEUS AND EUROPA

Edith Hamilton, *Mythology: Timeless Tales of Gods and Heroes.* First published 1942. New York: Grand Central Publishing, 2011, 100–5.

CUPID AND PSYCHE

Thomas Bulfinch, *Greek and Roman Mythology.* First published 1855. New York: Modern Library, 1998, 54–59.

THE GIRL WHO MARRIED A SNAKE

The Panchatantra, reconstructed from various sources by Maria Tatar.

HASAN OF BASRA

The Thousand and One Nights, summarized by Edwin Sidney Hartland, *The Science of Fairy Tales.* London: Walter Scott, 1891, 255–58.

BEAUTY AND THE BEAST

Jeanne-Marie Leprince de Beaumont, "La Belle et la Bête," in *Magasin des Enfants.* London: Haberkorn, 1756. Translated by Maria Tatar.

EAST OF THE SUN AND
WEST OF THE MOON

Adapted from Peter Christen Asbjørnsen and Jørgen Moe, *Popular Tales from the Norse*, translated by George Webbe Dasent. New York: D. Appleton and Co., 1859, 266–80.

KING PIG

Adapted from Giovan Francesco Straparola, "The Pig King," in *The Facetious Nights of Straparola,* translated by W. G. Waters. London: Society of Bibliophiles, 1891, 4, 58–66.

THE FROG KING, OR IRON HEINRICH

Jacob and Wilhelm Grimm, *Kinder- und Hausmärchen*, 7th ed. Berlin: Dieterich, 1857. First published Berlin: Realschulbuchhandlung, 1812, 1–5. Translated by Maria Tatar.

THE SWAN MAIDENS

Adapted from Joseph Jacobs, *Europa's Fairy Book*. New York: G. P. Putnam's Sons, 1916, 98–105.

PRINCESS FROG

Adapted from Verra Xenophontovna Kalamatiano de Blumenthal, *Folk Tales from the Russian*. Chicago: Rand, McNally, 1903, 13–26.

THE PERI WIFE

Adapted from Thomas Keightley, *The Fairy Mythology*. London: H. G. Bohn, 1870, 20–22. From: *Bahar Danush, or Garden of Knowledge*, written in 1650.

THE CONDOR AND THE SHEPHERDESS

M. Rigoberto Paredes, *El Arte Folklórico de Bolivia,* 2nd ed. La Paz: Talleres Graficos Gamarra, 1949. First published under the title *El Arte en la Altiplanicie,* 1913, 65–67. Translated by Leonard Neidorf.

THE PARROT PRINCE

Ramón A. Laval, *Contribución al Folklore de Carahue (Chile), segunda parte: Leyendas y Cuentos Populares.* Santiago: Imprenta Universitaria, 1920, 146–57. Translated by Leonard Neidorf.

NICHOLAS THE FISH

Gerardo Reichel-Dolmatoff and Alicia Reichel-Dolmatoff, *La Literatura Oral de una Aldea Colombiana.* Divulgaciones Etnológicas, vol. 5. Barranquilla, Colombia: Universidad del Atlantico, Instituto de Investigación Etnológica, 1956, 55–58. Translated by Leonard Neidorf.

THE MUSKRAT HUSBAND

Anthony C. Woodbury, compiler and editor, *Cev'armiut Qanemciit Qulirait-llu: Eskimo Narratives and Tales from Chevak, Alaska.* Fairbanks: Alaska Native Language Center, University of Alaska, 1984/1992, 59–63.

A BOARHOG FOR A HUSBAND

Roger D. Abrahams, *African American Folktales: Stories from Black Traditions in the New World.* New York: Pantheon, 1999, 108–10. From an informant in St. Vincent.

THE MONKEY BRIDEGROOM

Keigo Seki, *Folktales of Japan,* translated by Robert J. Adams. Chicago: University of Chicago Press, 1963, 167–70.

TALE OF THE GIRL AND
THE HYENA-MAN

Sir Allan Wolsey Cardinall, *Tales Told in Togoland*. New York: Oxford
University Press, 1931, 213–14.

THE STORY OF FIVE HEADS

Adapted from George McCall Theal, *Kaffir Folk-Lore: A Selection
from the Traditional Tales Current Among the People Living on
the Eastern Border of Cape Colony*. London: Swan Sonnenschein,
1886, 13–17.

THE GOLDEN CRAB

Adapted from Andrew Lang, editor, *The Yellow Fairy Book*. London
and New York: Longmans, Green & Co., 1894, 31–36.

THE GIRL WHO MARRIED A DOG

Tristram P. Coffin, editor, *Indian Tales of North America*. Philadelphia: American Folklore Society, 1961, 34–35.

THE SNAKE PRINCE

Adapted from Andrew Lang, editor, *The Olive Fairy Book*. London,
New York, Bombay, and Calcutta: Longmans, Green & Co.,
1907, 247–55.

THE SMALL-TOOTH DOG

Sidney O. Addy, *Household Tales with Other Traditional Remains,
Collected in the Counties of York, Lincoln, Derby, and Notting-
ham*. London: David Nutt, The Strand/Sheffield: Pawson & Brails-
ford, 1895, 1–4.

THE QUEEN OF THE PIGEONS

Adapted from Ethel L. McPherson, *Native Fairy Tales of South Africa*. London: Harrap, 1919, 44–61.

THE GRATEFUL CRANE

Adapted from William Elliot Griffis, *The Fire-Fly's Lovers, and Other Fairy Tales of Old Japan*. New York: T. Y. Crowell & Co., 1908, 140–46.

THE PIQUED BUFFALO-WIFE

Clark Wissler and D. C. Duvall, *Anthropological Papers of the American Museum of Natural History: Mythology of the Blackfoot Indians*. New York: Order of the Trustees, 1908, 117–19.

THE TURTLE AND THE CHICKPEA

Georgios A. Megas, editor, *Folktales of Greece,* translated by Helen Colaclides. Chicago: University of Chicago Press, 1970, 74–79.

THE FROG MAIDEN

Maung Htin Aung, *Burmese Folk-Tales*. London: Oxford University Press, 1948, 70–74.

CHONGUITA

Adapted from Dean S. Fansler, *Filipino Popular Tales. Memoirs of the American Folk-Lore Society*, vol. 12. Lancaster, Penn.: American Folk-Lore Society, 1921, 244–46.

URASHIMA TARO

Keigo Seki, *Folktales of Japan*. Chicago: University of Chicago Press, 1963. 111–14.

OISIN IN TIR NA N-OG

Adapted from Jeremiah Curtin, *Myths and Folk-Lore of Ireland*. Boston: Little, Brown, & Company, 1890, 230–33.

THE DOG BRIDE

Adapted from Cecil Henry Bompas, *Folklore of the Santal Parganas*. London: D. Nutt, 1909, 255–56.

THE SWAN MAIDEN

Herman Hofberg, editor, *Swedish Fairy Tales*. Chicago: Belford-Clarke Co., 1890, 35–38.

THE HUNTER AND THE TORTOISE

Adapted from W. H. Barker, *West African Folk-Tales*. London: George G. Harrap & Co., 1917, 119–21.

THE PEASANT AND ZEMYNE

Edmund Veckenstedt, *Die Mythen, Sagen und Legenden der Zamaiten, vol. II.* Heidelberg: C. Winter, 1883, 149–50. Translated by Boria Sax in *The Serpent and the Swan: The Animal Bride in Folklore and Literature*. Blacksburg, Va.: McDonald & Woodward, 1998, 248–49.

PUDDOCKY

Adapted from Andrew Lang, editor, *The Green Fairy Book*. London: Longmans, Green & Co., 1892.

THE MAN WHO MARRIED A BEAR

Adapted from Franz Boas, editor, *Folk-Tales of Salishan and Sahaptin Tribes. Memoirs of the American Folk-Lore Society*, vol. 11. Lancaster, Penn., and New York: American Folk-Lore Society, 1917, 198–200.

AVAILABLE FROM PENGUIN CLASSICS

The Turnip Princess
and Other Newly Discovered Fairy Tales

Franz Xaver von Schönwerth

Compiled and Edited with a Foreword by Erika Eichenseer
Translated with an Introduction and Notes by Maria Tatar
Illustrations by Engelbert Süss

A rare discovery in the world of fairy tales—now for the first time in English. With this volume, the holy trinity of fairy tales—the Brothers Grimm, Charles Perrault, and Hans Christian Andersen—becomes a quartet. Violent, dark, and full of action, these more than seventy newly discovered stories by a contemporary of the Brothers Grimm bring us closer than ever to the unadorned oral tradition in which fairy tales are rooted.

One of NPR's Best Books of the Year

PENGUIN CLASSICS

AVAILABLE FROM PENGUIN CLASSICS

The Tale of Tales

Giambattista Basile

Translated with an Introduction and Notes by Nancy L. Canepa
Foreword by Jack Zipes
Illustrations by Carmelo Lettere

The inspiration for the major motion picture starring Salma Hayek, John C. Reilly, Toby Jones, and Vincent Cassel, *The Tale of Tales* is a rollicking, bawdy, fantastical cycle of fifty fairy tales told by ten sharp-tongued women over five days, by an Italian poet whom the Brothers Grimm credit with recording the first national collection of fairy tales.

PENGUIN
CLASSICS

"Though [Basile] wrote for a literary elite, the dirt of an oral tradition clings to his telling, rich in legend and slang." —Anthony Lane, The New Yorker

Fairy Tales

Hans Christian Andersen

Translated by Tiina Nunnally
Edited with an Introduction by Jackie Wullschlager

The thirty stories here by Hans Christian Andersen, who gave us the now standard versions of many traditional fairy tales, range from exuberant early works such as "The Tinderbox" and "The Emperor's New Clothes" through poignant masterpieces such as "The Little Mermaid" and "The Ugly Duckling" to more subversive later tales such as "The Ice Maiden" and "The Wood Nymph."

**PENGUIN
CLASSICS**

AVAILABLE FROM PENGUIN CLASSICS

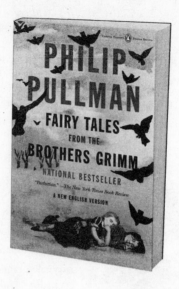

"*Perfection.*" —The New York Times Book Review

"*You didn't know you needed to reread Grimm. You do. This is a grand and great book. . . . I read it ravenously, rapturously.*"
—*Gregory Maguire, author of* Wicked

"*Pullman's* Fairy Tales *offers something unique: the chance to watch a master storyteller think through these most foundational of tales. . . . It is fascinating.*" —The New York Times

PENGUIN CLASSICS